DEAD
AIR

Liz,

Can you keep a secret?

DEAD
AIR

DEAD AIR

A NOVEL OF SUSPENSE

MICHAEL BRADLEY

CamCat
Books

CamCat Publishing, LLC
101 Creekside Crossing, Suite 280
Brentwood, Tennessee 37027
camcatpublishing.com

This is a work of fiction. Names, characters, places, and incidents are either products of the author's imagination or are used fictitiously.

Hardcover ISBN 9780744300062

Trade Paperback ISBN 9780744300017

eBook ISBN 9780744300031

Large Print Paperback 9780744300345

Audiobook ISBN 9780744300079

Library of Congress Control Number 2020934192

Cover design by Alicia Tatone

1 2 3 4 5 6 7 8 9 10

To Simon,

You were the best buddy a man could have asked for. I miss you.
Rest in peace.

1

SHE'D BEEN FOUND OUT. There was no other explanation.

On any other night, Kaitlyn Ashe would relish the breath-taking view of the Philadelphia cityscape. The twinkle of white streetlights, red, yellow, and green traffic lights, and the white and red hues from car lights on the streets below looked like a swirling star field, constantly changing as if at the whim of a fickle god. From the twentieth-floor broadcast studio, she could look down upon Center City, could see as far east as the Walt Whitman Bridge and across the Delaware River to the distant lights of Camden, New Jersey. Yes, every other night, this view was mesmerizing. But not tonight. Tonight, Kaitlyn Ashe trembled at the thought that someone out there knew her, knew her secret, and was making damn sure she didn't forget it.

The past had come a step closer each time another letter arrived. Her fingers tightened their grasp on the latest, a crumpled paper creased with crisscrossed lines and folds. It was a cliché. The mysterious correspondences consisted of letters and phrases torn from newspapers and magazines, crudely pasted onto plain paper. Always the same message, always the same signature.

Behind her, music played softly. She turned away from the window and moved around the L-shaped counter in the middle of the room to slide onto the tall stool behind the control console. Kaitlyn leaned forward, glancing at the needles on the VU meters that jumped and pulsed to the music's beat. She touched one of the ten slider controls and adjusted the volume to remove some mild distortion.

Kaitlyn watched the onscreen clock count down to the end of the current song. Fifteen seconds to go. She slid the headphones over her ears and drew the broadcast microphone to her mouth. She tapped the green button on the console and pushed the left-most slider upward.

Kaitlyn leaned into the microphone. "Taking things back to 2005 with Lifehouse on WPLX. That was 'You and Me,' going out to Jamie from Kristin, Tiffany from Steve, and to Tommy—Jackie still loves you." She glanced again at the clock in the upper corner of the computer screen. "It's ten past ten. I'm Kaitlyn Ashe with Love Songs at Ten. 888-555-WPLX is the number to get your dedication in tonight. I've got Adele lined up, as well as John Legend on the way next."

Her fingers darted over the control console, tapping buttons and moving sliders. Kaitlyn took the headphones off. As a commercial for Ambrosia—her favorite seafood restaurant in downtown Philadelphia—played, she stared at the crinkled letter that rested beside the console. She read it once again beneath the dim studio lights. Her eyes focused on the name at the bottom. *The Shallows.* She shivered. Who knew? And how much did they know?

Kaitlyn slipped a green Bic lighter from her pocket, lit the edge of the letter, and pinched the corner as the flames swept up the paper. She'd stolen the lighter from Kevin O'Neill's desk. She knew the midday DJ would never miss it. He had half a dozen more where that one came from.

She dropped the paper into the empty wastebasket, and watched the fire dwindle into nothingness, leaving behind blackened flakes. A faint trace of smoke hung in the air, then dissipated quickly. She wrung her hands and sighed. There'd be another waiting in her station mailbox tomorrow, just like the four others that she'd received, one each day this week. She was certain of it.

The flash of green lights caught her eye, and she looked down at the studio telephone. All four lines were lit up. She hesitated for a moment, then tapped the first line. "WPLX, do you have a dedication?"

"Yeah, I'd like to dedicate my weekend to kissing your body from head to toe." The smoky voice echoed through the darkened studio.

Kaitlyn laughed, and felt her face become warm with embarrassment. "Brad!"

"How goes it, babe? Having a good night?"

She forced a smile, trying to sound upbeat, just as she'd learned in her voice-over classes. "It's not too bad."

"What's wrong?"

She cursed under her breath. She never could hide things from Brad. "I got another letter today."

The line was silent for a moment. "Same message?"

She glanced at the computer, then back at the phone. "Yeah. Exactly the same."

"You should call the police."

It was the same suggestion he had made a month ago, when the letters started arriving on a weekly basis. With this week's sudden volley of letters, he had taken to repeating his advice nightly. Kaitlyn had shrugged it off as just some crank. "You get those in this business," she'd told him.

"Still no idea who sends these letters? Or what they are about?"

She hesitated for a second before replying. "No idea," she lied.

"You need to tell someone. If not the police, at least tell Scott."

Kaitlyn frowned at his remark. The last thing she wanted to do was tell her program director Scott Mackay about the letters. His overly protective nature would mean police involvement for certain. "I can't tell Scott. He'd place an armed guard on the studio door."

Brad laughed. "Would that be so bad?"

"There's no point. It's probably some infatuated teenager." She knew how ridiculous the words sounded even as they escaped her lips. No teenage listener would know about the Shallows.

"Do me a favor—watch yourself tonight when you go home." The concern in his voice was evident. If she asked, he'd be there in a moment to escort her home. But she couldn't do that to him. Not without revealing something she'd worked so hard to bury in her own past.

Kaitlyn said, "I will. Promise."

"How's the rest of the night going?"

"It's been crazy. Lots of lovers out there tonight. I can't even get them all in. Just not enough time."

"I wouldn't expect any less from the most listened-to night show in Philly."

With a glance at the computer screen, Kaitlyn noted where she was in the commercial break, and then turned back toward the phone. "What are you up to, sweetie?"

"Working my way through a couple briefs. I've got to have these ready for review by tomorrow."

"Sounds like a late night."

He sighed. "Probably."

Kaitlyn sensed fatigue and frustration in his voice. She knew nothing about corporate law other than what Brad had told her. The reams of paperwork and bewildering legalese seemed boring and unappealing. She knew he had a lot on his plate and hated to see him work as hard as he did. A mischievous smile crossed her lips. "If you want, I could slip over later tonight, and help you with your briefs."

Brad's chuckle echoed through the studio. "That'd be nice, really nice."

She leaned closer to the speaker phone and spoke almost in a whisper. "You know you want to." She added a sensual emphasis to each word. "It'll make you feel good."

"That's not fair." He paused, then asked, "Can I take a raincheck? I need to get these done."

Kaitlyn glanced again at the computer and reached for her headphones. "Hang on."

Her fingers clicked on the microphone, and, out of the commercial break, she gave a quick weather forecast before starting the next song. Then she turned off the microphone and turned back to the phone. "Are we still on for lunch tomorrow?"

"Absolutely. Just you and me in a dark corner at Toscana's."

Looking down at the phone, she noticed that the other three lines were still flashing. "I've got to go, sweetie. Love you."

"Love you too. Talk to you later."

When he'd hung up, Kaitlyn turned to face the window and gazed out across the cityscape. The lights below seemed brighter somehow, a little more stunning than before. She sighed with deep satisfaction. There was something about Brad's voice that always relaxed her and quelled her fears. He was trusting, gentle, and loving. She was lucky to have him. For four weeks, he had accepted her word that she knew nothing about *The Shallows*, or why anyone would send her these letters. Brad may have suspected that she was lying, but he never pushed her. It would all come out eventually. She couldn't go on being dishonest indefinitely. She just needed time. Time to figure out how to explain that she wasn't who she pretended to be.

Kaitlyn turned back to the computer to check the playlist. Her gaze froze, and she frowned. REO Speedwagon was coming up on the list. Her shoulders gave a momentary shudder.

She'd loved the band for as long as she could remember. While her high school friends were listening to likes of Justin Timberlake and Christina Aguilera, Kaitlyn had dug back a couple decades and discovered REO Speedwagon. She loved their songs, but this particular one held a spell over her. Its impact had diminished over the years. She'd almost reached the point of being able to play it as opposed to deleting it from the playlist whenever it showed up. Until recently, it only invoked the briefest of memories. She would twinge at the brief reminder and use the song's deletion as a way to purge herself of her past.

That, however, was then. The arrival of the letters had changed everything. Now, the sheer appearance of the song frightened Kaitlyn, reminded her that her past was catching up. Some secrets couldn't stay hidden forever. She'd hoped the anniversary would pass unnoticed again this year. But with only three weeks to go until that date, someone was making sure that she remembered every detail.

She jabbed the delete key and a sense of relief washed over her as the song vanished from the screen. Breathing slow and deep, she allowed her uneasiness to subside. Then, she leaned toward the phone and clicked the next blinking line. "WPLX, do you have a dedication?"

———

WHEN THE ELEVATOR DOORS OPENED, Kaitlyn stepped out into the building's attached parking garage. An hour's worth of commercial voice-over work had been waiting for her when she went off the air at midnight. It took longer than usual for her to plow through it. She was too distracted, making too many mistakes, leading to far more retakes than was her norm. On her way out, she'd stopped by the studio to tell Justin Kace, the overnight personality, that she was leaving. They talked for another hour. Between station IDs and weather forecasts, Justin showed her pictures of his latest girlfriend—his third this year— and explained how they met. Kaitlyn suggested a couple places he could take her. Longwood Gardens. The Art Museum. Justin shrugged them off, saying the girl "was more into the unusual and bizarre."

Kaitlyn rolled her eyes and laughed. "Then try the Mütter Museum. That should be bizarre enough for her." Then she said her farewells and left, imagining Justin and his new girl finding romance amidst anatomically correct wax figures, glass cases full of pathology specimens, and ancient medical equipment fit for a steampunk horror movie.

Pausing by the elevator doors for a moment, she scanned the empty parking garage, just as she'd done every other night for the past four weeks. The night air was crisp on her face and she caught the faint whiff of the city. It was a mix of odors almost unique to Philadelphia. Bitter and often pungent. She shivered in the chilled air and an unwanted memory flashed through her mind. Back then, on that fateful night, the air had been brisk as well.

She didn't see anyone around but couldn't shake the sense that she was being watched. For a while, she had chalked it up to paranoia induced by the letters, but their increased recurrence left her more anxious every day. Her fingers gripped a little more tightly on the pepper spray canister on her keychain.

Kaitlyn gave the parking garage one more inspection. No one was in sight and no sound came other than the hum of a nearby flickering fluorescent light. She strode toward her motorcycle. Her boot heels echoed throughout the empty garage. The chrome of the handlebars and exhaust pipes on the Harley-Davidson shone in the overhead lights. She smiled as her eyes glanced over the motorcycle's candy apple red fuel tank and fenders. She'd always wanted a Harley, even as a child. But a bike was a luxury that had eluded her until last year. When she topped the Arbitron ratings as the highest-rated nighttime on-air personality in Philadelphia, Kaitlyn had celebrated by fulfilling her childhood dream.

The promise of more spring-like temperatures for April was the catalyst she'd been waiting for to bring the motorcycle out of winter storage. Kaitlyn had changed the oil and washed and waxed it the previous weekend. Three days into the new week, she was re-experiencing the joy of riding she had longed for throughout the winter.

She straddled the black leather seat and zipped up her tan leather jacket. As the motorcycle rumbled to life, Kaitlyn raced the throttle a few times just to hear the engine's roar echo through the deserted parking garage. She got a rush every time from the engine vibrations racing from the handlebars up through her arms. She smiled, and for a moment, forgot about the letters. Then, she slid a black helmet over her head and drew the visor down over her eyes. Her foot pulled the kickstand up, and, revving the engine one more time, Kaitlyn sped down the ramp of the garage and onto the dark Philadelphia streets.

SHE LOOKS NERVOUS TONIGHT. A bit more pensive than usual. Standing in the elevator's threshold, she's keeping the doors open. Almost afraid to move out into the parking garage. Her reaction amuses me. No, amusing isn't the word. Ecstatic. Yes, that's the word. I'm ecstatic over the reaction my letters are having on her. Ecstatic to the point of being rapturous. Rapturous? Yes, I like that.

She's kept me waiting tonight, longer than usual. What time is it? After 2 a.m.? Shit. I've been here five hours. Far too much time to spend in this godforsaken city. I've grown to hate it over the years. The lights. The noise. The smells. I hate it all. Too many fractured memories and an overabundance of lingering grief.

I must have liked it at one time. After all, I grew up in its shadow. This city litters my childhood memories like newspapers blowing in the wind. Trips over the river to see Independence Hall and the Liberty Bell. Sitting on a bench for a picture with a smelly old man dressed like Ben Franklin. Springsteen in concert at the old Spectrum. All memories that should bring a warmth to my heart and soul. But I feel nothing beyond anger and hate. She's tainted everything. My memories, this city, my life . . . everything.

God . . . I need a cigarette.

I don't dare light up. She might see the flare of the match. Filthy habit. Not sure why I started smoking. It was something to do these past few months while I waited for her to emerge each night. There's a growing pile of discarded butts by my feet. Doesn't anyone clean up around here?

She didn't play the song again. I listened all night and nothing. Why can't she take a hint? I doubt she's forgotten. I just want to hear her play it once. Just once. That's all I wanted when this all began. To hear that song and know she remembers. Why won't she ever play it?

How many months have I stood here watching her, night in and night out? You'd think I'd be used to it by now, but I'm still apprehensive. Still jittery. Would she recognize me if she saw me? It has only been thirteen years, but I've changed so much in that time. Dropped a shitload of weight. Cut off most of my hair. I'm not a goddamn kid anymore. Will she know me when we finally meet?

She's on the move, crossing the garage to that bike of hers. Audacious piece of crap. Why would she ever want one of those things? Jesse would never have gone for a biker bitch. The damn thing is loud, especially in the parking garage. Its roar pierces my ears. She'll be leaving momentarily. If I want to follow her, I need to get back to the car two levels above. But I don't dare move. She mustn't see me. Not yet. Not until everything is in place. It'll be a reunion she won't forget until the day she dies.

At this hour, she'll only be going to one of two places. Her home or his apartment. I can catch up to her either way. The breath I've been holding escapes. I'm still trembling. I need a smoke.

There's nothing like the first drag off a freshly lit cigarette. I love the way it tickles my throat. God, I need this. It's soothing and steadies my nerves. A chill hangs in the air like the night Jesse died. Was it this cold back then, or did it just seem like that? I can't remember the details as clearly anymore.

Time heals all wounds, they say. That's such a lie.

The concrete is cold beneath my feet. As cold as my heart. As cold as she will be when I'm done. Just a couple more weeks, then it'll be time for Laura Hobson to return to the Shallows.

KAITLYN GROANED when the alarm clock buzzed at 9:30 the next morning. She'd returned to her Bala Cynwyd home, arriving just after 2:30. She vaguely recalled the clock saying that it was past three when she' finally made it to bed. Normally, the alarm wouldn't go off until closer to noon, but not this morning. Lunch with Brad meant her whole morning routine had to be moved up. It was one downside to working seven to midnight. Romantic meals were always relegated to lunch.

Kaitlyn kicked the paisley sheets off the bed, sat up, and ran her hands through her disheveled hair. She hadn't slept well; tattered images of her nightmare still clung to her subconscious: the dark pool of water engulfing her, cold hands clutching at her ankles . . . She shook her head and tried to shake off the wisps of memory once and for all.

She yawned, climbed from her king-size bed, and crossed to the window on the far wall. She pulled the curtains aside and looked up at the blue sky, squinting as the Friday morning sun filled the room with a fiery yellow hue. Kaitlyn's gaze dropped to her front yard and the street beyond. The Volkswagen Beetle she'd seen when she came home was gone. It likely belonged to one of her neighbors. Or maybe a regular guest? It'd been parked outside a couple times a week—sometimes further up the street, sometimes directly across from her house. But never in a driveway. Always on the street.

A grey Ford Focus pulled up along the curb near her driveway, and two elderly ladies—one African American and the other Caucasian—emerged from the car. Dressed in their Sunday best, each carried a large tote bag, overflowing with leaflets.

Jehovah's Witnesses, she thought as they started the short trek up her driveway. Kaitlyn pulled the curtains closed again as the doorbell rang. She made no move to answer it. *I'll have to slip out the back this morning.*

She walked down the hall to the bathroom. Flipping on the light, she glanced in the mirror over the sink. She ran both hands through her hair and pushed it back from her face. The dark shadows beneath her eyes looked more pronounced this morning. Just another sign that she hadn't been sleeping well over the past few weeks.

Was this really her? The same person who had been walking hand in hand out there, beside the Shallows? Just the two of them in the chilly evening. The innocence, the tranquility, and the love.

She turned on the faucet, cupped her hands under the cold water, and splashed her face. She smiled. The green toothbrush beside her pink one made her think of Brad. How late had he been up? He'd sounded pretty exhausted on the phone last night. Hopefully, he hadn't been forced to stay up too much longer after they'd hung up.

She hated deceiving Brad. In their two years together, there had been no secrets between them . . . except one. Her past, as far as he knew, had been as normal as anyone could hope for. No scandal, no remorse, and no death. She had hoped that he'd never have to know the truth, but she couldn't keep lying about the letters forever.

Back in the bedroom, she drew open the top drawer of the oak mission-style dresser to grab a sports bra. She caught a glimpse of the small box near the back and reached for it. Her hand hovered over it for a moment. She never should have kept it. With a force of will, she grabbed a bra and pushed the drawer closed. Then, Kaitlyn rummaged through the bottom drawer, pulling out black spandex running shorts and a pale blue tank top. She slipped a pair of Nikes onto her feet, tightened the white laces, and flexed her feet. The shoes were worn. Maybe it was time to get a new pair. She grabbed her iPhone from the dresser and slid it into the armband strapped to her right upper arm. She plugged the earbuds into the phone and crossed again to the window. The Ford Focus was still parked in the street, but there was no sign of the two women. She scooped her keys from the dresser, pausing to get a firm hold on the attached pepper spray canister.

——————

KAITLYN SNEEZED when she stepped out into the backyard. Fresh cut grass. She vaguely recalled hearing a lawn mower earlier in the morning. *Must have been Fred getting an early start on the yard work.* She sighed. She'd end up dragging grass clippings into the house on her shoes later. Her eyes fell upon the row of American Boxwoods that she'd planted two summers ago. They still hadn't grown tall enough to block her view of the cemetery beyond. Kaitlyn had thought she could live with a cemetery practically in her backyard, but it was far creepier than she'd anticipated. Perhaps if she couldn't see the cemetery, it wouldn't bother her. With earbuds in her ears, Kaitlyn cut across the lawn and jogged off toward the nearby street.

Her house, a split-level colonial with beige siding and chocolate-colored shutters, sat on the corner of Belmont Avenue and Garnet Lane. Her home was the smallest along the secluded lane; the others had more square footage, bigger yards, and better landscaping. Her neighbors were all married with children. None of this ever bothered her. She didn't mind still being single at thirty-two. Her early career in broadcasting had kept her moving from city to city every year or so, making it difficult to develop a long-term relationship. But she'd returned to the Philadelphia area three years ago, and now she was putting down roots.

Kaitlyn jogged along the road's shoulder and paid little attention to the passing cars and trucks. She was familiar with just about every inch of the path along this stretch of Belmont Avenue. She'd jogged the same route every morning since moving in. A few blocks down, Kaitlyn turned left onto East Levering Mill Road, which took her to the entrance of the Cynwyd Heritage Trail. The trail, which looped around the Westminster Cemetery, would eventually bring her back around to Belmont Avenue, just north of her house.

The wooded trail was a flurry of activity, far more than Kaitlyn expected for ten in the morning. Mothers pushing strollers—both walking and jogging—as well as retirees out for a leisurely stroll formed a human maze through which Kaitlyn weaved. She smiled. The beautiful Friday morning weather must have drawn the people out. Spring was in the air, which meant the flowers were in bloom, leaves were sprouting on the trees, and the fair-weather exercisers were coming out from their winter hibernation. Her smile widened as she remembered how she'd practically had the trail to herself in the bitter cold of January and February.

She continued along, absorbed in the music from her earbuds and paying little attention to what was around her. As the trail wound into the shade of the trees, the temperature dropped by a few degrees. Kaitlyn shivered at the sudden change. She passed a mother with two infants bundled up in a dual seat stroller. The woman looked haggard and frustrated, as if she'd spent all her energy just to get to the park. Kaitlyn returned the woman's nod and half-hearted smile with a wave, then pressed on.

The crowd thinned out, and Kaitlyn found herself alone on the trail. As she rounded a bend, she noticed a bench with a seated figure hunched forward, looking at a mobile phone. Dressed in a gray hoodie, the face was covered except for the long flowing chestnut-brown hair falling out from under the hood. No telling if it was a man or a woman. She tried not to pay much attention to the figure as she approached, but paranoia nagged at the back of her mind. *Be aware of your surroundings,* she reminded herself.

When Kaitlyn came alongside the bench, she turned her gaze toward it. The hood tilted upward, giving her a momentary glimpse of a shadowy face. It locked onto her and seemed to follow her as she passed. Before any of it could truly register in her mind, the hood tilted down again, and Kaitlyn continued to jog further up the trail.

Only after a few strides did she think again about the face she'd seen. She halted and turned back toward the bench. It was empty. There was no one around. Kaitlyn's hand trembled as she tightened her grip on the pepper spray canister.

———————

WHEN KAITLYN ENTERED TOSCANA ITALIANO, she inhaled the tantalizing aromas of garlic, homemade tomato sauce, Italian herbs, and freshly baked breads. She drew in a deep breath. The upscale bistro, located in the city's arts district, was on Spruce Street. It was elegantly decorated in dark woods and crimson fabrics. The tinted-plate glass windows and dim lighting created an intimate atmosphere, perfect for a romantic lunch.

She scanned the restaurant and spotted Brad's smile from across the lunch crowd. As she made her way through the scattering of occupied round tables, Kaitlyn admired the well-dressed man who waited for her. His coal black hair was brushed off to the right—not a single hair out of place. The chiseled jawline and tuft of hair on his chin gave Brad a rough look that Kaitlyn adored.

He rose from his seat as she approached, moving to pull out the chair beside his. Kaitlyn touched the arm of his pinstripe suit jacket and kissed him on the cheek. "Sorry I'm late."

"I only just arrived a few moments ago myself." His deep voice sounded far more relaxed than the night before.

Kaitlyn noticed the shadows beneath his blue eyes. "Were you up late last night?"

"More like early in the morning. That Radcliffe-Hesterton brief was a nightmare," he said. "Took me three hours just to get through that one alone."

Kaitlyn frowned, and reached across the table, touching his hand. "Probably good that I didn't come over after work."

A young, petite waitress in black blouse and trousers approached the table to take their order. A salad—grilled chicken Caesar—with an iced tea for Kaitlyn, and chicken piccata with a glass of water for Brad.

"Did you hear that GBT struck again last night?" Brad said when the waitress stepped away.

Kaitlyn closed her eyes and shook her head. "Strangled. What a horrible way to die." *Almost as bad as drowning*, she thought.

"Heard it on the morning news. They said his latest victim put up a fight before being killed. Police found the body behind Pegasus—that nightclub at Penns Landing."

Kaitlyn set her fork down on her plate. "I heard an announcer from Faith FM said this was God's punishment on the city for allowing homosexuality to flourish."

"Some religious fanatic trying to make a point. . . . That's probably who GBT is. It's a hate crime. Pure and simple."

"I hope they catch him soon." She took a long sip of iced tea.

They fell silent. The space between them became a vast wasteland of reticence that made Kaitlyn feel uncomfortable. She didn't like these moments, which had become more frequent of late.

"How'd the rest of your show go?" Brad asked, probably just as uncomfortable as Kaitlyn but much better at lightening the mood.

"Same as it does every night. The phones rang off the hook. I'm doing the anti-dedication song tonight. It'll be even crazier."

"Which song are you using tonight?"

"I took your suggestion. 'Love Stinks.'"

Brad nodded his head. "Classic J. Geils Band."

Kaitlyn smiled. Brad's knowledge of '80s music bordered on the obsessive. His music library was crammed with songs that even she had never heard of. She'd always considered herself to be an expert on popular music, a trait that went with the job. But Brad always had her beat when it came to music from that era.

The waitress returned with their meals. As they ate, she looked across the table and smiled. He turned his gaze away from her. Kaitlyn shifted in her seat and studied him. There were shadows beneath his eyes and the slouch in his shoulders was more pronounced. She felt a pang of compassion for him. Unlike her, he wasn't accustomed to working late into the evening, and she could tell just by looking at him that he wasn't tolerating his late night very well.

"I need a weekend away," he said suddenly. "A long weekend. Are you interested?"

She felt a surge of excitement within her. A getaway sounded like a tremendous idea. Get away from work. Get away from the letters. She locked eyes with him and grinned. "What'd you have in mind?"

"Three days in the Poconos."

"Sounds nice."

"There's a little resort up there, just for couples," he said between mouthfuls of his meal. "We could go up on a Thursday after your show and stay through Monday."

"I love it. When?" she said.

"I'll have to see what availability the resort has, but maybe two weeks from now?"

"Can we get one of those rooms with a tub shaped like a champagne glass?" Kaitlyn laughed. "I've always wanted to try one of those."

"I'll see what I can do."

Although the restaurant was bustling with the lunchtime crowd, their corner table was isolated in a silent bubble. An awkwardness hung over the table. Brad toyed with his food, using his fork to push it around the plate.

"About these letters . . ." he said.

Kaitlyn set her fork down. It clinked against the plate a bit louder than she wanted. "Do we have to talk about this again?"

"Again? We've barely talked about it at all. You always shrug it off like it's nothing."

Kaitlyn folded her arms and glared at him. "It *is* nothing."

"Then why the nightmares?" His words rumbled across the table like subdued thunder.

The topic wasn't new with them. But Brad had never been as fervent before. Maybe he was just tired. Kaitlyn furtively glanced around the restaurant to see if anyone was watching. Then she leaned forward and spoke softly. "Please . . . let's not talk about this now."

"Then when do we talk about it?"

She opened her mouth to speak, then thought better of it. If she wasn't ready to tell him the truth, then there was nothing she could say to make matters better. She looked down at her meal and jabbed at some lettuce with her fork. The Shallows was weaving its way into her love life like virulent poison ivy.

———

AS THEY CROSSED the restaurant to leave, Kaitlyn took hold of Brad's hand, giving it a tight squeeze. They paused just inside the entrance. She leaned toward him and kissed his lips. As she pulled away, something smacked against her shoulder, jostling Kaitlyn back into Brad's arms.

She heard the rough feminine voice utter apologies as the woman pushed open the door and exited with great haste. Kaitlyn caught the merest glimpse of chestnut brown shoulder length hair as the woman rushed from sight on the busy street.

"That was rude," Brad said, still holding Kaitlyn in his arms. "You okay?"

Kaitlyn eased herself out of his arms. "I'm fine." She gazed through the window at the street. The hair on her neck stood up but she couldn't explain why. There was something familiar, but she couldn't tell what. Was it the woman? Was it her voice? Or, was it something else completely? Everything else around her became white noise as *déjà vu* swept over her. It was the hair; she was certain of it. She'd seen it before. Where? The trail, on the bench, earlier in the morning. But could it be the same person? Was she being followed?

"Kate? You there?"

She jerked her head around to stare at Brad. "What? Yeah, yeah I'm here."

"You were off in Lala Land for a moment," he said. "What's up?"

Kaitlyn turned to look out on the street once more. "I thought . . . It was nothing."

"You sure?"

She nodded. "Yeah. Let's go."

Kaitlyn grasped his hand, leading him through the door onto the sidewalk beyond. They embraced, and she held him tightly for just a moment longer than usual. His arms around her helped to push away the uneasy feeling the collision had stirred within her. When she pulled away, Kaitlyn gave him a quick kiss. "I'll come over after my show. See you tonight."

4

KAITLYN ARRIVED at the WPLX studios just before five, pushed the door open and stepped into the station reception area. She stopped before the high mahogany reception counter. Resting her elbows on it, she leaned over and peered at Samantha Devonport, who was seated on the other side. Her head was tilted down, and her pudgy face was partially obscured by wavy blonde hair. A phone headset hung around her neck, the thin black wire snaked down her shoulder and across the desk to the phone. Attention fixated on the *National Enquirer* open on her desk, the receptionist chewed a piece of gum to the ends of its life.

"Anything good in there this week?" Kaitlyn said.

Sammy's gaze broke from the magazine and shifted to Kaitlyn. She smiled and flipped the magazine closed.

"Nah, nothing worth the cover charge."

Kaitlyn rested her chin in the palms of her hands and laughed. She glanced at the cover. An out-of-focus photo with a headline about a Kardashian being caught topless on the beach again. "What else is happening?"

Sammy glanced from side to side, as if checking to make sure no one else was around. "Did you hear about Justin? Rumor has it —and this is totally unconfirmed—that he's been havin' conjugal visits with some young redhead during the overnights." She made air quotes with her fingers around the word "conjugal."

Kaitlyn smiled but wasn't at all surprised. There had been nights when Justin Kace had been anxious for Kaitlyn to leave as soon as her shift had ended, even going as far as to offer to do her production voiceover work for her. Thinking about Justin's description of his latest conquest's off-beat interests, she swallowed a snicker. "Really?"

"Michael said he came in early on Thursday morning and saw a woman run down the back hallway. She was buck ass naked."

Kaitlyn was amused by the image that formed in her mind. Michael Tyler, the morning show host at WPLX, was deeply religious, and she could only imagine how he would've responded to seeing a young pair of naked butt cheeks dashing through the hallways in the wee hours of the morning. He probably shared his indignation with everyone he spoke to from his morning show co-host Dana Burns all the way to Scott. "Does Scott know?"

"Are you kidding?" Sammy said. "That's where Mr. Holy Roller went as soon as he was off the air."

"And?"

Sammy shrugged. "I don't know. Scott hasn't said anything about it, but you know how things work around here."

"In one ear and out the other." Kaitlyn snickered, knowing that Scott would make the obligatory call to Justin, give him the cursory hand slap, and forget about it all. Justin might be young and new to the business, but he had raw talent, and that wasn't something a station manager gave up easily. "Got any plans this weekend?"

"Gotta get my phone fixed. Got Oreos in the charging port."

"How'd you—" Kaitlyn stopped and shook her head. "Never mind. I don't want to know. You coming to O'Toole's tomorrow night?"

"Not sure. My old man has to work."

Kaitlyn thought it was funny to hear Sammy call her husband her "old man." The young woman couldn't be more than twenty-three and had only been married a little over a year. Kaitlyn had helped them move into their new Fishtown apartment, which was the first time she'd met Sammy's husband. Meeting him only confirmed that Sammy wore the pants in their family. "You should come anyway. What else you going to do on a Saturday night?" Kaitlyn said, lifting her arms off the counter. "I've got to go prep. See you tomorrow night."

As Kaitlyn passed through the double doors that led to the WPLX offices and studios, she heard Sammy yell, "Maybe. I said maybe."

———————

KAITLYN PASSED the sales office and production studio, entering the office set aside for the air personalities. The large open space, nicknamed the "Bullpen," featured six office desks in two rows set end to end across the room. The desks were basic, each with an aluminum frame, drawers, and laminate desktop.

Kevin O'Neill looked up from his laptop and gave Kaitlyn a quick wave from across the room. His caramel-colored hair was brushed back from his forehead, draping down behind his ears. Kaitlyn halted, staring at the thick strip of white surgical tape that covered his nose. "Kevin! What happened?"

He gave her a tentative smile. "Racquetball accident." His voice had a nasal twang to it. "Spent half the night in the ER."

She tilted her head for a moment. She never knew Kevin played racquetball. "Looks painful."

"Not like it was when it happened. The doc said the swelling should go down in twenty-four hours. The stitches should come out in two weeks."

She pointed at the bandage. "How long have you got to walk around with that on your nose?"

He rose from his seat, stepping around the desk. His biceps flexed beneath the sleeves of his polo as he crossed his arms. "A few days."

Kaitlyn laughed at the nasal tone in his voice. "It's done wonders for your voice."

His eyes flashed dark for a moment. "It doesn't sound that bad, does it?"

She crossed the room and stopped at the small square shelves that served as mailboxes for the staff. "I'm sure no one noticed."

Kaitlyn reached into her mailbox, and extracted the latest copy of Billboard magazine, two envelopes—one white and one Manila —and a compact disc. The label on the CD said it contained new jingles and commercials for Walmart. She slid the CD back into her mailbox. She'd enter them into the computer later. Kaitlyn rolled up the magazine and slipped it under her arm. Then she glanced at the two envelopes. The return address of the white envelope was a local charity, probably looking for free publicity. Kaitlyn shuddered when she glanced at the Manila envelope. She'd seen the hand-printed label numerous times before, and she knew what she'd find within it. She leaned back against the nearby desk. The envelope trembled in her hand.

Kevin crossed the room and stepped behind her. She felt his warm breath on her neck as he looked over her shoulder. He reeked of stale cigarette smoke, and she tried to not cringe.

"Anything the matter?" he said.

Kaitlyn's loss of composure was only momentary, then she smiled, sliding the envelope under her arm with the magazine. She turned to find him standing inches from her. Just a tad too close to be comfortable. She stepped back. "It's nothing. Just junk mail."

Kevin gazed at her for a moment, shrugged his shoulders, and returned to his desk. Once seated, his fingers danced across the laptop keyboard. Kaitlyn moved to her desk at the opposite end of the office and set down the mail she'd just collected.

"Anti-dedication tonight?" Kevin stopped typing and glanced across the office.

"Yep," said Kaitlyn, pulling open the lower left drawer of her desk.

"What're you using this week?"

Kaitlyn smiled as she lowered her leather purse into the drawer. "J. Geils Band."

"'Love Stinks?' Nice one."

Kaitlyn pushed the desk drawer closed. "Glad you approve."

As Kevin returned to his typing, Kaitlyn lowered herself into her desk chair and slid the Manila envelope across the desktop until it rested before her. A chill crept up her spine. Her eyes traced the black ink of each letter on the address label. The pinpoint lines were straight and sharp, the curves and corners precise. The same handwriting on every one of these envelopes she'd received over the past month. She took a deep breath and slid her fingers along the top edge to break the seal. The sheet of paper within was folded, just as all the others had been. Laying the paper flat on the desk, her eyes danced over the random magazine clippings that made up the message. Although the clippings were different this time, the words were not.

Play REO Speedwagon for me. You know the song.
The Shallows.

In an instant, she was there. Standing by the water's edge, watching a flashlight sweep over the water's surface. A frantic search in the darkness that she knew would yield nothing.

"A fan letter?" said Kevin.

Kaitlyn whirled around, startled by his voice. She'd hadn't heard him approach her desk. She refolded the letter, trying to hide its message. He leaned in over her shoulder. His breath was hot on her neck again. It sent a shiver along her spine.

"Just some crank," she said.

He lifted the letter from between her fingers. She didn't have time to resist and bit her lip as he gave the message a quick review. "REO Speedwagon? Whoever it is, they've got no taste in music."

"There's nothing wrong with Cronin and company," she responded as she tried to put some space between them, glad to latch onto a conversation about music.

"Bah! Dreaded love mush." Kevin dismissed her comment with a wave of his hand as he tossed the letter back on her desk.

"That's not true. What about 'Take It On The Run' or 'Keep On Loving You?' They had some great stuff in their heyday."

"Pish Posh. I can't think of a worse batch of songs than the crap they turned out in the '80s." He gestured toward the letter. "But if someone goes to all that trouble to make a request, you'd better play it for them." Kevin crossed to his desk. He grabbed his coat off the back of the chair. "I've gotta go. Have a good show."

He reached the office door and paused. "I'll be listening for REO tonight." Then he disappeared through the door.

She watched him leave, glad to be alone for a few minutes. She glanced at the unfolded letter, rereading the words. She knew the song. REO Speedwagon's "Can't Fight This Feeling." It had been *their* song. Who could possibly know the connection between that song and the Shallows? Who the hell was sending these letters?

Kaitlyn gathered up the letter and crossed the room to the office shredder. A few moments later, the letter was gone.

———

". . . and from Robby to Pookie—'I still hate you.' Here's tonight's WPLX anti-dedication, 'Love Stinks,'" Kaitlyn said.

She slid her headphones off as the song began to play. It'd been the longest anti-dedication she ever remembered having to read out. She glanced at her notepad. The list of names almost reached the bottom of the page. She tore off the sheet, crumpled the paper into a ball, and tossed it at the trash can by the door. It bounced off the wall and landed a foot from its intended target.

She stared out the studio window, gazing across the Philadelphia skyline. It always amazed her how many people called to express their hate for someone with the anti-dedication song. The Friday night feature on her show was growing in popularity. Soon, she wouldn't have time to read all the dedications. So much for the City of Brotherly Love.

All the request lines were still blinking. Listeners trying to get in a last-minute message for the anti-dedication, no doubt. Kaitlyn ignored the flashing green lights. Her head bobbed to the music's beat. She glanced at the clock. A few minutes after ten. Leaning forward, she answered one of the blinking phone lines.

"Is it too late to get my name in for the anti-love song?" said a young-sounding voice. Probably a teenager.

"It is, sorry," replied Kaitlyn.

She heard the abrupt click as the caller hung up. Snickering, she reached to answer the next blinking line. "Hello, WPLX."

"Hey babe."

Kaitlyn smiled at the sound of Brad's voice. "Oh, I'm glad it's you. Far too many scorned lovers out there tonight."

"That's why I called. I wanted to bring a little love into your otherwise loveless evening."

Kaitlyn giggled. "How are you planning to do that?"

"By telling you that I've got a chilled bottle of Chardonnay awaiting your arrival. You are still planning to come over?"

Kaitlyn's heart fluttered at the thought. A bottle of wine and Brad. She couldn't think of a better combination. She glanced at the computer screen to keep tabs on how much time she had before the next song. "Of course. I wouldn't miss out on a good glass of wine."

"And good company, I hope?"

She laughed. "Well, if I have to be in good company to get my glass of wine . . ." She heard Brad sigh. She loved teasing him.

"I could just leave the bottle at the front desk. You could pick it up on your way home," he said. Kaitlyn imagined the feigned pout on his lips. Then she imagined kissing them and her heart skipped a beat.

"I should be there by one."

There was a moment of silence on the phone and Kaitlyn wondered if he'd hung up. He hadn't. "Did you get another letter?"

Kaitlyn wanted to ignore his question. She didn't want to worry him anymore than he already was. He'd offered a dozen times to come to the station after her show and escort her home. She refused again and again, claiming the impracticality of the idea made it a foolish gesture. She played down the importance of the letters and told him he needed his sleep more than she needed to be chauffeured to and from work. "Yeah," she finally said.

"Damn it, Kate," he said. "You've got to tell someone."

"Please, let's not talk about this now. I want to enjoy that bottle of wine . . . and I want to enjoy it with you."

He sighed. "Fine. But we need to talk. If not now, sometime this weekend."

He was frustrated. She could hear it in his voice. She couldn't keep putting off this discussion for much longer. "Okay . . . but not tonight. Let's talk about it later this weekend."

To her relief, he agreed.

"I'll head over as soon as I'm off the air," she said.

"Good. I'll be waiting." There was a click as Brad hung up.

Kaitlyn gazed out the window at the lights of the Philadelphia skyline; the swirling and flickering colors soothed her anxious mind. Every time she thought about how long she'd been dating Brad—two years—she was amazed. She'd made a conscious decision to steer clear of long-term relationships ever since high school. Ever since the Shallows.

Growing up, her dream was to have a family. Perhaps a couple kids. But after the Shallows, she decided—no, was compelled—to relinquish those dreams. Her guilt would not allow her to ever be happy. She touched her upper arm and traced the scar that ran down to her elbow. It had faded over time, but she could still feel it. She closed her eyes and could almost see the rusted nail that had caught her arm years ago. Like Hester, the mark served as Kaitlyn's scarlet letter, a constant reminder of her shame and regret.

Moving from city to city every year or so had never been conducive for romantic involvement. At least that was her excuse when any man wanted to get serious. When she'd returned to the Philadelphia area, Kaitlyn had intended to continue her self-imposed embargo on serious relationships. Casual dating with little-to-no attachment had been fine by her. Then she'd met Brad.

They'd met at a black-tie event for the Philadelphia Auto Show. Kaitlyn had been broadcasting live from the event at the convention center. During a break, she wandered over to a small display of classic motorcycles. While she admired a Harley-Davidson WLA from World War II, Brad stepped up to the velvet rope and stood a few feet from her. His gaze never wavered from the forest green motorcycle. He gestured with the champagne glass he was holding. "My grandfather rode one of those in the war."

Kaitlyn glanced at him and gave his black suit a quick once over. The sharp creases down his pant legs were immaculate, his white shirt looked overly starched, but the knot in his bow tie had come undone.

She laughed. "Let me fix that." She turned, then reached up and retied his bow tie. "That's better."

Brad, surprised by her sudden adjustment to his wardrobe, touched the straightened tie, then smiled. "Thanks. I'm rubbish at these things."

Kaitlyn returned his smile and extended her hand. "Kaitlyn Ashe."

He looked out of place and uncomfortable in his tux. Her forwardness seemed to catch him off guard. "Uh . . . What?"

"My name. And you are?"

He took hold of her hand and shook it. "Brad. Uh, Ludlow. Brad Ludlow."

She giggled. "Nice to meet you, Brad Uh Ludlow Brad Ludlow."

He stared at her for a long moment, a perplexing look in his eyes. "Uh . . ."

With another smile, she said, "It's a joke."

From there, the conversation became more relaxed. Brad explained that he'd come as part of an entourage from his law firm, one of the sponsors of the event. He wasn't a big gear head, but he was enjoying himself, nonetheless. Their small talk turned to flirting and continued through the remainder of the evening, interrupted often, whenever Kaitlyn needed to go back on the air. By the end of the night, they'd exchanged phone numbers with the prospect of having dinner sometime in the near future.

Kaitlyn's heartbeat quickened at the memory, and she calculated how long before she would be with him at his apartment. A couple hours at most. For the first time since high school, she was willing to admit that she was in love. She'd opened herself up to him, allowing Brad to become a part of her life in ways that she'd never allowed anyone else before . . . well, almost anyone. Brad made her happy . . . and made her forget. *Maybe he's the one.* Maybe there was a family in her future after all.

As the song ended, Kaitlyn played a station ID, and then leaned forward to answer another request line.

"Hello, WPLX," she said.

The voice was a distorted whisper. "Play REO Speedwagon for me. You know the song."

Kaitlyn jabbed at the button to hang up. She clenched her hands into fists as she turned to look out across the cityscape, but the mesmerizing view could no longer quell her growing hysteria.

5

I KICK at the pile of cigarette butts. How many are scattered on the concrete? There must be forty or more. Each bent and crushed, some even browning with age. It won't be long before the one dangling between my fingers joins the others. What time is it? 1:30 in the morning. Where is she?

The silence in the garage at this hour is eerie. It's no wonder Laura looks frightened every night when she emerges from the elevator. Even without my letters and calls, it can't be easy to make that short trek to her motorcycle without some anxiety. I felt it the first few times I stood here. But the angst of those early days is long gone.

The night air is crisp and reminds me of the first night I waited for her to emerge. When was that? Late December? I stood in below-freezing temperatures just to get a glimpse of her. The first time in over a decade. When she came out, I tried to call her name, but the words stuck in my throat. What could I say to her? "Remember me? Remember Jesse Riley?" No, that wouldn't do at all.

Another drag from my cigarette. The elevator doors slide open; the sound echoing through the otherwise oppressive silence. She hovers in the doorway. Her face is a bit pale tonight. What's that in her hand? Pepper spray? Ha! Like that's going to stop me. As exhausting as the past few months have been, there's something to be said for the genuine pleasure I've received watching her anxiety mount every night. Seeing the subtle changes in her as apprehension and fear slowly engulf her. To make this quick would be to shortchange justice.

She crosses to the motorcycle, mounts it, and drives off. I'm not far behind. She's probably heading to his apartment. It's a ten-minute drive at this hour.

———

SHE PARKS in the visitor's lot in front of the building and goes inside. I pull up to the curb across the street. It's one of those older apartment complexes that's been renovated with all the latest amenities. But the brick facade still gives it that old city look. An indoor pool. Fitness center. Private parking. Guarded entrance. And ridiculously high rent. Not the kind of place I'd be happy with or could afford.

The front desk security must know her. She cruises right on in. Through the glass doors, I can see her wave at the burly guard. She acts like she owns the place. She disappears in the elevator. I need another cigarette.

I remember the first time I realized who she was. It was seven, maybe eight months ago. I arrived on time for my therapy appointment, but Dr. Lloyd, as usual, was running behind. He was a decent enough psychologist. Just a bit disorganized. I've been seeing him for over twelve years. Damn, has it really been that long? He probably knows more about me than anyone else. He knows better than anyone how I feel about Laura.

While I was waiting, I picked up one of the obligatory magazines that were scattered throughout the waiting room. *Philadelphia Magazine*'s "Best of Philly" issue. Maybe a month or two old, but not so out of date that I'd read it already. I scanned the pages, reading the headlines but missing most of the words. I didn't even see the pictures. I mean I saw them, of course, but what they showed didn't register. But then that one picture caught my eyes. Tickled something in the back of my mind. Wisps of better, happier days. I wasn't sure at first, but something was so familiar about the face staring at me from the pages of Philadelphia magazine. Was it her? Could it be her? Different name, different hairstyle. But that smile. I couldn't mistake that smile. It had to be her. Ironic that she'd be called the "best of Philly."

If I could have spoken to her . . . just for a moment. To know that she hadn't forgotten. Maybe she was just as shattered as I was, just as broken. Perhaps we could share a drink and raise a glass in memory of what we lost. But . . .

It was hard to hide my excitement during my therapy session. Lloyd may not have it all together, but he's damn good at picking up changes in my behavior.

"You seem a bit agitated today," he said.

"No. What made you think that?"

He reclined back in his chair and looked at me across the small office. "Just a few small things. Your foot is working like a piston. You keep wringing your hands. And you've avoided my gaze for the past ten minutes."

I did some fast-talking and serious lying to avoid telling him what was setting out in his waiting room. I doubt he believed me, but he jotted a few notes on his notepad and let the matter drop. Forty minutes later, I was out of his office and racing out of the city. I now had a purpose. I needed to find out all I could about Laura Hobson.

That was the last time I saw him, or any other therapist. She is the only therapy I need.

I take another long drag on my cigarette and let the smoke drift out the partially open window. She'll be here for the rest of the night. No point in sticking around. Best to head home and grab a couple hours of sleep. I'll catch up with her in the morning.

Maybe this would be a good night to crank things up a notch. An escalation, as the profilers would call it. Perhaps a little surprise at home would do the trick. I need to make another visit there anyway. The bedroom's out of focus. Need to make a quick adjustment. Yes, a little surprise at home would be just the thing. Something to say I know where she lives. The clock on the car stereo says it's 1:45. I've got a few hours before daybreak. Plenty of time to run over to her house.

6

RODNEY SHAPIRO CURSED at the driver in front of him in the pale blue Ford Escort. His headache left him with a shortage of patience and an even shorter temper. With a hangover drumming on his temples, the last thing he wanted to do on a Saturday morning was get stuck behind a driver who actually obeyed the speed limit. Perhaps he should have tossed the teardrop light on the roof after all.

He tried to remember how much he'd had to drink the previous night . . . and how much money he'd lost. The monthly Friday night poker game with his old college buddies had gone on later than usual, and now he was paying the price. Thank god he wasn't headed to a murder scene. He was certain he'd not be able to handle a murder on a morning like this.

Thumping his thumbs on the steering wheel, Rodney tossed the previous night around in his head. He'd been on a roll. He remembered that much. A full house, a couple straights, and a straight flush had put him up early in the evening. But he couldn't quite remember where it had all gone wrong. He really needed to lay off the Jim Beam while playing poker. He must've lost at least a few hundred last night. *What was that quote from F. Scott Fitzgerald?* He smiled as he remembered. "First you take a drink, then the drink takes a drink, then the drink takes you." *Yep, that was just about how it happened.*

The morning's call from the dispatcher had jarred him awake. A possible stalking case. He'd been tempted to hang up and go back to bed. Couldn't uniform handle a stalker? A minor celebrity, the dispatcher had told him. Fifteen years on the force, and this is what it got him. Celebrity stalking cases. Probably some overreacting rich businessman whose donations have earned him the mayor's personal phone number. He knew the kind, demanding twenty-four-hour protection because they received some junk mail. What a way to spend the weekend, and with a hangover none the less.

There was a silver lining, he figured. At least he didn't work for the Philadelphia Police. With a serial killer on the loose, he heard Philly detectives were working around the clock with no end in sight. The search for the GBT Strangler headlined the news every night. The latest victim—a twenty-three-year-old gay man—had been found in an alley near Penns Landing yesterday morning. That was seven in the past five months. Rodney didn't envy Philly police. Not one bit.

To his relief, the Ford Escort turned onto a side road. Rodney pushed on the accelerator, and he stuck his hand out the window, about to wave his middle finger high in the air. But after a moment's thought, he drew his hand back in the car. It was the hangover talking, nothing more.

———

AS RODNEY DREW his car up to the house on Garnet Lane, he saw Detective Julie Lewis leaning against one of the two police cars parked in the driveway. She chatted with a young uniformed officer he didn't recognize. Must be one of the rookies. When he turned off his car, Julie nodded in his direction and the officer followed her gaze. They both laughed for a moment before she stepped away from the car and moved down the driveway toward him. He wondered what she'd said to make the rookie laugh. Probably told him about last year's Christmas party. God, will she never let him hear the end of that?

As he stepped from the car, he noticed the steaming Starbucks cup in her hand. He smiled. Perhaps he could forgive her just this once. As Julie approached, she extended the cup toward him. He took it in both hands and drew it up to his face. He sighed.

"I figured you'd need that," she said. "Last night was poker night, wasn't it?"

Rodney nodded, taking a long sip from the cup. One cream, two sugars. It was perfect. "Thanks for this. I really needed it."

"How much did you lose?"

He shook his head. "I'm not sure."

Julie laughed. "That bad, huh?"

As he took another sip, he gave Julie a quick once-over. Black knee-high boots, grey slacks, and navy blouse, all covered with a light windbreaker. Her short hair—dyed cranberry red—was immaculate. Even on a weekend call out, she managed to look professional. Particularly when compared to his Villanova sweatshirt, blue jeans, and Nike sneakers. At least he managed to remember his badge. It hung from his neck on a silver chain.

"Did you hear about GBT?"

"Yeah. That's the second one this month. He's upping his game." Rodney nodded toward the house. "What've we got?"

Julie pulled a notepad from her coat pocket. She flipped through a few pages until she found what she was looking for. "Victim's name is Kaitlyn Ashe. Have you heard of her?"

The name sounded familiar, but he didn't know why. He shrugged his shoulders. "Should I have?"

"WPLX. She does the evening show." She looked at him as if waiting for a sign of recognition. When none came, she added, "Love Songs at Ten?"

He shrugged again. "I got nothing."

Julie looked disappointed. He waited for the usual diatribe that followed any of his "geographic lapses." She was always critical of his lack of interest in the community around him.

"How can you have lived here for twenty-five years and not know the area radio stations?"

"I don't listen to the radio."

"I know, you've said. You don't listen to the radio. You barely watch TV. What the hell do you do in your spare time?"

"Lose money at poker." He took another sip from his coffee. "Can we get back to Ms. Ashe?"

She looked back down at her notepad. "Kaitlyn Ashe came home this morning to find a threatening letter taped to her front door."

Draining the remaining coffee from his cup, Rodney gestured toward the house. "One letter? One letter does not a stalker make."

Julie raised an eyebrow. "Sounds like Yoda."

"Aristotle."

She placed a hand on her hip, tilting her head to the side. "What the hell do you know about Aristotle?"

Rodney only grinned. They'd worked together for two years, but there was plenty she didn't know about him. He'd always been guarded when it came to the details of his personal life. Over time, she'd picked up bits and pieces—like the poker game—but it was rare that his personal and professional lives ever crossed paths. It was the way he liked it.

Rodney rubbed his cheek and felt the roughness of day-old stubble. He could only imagine what he must look like. He'd rolled out of bed, thrown on some clothes, and headed out the door, never even stopping to comb his hair. At least the coffee took the edge off the headache. He glanced at Julie. "You got a Tic Tac? My breath's probably strong enough to cut through bank vaults."

She pulled a box of mints from her pocket, dumping a few into his outstretched hand. "The letter consisted of magazine clippings pasted on a sheet of paper. Uniform bagged and tagged it before I got here."

"You spoken to her yet?"

She shook her head. "Not yet. I just arrived a few minutes before you."

He ran his hand through his hair. "Then let's go speak to Ms. Ashe."

———

THE YOUNG WOMAN seated on the beige leather sofa was leaning forward, her head bowed, and hands folded between her knees. Her long auburn hair fell forward and concealed her face. Rodney nodded to the man seated next to her. His dark hair was disheveled, looking as if he'd just rolled out of bed. *God, I hope mine doesn't look that bad.*

When the young woman lifted her head, he was momentarily taken aback. The hair, the face. She looked a lot like Carol. The auburn hair was longer than his daughter's, and the face was filled out a little more. The woman was older, but the distinct resemblance was uncanny. She could be Carol's doppelgänger. Rodney drew in a deep breath. How long had it been since he'd visited her? A year, maybe two?

The young woman's eyes were bloodshot and her cheeks blotchy. She'd been crying. Pushing the hair back from her face, she tried to smile, but he could tell it was half-hearted. She began to rise to her feet, but he quickly waved for her to remain seated. Rodney's gaze fell on the third person in the room. Craig Peterson, a uniformed officer, stood in the far corner. Rodney gave a brief wave of his hand to Peterson, and then approached the couple on the sofa.

"I'm Detective Rodney Shapiro from the Lower Merion Township police," he said. Gesturing behind him, he added, "And this is Detective Julie Lewis."

Julie drew up beside him, nodding toward the couple. The man sitting on the sofa ran a hand through his hair, then said, "Brad Ludlow. This is my girlfriend, Kaitlyn Ashe. Thanks for coming."

As Rodney lowered himself onto the leather love seat across from the couple, he noticed Brad reach over to take hold of Kaitlyn's hand. The loving grasp of reassurance. He'd seen it so many times between loved ones. A quick squeeze to bolster the courage of a grieving or injured friend or family member. He'd often wondered if it really worked.

"Ms. Ashe. Can you tell me what happened? How you found the letter?" he said.

Kaitlyn's gaze drifted from him to Julie, where it lingered for a long moment. "I was staying at Brad's place last night."

"I have an apartment in downtown Philly," Brad added.

"We were sharing a bottle of wine to unwind—it was anti-dedication night," Kaitlyn said.

Rodney closed his eyes for a moment. *Maybe the coffee's worn off.* He was already lost in the conversation. Maybe Julie was right. He needed to pay more attention to the community around him. "Anti-dedication?"

Julie leaned over his shoulder. "She plays a song that's basically the opposite of a love song, and people can call in their dedications for it."

"I only do it on Friday nights." Kaitlyn took a longer-than-usual look at Julie, perhaps out of appreciation that, unlike him, she knew of her work. "Sorry, have we met before?"

"No," Julie said, shaking her head. "I don't think so."

Rodney cleared his throat. "Can we get back to the letter? You said you stayed in Philly last night."

Kaitlyn turned toward him. "That's right. This morning, I drove home to find a letter taped to my door."

Her gaze locked on his. Rodney was unable to shake her singular likeness to his daughter. This was how he'd hoped his daughter would've looked in ten years, but after his last visit to see Carol, he'd given up on that dream. "What time did you leave Brad's apartment?"

"We had breakfast around nine, and she left close to ten," Brad said.

Rodney gave the man a half-smile. He couldn't stand loved ones who answered questions for the victim. Too controlling in his mind. *Have to be patient*, he thought. *I'm sure he means well.*

"I got back here about ten-thirty. I knew what it was as soon as I saw it on the door," said Kaitlyn.

"She called me in a panic," Brad said. "I rushed over immediately."

Rodney turned her words over in his head. Something she'd just said had caught his attention. "How did you know?"

Kaitlyn looked puzzled for a moment. "What?"

"You said you knew right away what it was," Rodney said. "How did you know?"

"There've been other letters."

7

RODNEY WATCHED the silver BMW as it backed out of the driveway, moved along Garnet Drive, and then turned onto Belmont Avenue. As the car sped off, he caught a brief wave from Brad. Kaitlyn slouched in the passenger seat, looking despondent. Her fidgeting throughout their interview revealed how uncomfortable she was with his questioning. She was visibly shaken by recent events. Spending the rest of the weekend at Brad's apartment had seemed to come as a welcome suggestion. Rodney had waited with the others in the living room while Kaitlyn went upstairs to pack a few things in an overnight bag.

While she was upstairs, he studied the bookshelves in the living room. He smiled as his eyes scanned the titles. *War and Peace. Anna Karenina.* Milton's *Paradise Lost. Pride and Prejudice.* This was where the resemblance between Kaitlyn and his daughter ended. Carol could never stand the classics. He shook his head slowly. The last time he'd seen her, Carol had lost a lot of weight. She'd looked bony and emaciated. Her once auburn hair had been dyed jet black and looked like it hadn't been washed in days. The red marks on her arm had been a dead giveaway. She was on drugs, he was sure. He had resolved to talk to the warden and bring this to his attention, knowing full well that drugs seemed even easier to get and harder to combat inside than on the street. That last meeting hadn't gone well, with his daughter seeming more resentful than ever. She'd spewed a litany of scornful words across the cold, metal table while he sat silent, feeling her every vicious word like a dagger to the heart. When Carol was escorted back to her cell, he could do nothing but remain motionless and watch her vanish back into the prison.

Rodney glanced at his watch. 2:35. He leaned against his car and folded his arms. "What do you think?"

Julie stood before him, gazing over the pages of her notepad. They'd spent two hours talking to Brad and Kaitlyn. It hadn't been anywhere near as fruitful as he would have liked it to be.

"Not a lot to go on," Julie said.

"I know. Eight other letters," he said. "All in the trash. If forensics can't find a fingerprint on this latest one, we'll have damn near nothing to work with."

"Since the other seven were delivered to the radio station, should I liaise with Philly police to see what they can do?"

Rodney nodded. "Talk to them. I doubt there'll be much they can do unless things escalate further. They've got enough going on with the GBT Strangler running amok in the city."

Julie flipped to another notepad page. "What about getting a trace set up on the request lines? Just in case this creep calls in again."

Rodney stroked his chin for a moment, and then shook his head. "Beside the fact that the radio station is out of our jurisdiction, we'll be hard pressed to get permission to do that. Especially since there's only been one call."

Nine letters in total. All of them identical in structure. Magazine clippings pasted on eight and a half by eleven sheets of paper. Until this latest one, the message had always been the same. A request to play an REO Speedwagon song, but never stating which one. Creating a letter in that fashion seemed a bit too time consuming to Rodney. Why go through all the trouble? And what was up with that signature? The Shallows?

Kaitlyn had explained that the first letter arrived over a month ago, with a new one arriving each consecutive Friday since. The frequency accelerated this past week with one letter every day in her mailbox at the radio station.

"Why didn't you report this to someone sooner?" he'd asked.

"I didn't take it seriously. In my line of work, we get the occasional enthusiastic fan." She made air quotes with her fingers for the word "enthusiastic."

Rodney narrowed his eyes. Her rationale was naive, and a bit far-fetched. "Enthusiastic fan?"

Kaitlyn looked down at the floor. "At first, it seemed innocent enough. Just someone playing a prank. I started to get worried this week." She glanced at Brad. "We talked last night. I'd decided to speak to the police on Monday."

"And the letter you received yesterday? Where is that?"

"Gone, just like the others."

Rodney had cringed when she said it. That was vital evidence lost forever. Forensics might be able to pull something from the most recent letter, but they'd have stood a better chance if they had more to work with. What about those magazine clippings? It sounded more like a bad cliché. Why not print a letter from a computer? Surely that would be easier.

"What about the boyfriend?" Julie asked, snapping his thoughts back to the present.

Rodney remained silent for a moment. Brad Ludlow looked genuine enough, but it wouldn't have been the first time a man played head games with his girlfriend. "Not sure yet. We've got to play it cool with him. He'll know the law better than we do. Including every loophole. If it is him, I don't want him getting away because of some technicality."

"He's a business attorney, not a trial lawyer."

"Doesn't matter," he said. "Let's run a check on both of them. Him in particular. I doubt that it will turn up anything, but you never know."

While Julie scribbled in her notepad, Rodney acknowledged

his nagging misgivings about his conversation with Kaitlyn. There'd been a reluctance in her answers that he couldn't explain.

"These letters keep referring to a song, as if you know what it is. Any idea why?" he had asked.

Kaitlyn turned her gaze away from him to study the spines of the books on the shelf along the far wall. "No, I don't know why."

He sighed. "What about from your past? Anything that you can think of that might even remotely involve REO Speedwagon?"

She rose from the sofa, crossed to the bow window and looked out over the front yard. She looked at her hands, seeming preoccupied with her fingernails. "I can't . . ." She slid her hands into her back pockets and stared out at the street. "There's nothing that I can think of."

"Nothing at all? Think carefully. Even the smallest detail could help us."

With her gaze turned toward the window, Kaitlyn appeared reticent, either unable or unwilling to speak. Rodney studied her carefully, noting the slight tremor in her arms. He was struck by the similarity between this moment and the moment when he'd confronted his daughter about the accident. Carol had avoided eye contact as well.

"Detective, I'm sure she'd tell you if she knew what this was about," said Brad. "She wants to get to the bottom of this as much as you do."

Spoken like an attorney.

There was something off with Kaitlyn's behavior. She'd been visibly upset when he'd arrived, but by the time she had left with her boyfriend, Kaitlyn had become resolute that it was nothing more than a harmless prank. She knew more about this than she was letting on. He was certain of it.

"Where's that letter?" he said to Julie.

She reached into the leather bag at her feet. "I've got it here." She handed him a clear plastic bag, the letter sealed inside.

Rodney held it before him, gazing at the sheet of paper. At first glance, the placement of the magazine clippings appeared to be random. Small lettering—perhaps from within an article—intermixed with larger letters from headlines and article titles. It was almost juvenile. He reread the text, finding that the message made no more sense to him now than it did the first time he read it.

Can't remember the song? You'll pay for your forgetfulness.
The Shallows holds no more love for you.

As he reread the words, Rodney pressed his tongue to the roof of his mouth, making a clicking noise. He didn't need to look at Julie to know that she'd be cringing. She hated when he did that. He leaned toward her and pointed at the letter. "The Shallows must be a person or a place. Look at the other words. Each is its own clipping. But, the Shallows, that's pieced together from multiple clippings, like he couldn't find it on its own."

Julie nodded. "Not surprising. It's not a word you see often in magazines." She smiled. "Not that you'd know."

He handed the plastic-wrapped letter back to her. "See if forensics can tell us what magazines the clippings came from. I doubt it will help us, but you never know." Rodney thought once again about Kaitlyn Ashe. "She knows more than she's telling us."

Julie flipped her notepad closed, slipping it into her pocket. "You going to the station?"

"Eventually. I missed breakfast and lunch. I've got to grab something to eat. I'll meet you there in an hour."

Julie picked up her leather bag and crossed the street, heading for her blue Volkswagen parked along the opposite curb. As he watched her pull away, Rodney folded his arms, leaning back against his car. His eyes roamed up and down the street. Upscale homes. Middle-class families enjoying life in the suburbs. A nice, quiet neighborhood. Why did he feel like that was about to all change?

8

BRAD HELD the door for Kaitlyn and ushered her into O'Toole's Brew Pub. A Saturday night crowd crammed into the Walnut Street taproom. The bar was packed to capacity, every table occupied. An inverted cone-shaped light hung over each booth, illuminating the occupants in the otherwise gloomy light of the pub. Conversations blended into a cacophony of voices that practically drowned out the music from the jukebox. Despite the din, Kaitlyn picked up the familiar melody of the Gin Blossoms and smiled. Someone had good taste in music. The hostess by the door waved, then gestured toward the back of the bar. Kaitlyn grabbed Brad's hand and weaved her way through the crowd.

A round of drinks was already on the table when they approached the three-square tables that had been pushed together to make room for the gang. Sammy leapt from her seat and threw her arms around Kaitlyn in a tight embrace.

"You're late," she said. "I was startin' to think you weren't comin'." Sammy released Kaitlyn and moved toward Brad, wrapping her arms around his neck. "How goes it, Legal Eagle?"

He gave her a tentative pat on the back. "I'm good."

Kaitlyn heard the awkwardness in his voice and saw the forced familiarity of his gesture. Brad wasn't yet comfortable with

Sammy's forthrightness. "You'll get used to it," she'd told him the last time they'd been out together. Kaitlyn remembered when they first started dating, how long it took him to get comfortable with Kaitlyn herself. Sammy was twice as outgoing.

Scott Mackay, who sat across the table, lifted a Corona bottle and used it to point toward two empty chairs at the table. His salt-and-pepper, shoulder-length hair was pulled back in a ponytail. There was a trace of fatherly affection in his smile and a sparkle in his eyes. The fifty-two-year-old program director had been like a father to her from the first day she started working at WPLX. He took her under his wing and was just as responsible for her success in Philadelphia as she was. Scott's wife Amanda sat beside him and gave a vehement wave. Kaitlyn smiled in return and took a seat at the table next to Brad.

Kevin O'Neill, who was sitting across the table, stared at her long enough to make Kaitlyn notice.

"What?" she asked.

"What're you drinking?"

"White wine," she said, slightly irritated that Kevin seemed to suggest she couldn't order for herself.

"I'll have what he's having." Brad pointed at Scott, but Kevin didn't seem to acknowledge Brad's order and kept his gaze on her.

"White wine," Kevin said, then slowly turned toward Brad. "And a Corona. Coming right up." Kevin rose from the table and walked to the bar.

Kaitlyn shook her head and admonished herself silently not to take out her frazzled state on an innocent colleague. It wasn't Kevin's fault that her equilibrium had vanished.

"Where's Zeek?" she asked, ready to enjoy the moment.

Sammy sipped from her Guinness, then said, "Workin'."

"No Justin?"

Sammy shrugged. "Said he was coming."

An arm flashed in front of Kaitlyn's face and set a wine glass down before her. Kevin's fingers brushed across her shoulder as he handed a Corona to Brad. She flinched at his touch. Kevin didn't

seem to notice and returned to his seat with a fresh Bud Light of
his own.

Scott raised his bottle. "Here's to the end of another week."

The small group chatted, laughed, and drank. They ordered
appetizers and Kaitlyn relaxed, pushing thoughts about the mysterious letters into the recesses of her mind. These biweekly get-
togethers were a longstanding tradition among the station staff, an
open invitation to anyone who wanted to show up. Attendance
often varied, sometimes with a large contingent from the sales staff
as well as the on-air DJs making an appearance. But, more often
than not, it was the DJs who could be considered "regulars."

Kaitlyn enjoyed nights like this. The people around the table
were the closest thing she had to friends. It had been the same at
every radio station where she worked. Broadcasting was a close-
knit community, because the odd working hours often prohibited
what many would consider a normal social life. The sense of family
that arose among station staff frequently took the place of friend-
ships outside of work. This was Kaitlyn's comfort zone. Each
person at the table was dear to her in some way.

It was shortly after ten when Justin Kace wandered up to the
table. With hands buried deep in the pockets of his jeans, he
hunched forward over the table, nodding a greeting to everyone.
His bare forearms were long and bony. A faded Van Halen T-shirt
hung off his pointed shoulders and draped down over his scrawny
body.

"Hey all, sup?" he said.

"About time," Kevin said, glancing at his watch. "Who was
she?"

Justin straddled the nearest chair, rested his arms on the back.
"What're you on about?"

"The only time you're late for something is when a woman's
involved."

Justin pushed a few stray strands of jet-black hair back from his
face. "Why you gotta get on my case?" He smiled, then looked
around the table. "No Holy Roller Tyler again?"

Kevin laughed. "Nope. Probably doesn't want to run the risk that he might start having fun in a bar."

Scott frowned and shook his head. "Come on, guys. Lay off him." His tone was very much that of a parent scolding a child.

"Whatever." Justin gave a wave to dismiss the rebuke. "How does one get a drink around here?"

Kevin stood and said, "I'll get it. What're you having?"

"Jack and Coke on the rocks."

When Kevin returned with the drink, Justin raised the glass. "Ah, the elixir of life."

As the group fell back into friendly banter, Kaitlyn sipped her wine and allowed her mind to drift. Discussions flew back and forth across the table. Justin talked more with his hands than in words as he recounted some amusing childhood story to Scott. Amanda laughed as Sammy mimicked the reaction Dale Jamison—the station's sales manager—had to the news that he was being moved to a smaller office to make room for a new production studio. Brad drank in the conversations in silence, his arm wrapped around the back of Kaitlyn's chair. Perhaps it was the camaraderie or maybe just the wine, but Kaitlyn felt a warm, comforting sense of calm wash over her. No past to worry about. No future to fret over. Just another Saturday night with a few drinks and good friends.

When the first few chords of the next song reached her ears, she gasped. The slow, melodic piano cut through the cacophony in the bar. Each note drove a dagger of fear into her heart. Someone was playing REO Speedwagon on the jukebox.

She glanced across the table and caught Kevin staring in her direction. His eyes were piercing and dark. He had a half-smile and winked at her as he placed his beer bottle to his lips to take a drink. A chill crept down her spine. He turned his gaze away from her, but she couldn't help but feel as if he were still watching her from the corner of his eye.

She reached for Brad's hand. He was laughing along with the others over some joke Scott had just told. Kaitlyn had missed it.

She looked over her shoulder, scanning the faces of those nearby. Perhaps she would recognize someone. No one was paying her the least bit of attention. She glanced back across the table. Kevin was talking, but she didn't hear his words. All she heard was the song, sharp and clear in her head.

As the chorus played over the speakers, a chaotic flood of images sent her head spinning. Splashing in the water. Jesse's touch. His lips on hers. A cuddle by the bonfire. Then, darker images. A tight grip on her arm. A slap across the face. Jesse's face disappearing . . .

Kaitlyn shuddered. Her hands, resting in her lap, trembled. Someone was watching her. It felt as if a set of eyes was boring into the back of her head. Another quick glance behind her revealed nothing out of the ordinary. It was more than she could stand.

She leaned toward Brad. "I'm not feeling well. Do you mind if we leave?"

He looked at her, deep concern in his eyes. "You okay?"

As the chorus repeated, she reached over and took his hand. "I just want to go."

9

SHE SCREAMED. Flailing her arms, Kaitlyn struggled to free herself from the hands that grasped her shoulders. Her eyes darted from side to side, peering around the dark room. She fought for air as she wrestled with the tangle of sheets around her body. She bolted upright and tried to clamber from the bed. Two hands gripped her shoulders, pulling her back.

"Kaitlyn. Wake up," she heard from behind her. "It's just a nightmare."

She continued to struggle, desperate to pry herself free.

"Kaitlyn!" The voice sounded more urgent this time, more insistent. "Wake up!"

Closing her eyes, she leaned forward and lowered her face into her palms. Was it another nightmare or was it real? It was becoming harder to tell. The water, the darkness. The lines between reality and fantasy blurred. Then, brushing her hair back from her face, she opened her eyes. A light clicked on behind her, illuminating the room in a faint glow. Brad's bedroom. She drew in a deep breath. Brad sat in the middle of the bed, staring at her. His furrowed forehead was creased with shadows from the bedside lamp.

"Babe, you okay?"

Kaitlyn didn't speak. Her mind still fought with the lingering images of dark icy waters and grey hands clawing at her legs. She was chilled by the frigid sweat that had soaked into her pink T-shirt. When Brad touched her shoulder, she recoiled.

"Relax. You're safe," he said.

She turned away from him and stared into the corner, watching the light dance with the darkness, forming intricate silhouettes of indeterminate shape. Did one of the shadows look like a hand reaching toward her? Kaitlyn touched the back of her neck. The skin was cold and clammy. "What time is it?"

"3:30."

Kaitlyn sighed, still watching the shadows. "Sorry. I didn't mean to wake you."

Brad reached for her. This time, she didn't flinch. "Must have been some nightmare," he said. "You were screaming your head off."

She reclined into his arms and felt the warmth of his embrace. But it didn't do much to relieve her trembling. "Hold me."

"We need to talk about this."

She looked away. Talking would only mean having to either lie to him or tell him the truth. She didn't want to do either at the moment. "There's nothing to talk about." They'd had this argument several times before. *Not tonight. Please, not tonight.*

"There is something to talk about." The irritation in his voice was unmistakable. "I can't help you if you won't tell me what these letters are about."

"They're nothing." She stared across the bedroom, watching the shadows in the far corner. Anything to keep from looking him in the eye.

"Kaitlyn . . ."

She spun around to face him, but kept her eyes looking down. "Can't you believe me? Just let me deal with this in my own way? Is that too hard for you?" The outburst surprised her. She hadn't intended to snap at him.

Brad was silent for a moment. "I'm trying to help."

She leaned forward and took his hand. "Just hold me tight."

As his arms tightened around her, Kaitlyn closed her eyes and sank deeper into his embrace. The nightmare was still vivid in the recesses of her mind. Murky water around her. A small point of light above her that she had so desperately tried to reach. Cold hands held her back. She'd kicked her legs, trying to free herself. But, as soon as she freed herself from the grip of one hand, another would find a hold and drag her deeper into the water.

Just let me deal with this in my own way. Her own words trickled back to her. No, not her own words. Jesse's words. Fragments from the past. Words spoken to her in anger only days before his death. She'd only been concerned about his health, but he'd snapped at her. Frightened her.

Feeling Brad's fingers stroking her hair, Kaitlyn opened her eyes and looked up into his concerned face. He gave her a reassuring smile, but it did little to ease her fear. She looked into his eyes and wished that she could get lost in the deep blue pools. But no sooner had the thought entered her mind than she was reminded of the waters that had engulfed her in the nightmare. She looked away, shuddering.

"Babe?" he said.

"I'll be okay." She fought back the tears. "Just hold me."

———

KAITLYN RESTED her elbows on the round table, holding an aimless gaze across the small kitchen in Brad's apartment. With her chin in her cupped hands, she allowed her eyes to close. Breathing deeply, she smelled the frying bacon. Brad was busy in the kitchen, fixing her an omelet for breakfast. She heard him sniff. The onions he was chopping must have gotten the better of him.

She was grateful. Brad had held her in his arms until she finally drifted off. Her slumber for the rest of the night, although fitful, had been uninterrupted.

When she awakened at 8:30, he was already awake, sitting in

the bed beside her. He gently stroked her hair and Kaitlyn rolled over to smile at him. His eyes were tight and worried.

"Did you sleep better?" he asked.

"How could I not, with you here?"

He leaned over, kissing her on the forehead. "How about breakfast?"

As Brad diced a tomato, Kaitlyn thought about the letter she'd found on her door the previous morning. It must have been what had triggered the nightmare. Or perhaps the REO Speedwagon song at the bar. It'd been almost ten years since she'd had any of those dreams and now, with the arrival of the letters, they were frequent and getting worse progressively. Why did whoever wrote these letters have to dredge up the past? Didn't Jesse deserve to rest in peace?

Her mind drifted to an autumn evening years before. She recalled Jesse chasing her through the cornfield maze his father created in the field on the farm. She giggled and frolicked through the maze, and occasionally glanced to see if he was behind her. Kaitlyn turned a corner and raced between the walls of brown corn stalks.

"Catch me if you can," she shouted.

A fun game of hide-and-seek with her boyfriend. What more could a sixteen-year-old girl ask for? It was a time of innocence, of young love, without a care in the world. The aging corn stalks rustled as she rushed along the narrow path; her elbows grazed the wilting, brown leaves. She rounded another corner and halted soon after at a dead-end. She'd have to double back. Listening for a moment, Kaitlyn tried to determine where Jesse was in the maze. The only sound to reach her was a flock of geese overhead, probably heading south for the winter. She was about to head back along the path when a hand reached out and gripped her arm. She screamed and spun around in time to find Jesse push through the wall of corn stalks.

"Gotcha," he said.

"Not fair! You cheated!"

Jesse pulled her close, smiled, and then kissed her.

The sizzle of onions in the pan drew her attention back to the kitchen. Her gaze lingered on Brad. He didn't know about the Shallows, but she knew it wouldn't be long before he asked. Especially if more letters arrived. She'd never intended to hide anything from him. The topic simply had never come up until now, and she'd seen no reason to bring it up herself. What happened at the Shallows was ancient history, and she wanted to keep it that way.

Brad approached the table, carrying two plates. He set one down before her. The omelet was cooked to perfection. The bacon was crisp. The aroma tantalized her senses. Kaitlyn grinned at him, wondering for a moment what she'd done to deserve his affections. "You spoil me."

"Yes, I do," Brad said. "And I'm going to keep on spoiling you."

He took a seat across the table from her. He toyed with his own omelet, pushing a piece around the edge of the plate. Kaitlyn felt his eyes on her, watching as she ate. She felt her cheeks flush red. Brad must have known how embarrassed she was, because he laughed when she glanced up at him.

"What?" she asked.

"Can't I look endearingly at the woman I love?"

"No." Kaitlyn shook her head and laughed. "Not when I'm eating."

His eyes held her in a contemplative stare. "Do you want to talk about it?"

Kaitlyn pretended that she didn't hear the question and continued to eat, but when she glanced up, he was still staring at her.

"There's nothing to talk about," she said.

"You've been having nightmares for a few weeks, ever since you got the first letter."

Damn, he noticed. She shook her head. "That can't be true." She knew he was right.

"I wish you'd tell me what this is all about. I feel helpless watching you go through this alone."

She ignored his remark and picked at her food. *How would he react if he knew the truth?* She measured her fear of losing him against the weight of her own shame. For all his love and compassion, would he truly understand if she told him the truth?

"I understand if you don't want to talk about it," he said, looking down at his plate. "Just remember, I'm here when you're ready."

Her guilt weighed heavy as Kaitlyn tried to shrug off his concern. She made no response other than a brief nod. He continued to pick at his food, not showing much interest in what was on his plate. He was hurt by her reluctance to talk; she could tell. They'd both been happy, but the letters—and now the nightmares—were stealing that happiness away. She didn't want to lose that happiness. She didn't want to lose Brad.

"I hate seeing you like this." He set the fork down on the table. "You seem so sad. I wish there was something I could do."

Kaitlyn couldn't bear to look in his eyes. "Just a bad night," she said, her eyes glued to the plate. "I'll be fine."

"Are you sure? This business is more than just one bad night."

She nodded and picked at her omelet, taking small bites despite not having an appetite. Silence fell over the table.

Then, with sudden determination, Brad rose from the table, and walked from the kitchen.

"Where are you going?" she asked.

"I'll be back in a sec."

Kaitlyn set the fork down on the edge of her plate. Any other day, she would have devoured the omelet. Brad's culinary skills notwithstanding, she had no stomach for food at the moment. She looked across at Brad's empty chair, wondering why he rushed from the room. With arms crossed tight over her chest, she leaned back. Was it possible he knew the truth about her past? Could this be the moment he brought forth a record of all her sins and demanded an explanation?

The Shallows. What happened there had been buried so deep in her memory for so many years that it had felt like someone else's memory. But she couldn't push it away any longer, and it wasn't fair to keep it from Brad. He deserved to know the truth. *What would he think? What would he say? Would he understand why she did what she did?* With a resolute air, Kaitlyn placed her fork down, crossed her arms, and leaned back in the chair. *It's time to tell Brad. When he comes back in the room*, she decided, *I'll tell him everything*.

Brad returned to the kitchen. He stood before the table, his hands behind his back. She recognized the mischievous smile on his face. He was up to something. She rested her arms on the table and raised her eyebrows. "What's going on?"

"I hope this will cheer you up," he said. "I was going to wait until our Pocono getaway next weekend, but . . . well, now is as good a time as any."

Brad dropped to one knee before her, bringing his hands out from behind his back. Kaitlyn gasped when she saw the velvet-covered ring box in his hand. Her cheeks felt warm and flush. She struggled to catch her breath. Her mouth gaped open; her hands jumped to cover it. "Oh my god. Oh my god. Oh my god."

Brad held the ring box toward her. "Kaitlyn Ashe. Will you marry me?"

She wanted to scream, wanted to fall into his arms. She opened her mouth, and then closed it, struggling to find the words to answer. The thumping of her heart was loud, echoing in her ears. *Can he hear it?* He'd flipped the lid open on the ring box. Her eyes caught the dazzle of the large diamond, and the smaller ones that encircled it, atop the ring; the sparkle was brilliant and mesmerizing. She looked from the ring to him, and locked eyes with his. His face beamed with expectation, and she realized that she hadn't answered him yet.

"Yes," she shouted. "Of course, I will."

Removing the ring from the box, he slipped it onto Kaitlyn's finger. She fell forward into his arms, bowling him over onto the floor. He drew her down, kissing her long and hard. The floor was cold and hard on her knees, but she didn't care. When their lips parted, she held up her hand to gaze at the ring.

"It's beautiful," she said.

"So are you," he said, pulling her close to kiss her again. Kaitlyn gave in to the moment's passion, and the Shallows withdrew to the edge of her conscious thoughts. She'd tell him another day.

10

RODNEY CARRIED the bulky leather-bound book across the room and settled into the beige Lazy Boy in the far corner. He set the book on his lap, glancing at the gold lettering on the cover. *A History of Western Philosophy*. He'd been meaning to read the Bertrand Russell book for more than a year, but it sat untouched on his shelf. He opened the book, catching a faint whiff of dust from the yellowing pages. The first edition set him back several hundred dollars, but Rodney was certain it would be worth it.

He'd been reading for twenty minutes when his mobile phone rang. Setting the book down on the table beside the recliner, he rose from the chair and crossed the room to answer the phone.

"Rod, it's Julie."

Rodney smiled, knowing this wouldn't be a social call. Julie never called just to chat. Her calls were always related to an ongoing investigation. *Did she ever take a day off?*

"What've you got?" he said.

"Did you get the email I sent you?"

He shook his head. This was typical of her. "When did you send it?"

"An hour ago."

Rodney frowned and remained silent for a moment. This line

of conversation was far too familiar. He'd tried time and again to break her of the assumption that he was waiting with bated breath for her next email. Yet she persisted with calling him when she didn't receive a response within what she perceived as an acceptable amount of time. "No. Didn't see it," he said. "Julie, it's Sunday. What are you doing?"

"Following up on a couple things with the Ashe case. I can wait while you check your email."

He bowed his head, rubbing the forehead with his fingers. "What's so important that it can't wait until tomorrow morning?"

"I ran that background check on Kaitlyn Ashe. It came back with some interesting results."

Rodney sighed, glancing back at his book. So much for spending the afternoon enthralled in Western Philosophy. "Hang on, give me a second to get to my laptop."

It took him five minutes to get logged in to his email, and another two to find the one Julie had sent him. He opened the attachment and scanned the screen. "Looks clean to me."

"Do the math. She told us she was thirty-two, but her records stretch back only fourteen years."

Rodney chewed his lip as he reread the document on the screen. "Could be a glitch."

"I ran the check three times."

He frowned. It was just like Julie to find anomalies where there likely were none. That was part of what made her such a good detective. "Maybe she kept her nose clean when she was a kid. Not everyone comes under the attention of the police when they're young."

"That's what I wondered at first," she said.

Rodney knew what was coming next. Not satisfied with what she found, he knew Julie would have continued to probe until she could either reconcile the so-perceived discrepancy or found some new bit of information. He wondered which it would be.

"Kaitlyn Ashe isn't her birth name," Julie said. "She was born Laura Hobson. Changed her name when she turned eighteen."

"So?"

"So, she must have changed her name for a reason."

Rodney stepped away from his laptop and crossed the living room to stare out the front window of his townhouse. The leaves were budding on the young oak tree he'd planted five years ago. He might need to trim the branches a bit. "Again, so? Most people have a reason for changing their name. Otherwise, why bother?"

"Exactly."

Rodney didn't respond. He knew there was more. Best to let her weave together her conspiracy before commenting. He'd learned that it was better that way. Easier for everyone involved.

"Once I found her birth name, I dug a little deeper," she said. "Something of interest came up for Laura Hobson."

Rodney looked at his front yard. The grass was waking from its winter hibernation. He'd have to get out the lawnmower soon, probably next weekend. "What did you find?"

"There was an incident in New Jersey. Kaitlyn Ashe, aka Laura Hobson, was involved. I sent you the police report. It's from a department in New Jersey. Real rural area. The report wasn't even in their computer. They had to dig it out of the back of a file cabinet somewhere."

Rodney wondered what she must have told them to get an officer to dig through some old storage room on a weekend. They'd never do it on a Sunday for a simple stalking case. Probably told them it was a murder inquiry. "Okay. I'll give it a read. Anything else?"

"What? Uh, no. I guess not."

He heard the disappointment in her voice. He knew she'd have preferred that he read it while she was on the phone. But Rodney didn't feel like listening to her running commentary. His Saturday had been disrupted by this case. He didn't want to lose his Sunday too.

"Right. Then I'll see you tomorrow," he said. "Thanks for calling."

After they'd hung up, he shook his head and laughed. For all her faults, Julie was a good detective. Very thorough, but very headstrong. Once she found a loose thread, she would track it to its end, no matter how many obstacles stood in her way. Rodney had a great deal of respect for her, even if he didn't often show it.

As he moved back toward the Lazy Boy, he stopped by the bookshelf, reaching for a small, framed photograph. He stared at the photo's subject, a young auburn-haired girl. Carol had been sixteen when it was taken. Young and vivacious. A brilliant student with a great future ahead of her. Two years later, she'd stood before a judge accused of a long list of charges, including manslaughter. He wondered where he'd gone wrong.

Rodney recalled the morning he'd found the front-end damage on her Nissan Sentra. She'd been vehement in her denials, claiming to not know anything about it. Later that day, he heard about the mother and daughter killed in a hit-and-run the previous night. His heart was broken as he rushed home from the police station to confront Carol.

His daughter admitted to doing shots during a party at a friend's house. She barely remembered getting behind the wheel or driving home. Carol, as well as his wife Stephanie, had begged him to turn a blind eye, but Rodney had no choice. By the late afternoon, the police arrived to tow the car and arrest his daughter. She'd only turned eighteen two months before.

Placing the photo back on the shelf, he moved back to his Lazy Boy and picked up the book he'd started earlier. But, as Rodney tried to settle back into reading, he couldn't shake his curiosity over what Julie had found. He turned the page, trying to focus on the book, but his gaze drifted back toward his open laptop. He reread the page from the top, attempting to digest Russell's commentary on Plato, but the words ran together. His eyes returned to the top of the page for a third read.

"Damn," he muttered, slamming the book closed and rising from the chair.

He opened the police report and began to read. The sixteen-year-old report came from the Woolwich Township Police Department. He'd never heard of the township but figured it must be somewhere in rural southern New Jersey. Julie dug pretty damn deep for this one. He read every word of the report, and then read it again just to be sure he understood the incident.

Stepping away from the laptop, he wandered around the room, past the bookcase on the far wall. He picked up the small ceramic bust of Aristotle from the upper shelf. He looked down at the lifeless eyes, and carried the bust with him as he drifted aimlessly around the room.

"Interesting turn of events, Ari," he said. "What do you make of it?"

He stared at the bust for a moment, as if listening for a response. "Could this be what this whole business is about?"

He tossed the bust back and forth between hands. He'd been a good juggler in college, able to keep as many as five objects in the air at once. Now he was lucky if he could manage one thing at a time. Holding the bust out in front of him, he resisted the urge to quote Macbeth. "There's one thing I don't get, Ari. Well, one of many things. What are the Shallows? What does it have to do with a drowned teenager in Woolwich?"

He crossed back to the bookshelf, placing the bust back in its place. He picked up his mobile phone. He had a call to make to rural New Jersey. As he looked up the number for Woolwich Township Police, he glanced back at the book that rested in the Lazy Boy. Western philosophy would have to wait.

11

KAITLYN WALKED around the BMW and knelt down by the driver-side window, dropping the small black duffel bag she carried on the curb. Brad rested his hands on the steering wheel. For a moment, she was struck again with how handsome he looked in his navy suit. It amused her to think of herself in contrast with faded jeans and a Phillies sweatshirt.

"I'm sorry you had to get up so early to get me home before going to work," she said. "I hope the traffic isn't bad."

Brad smiled. "No worries. The pleasure's all mine for my fiancée."

She drew her arms in around her body, trying to stave off the crisp morning chill. "That's going to take some getting used to." She laughed. "Mrs. Kaitlyn Ludlow. Has a nice ring to it."

Brad's momentary laugh faded, and his eyes narrowed. "You sure you'll be okay?"

Kaitlyn leaned into the window and kissed him on the cheek. "I'll be fine. Don't worry about me."

"Call me tonight."

Kaitlyn stood on the curb and watched as the car pulled away. She glanced at her watch, frowning at the time. 6:35. *Poor Brad,* she thought. It would to be a long day for him. All because of her.

As the BMW disappeared up Belmont Avenue, she picked up the duffel bag and walked up the driveway to her house. At the front door, she fished in the bag's side pocket, looking for her keys. A car door slamming shut somewhere behind her barely registered, but the sound of footsteps approaching along the driveway caught her attention. There was a prickle on the back of her neck. The confidence she had felt with Brad evaporated and left her with a racing heart and trembling hands. *Who could it be?* A neighbor? Not at this hour. *Turn around,* she told herself. *Face whoever it might be. End this.* But paralysis had set in. She was unable to move. Maybe she could open the door and get in the house? She'd be safe inside. She fumbled with the key ring. The jangle of keys suddenly seemed deafening. Why couldn't she find the right one?

The footsteps drew up behind her, and then all went silent. Kaitlyn straightened her back, her muscles tensed in anticipation.

"Ms. Ashe?"

Kaitlyn turned, breathing a sigh of relief. She felt the tautness in her shoulders fade. Julie Lewis, brushing a few rogue strands of black hair out of her eyes, matched Kaitlyn's smile.

"Detective Lewis? You startled me."

Julie slipped her hands from the pockets of her grey overcoat. "Sorry. That wasn't my intention."

"I'm a bit freaked out over those letters." Kaitlyn paused, then added, "Can I help you with anything?"

"No. We had a report of a suspicious vehicle in the area. I was just checking it out."

Kaitlyn couldn't stop herself from making a nervous glance up and down the street. She saw nothing out of the ordinary. "Oh. Did you find anything?"

Julie shook her head.

Kaitlyn couldn't shake the residual nervous anxiety. Her trembling hand made it difficult to slip the house key into the door lock. She hoped the detective didn't notice. "I was going to make myself a mug of hot tea. Want to come in and join me?"

"Sure. Thanks."

Once inside the house, Kaitlyn tossed the duffel bag on the sofa as she passed the living room and led Julie toward the kitchen at the back of the house. She gestured for the detective to have a seat at the kitchen table, then filled a red tea pot and placed it on the stove. "It'll just be a few minutes."

Sitting down at the table, Kaitlyn rested her elbow on the tabletop and supported her head with her hand tapping her fingers on her cheek. "Have you had any luck with that letter?"

Julie returned her gaze. Kaitlyn noticed a coolness beyond their icy blue hue. When the detective smiled, the coolness seemed to fade. "Nothing yet. Forensics is still looking over it."

"Do you think they'll find anything?"

Julie shrugged. "In all honesty, it's doubtful." She placed her hands on the table, intertwining her fingers. "We might have gotten more if we had the other letters."

Kaitlyn turned her eyes away. "Sorry."

"You had no way of knowing this would escalate."

All went silent for a moment. Kaitlyn wondered if this had been a good idea. Why had she invited Julie in for tea? Was it because she couldn't bear to be in her house alone? She'd put on a brave face for Brad to quell his concern. Deep inside, however, she was terrified.

Julie broke the silence. "Are congratulations in order?"

"What?"

Julie gestured across the table. "The ring. You weren't wearing it the other day."

Kaitlyn felt a spark of excitement as she recalled Brad's proposal. "Oh my god! Yes. He asked me yesterday morning."

Julie smiled. "Congrats! How long have you two been dating?"

"A little over a year."

"Did you know he was going to ask you?"

Kaitlyn shook her head. "No. He'd planned to ask me next weekend while we're in the Poconos, but . . ."

"But he couldn't wait?" Julie laughed. "Typical man. Utterly impatient."

Kaitlyn rose from the table to answer the call of the whistling tea pot. "I know. I know."

"Where in the Poconos?"

"I don't know. He's made the reservations. One of those 'couples only' resorts, I think. I don't really care as long as it's got one of those hot tubs shaped like a champagne glass." Kaitlyn pulled two mugs from a nearby cabinet. "What kind of tea? I've got Earl Grey, and herbal."

"What kind of herbal?"

She pulled two boxes from the cabinet. "Apple cinnamon, and chamomile."

"Definitely the apple cinnamon. I've got to work all day."

Kaitlyn poured hot water into two mugs, then dropped a tea bag into each.

"The Poconos are nice this time of year. You going up on Friday night?" Julie asked.

"No, Thursday night after my show. He's going to pick me up at the station. A nice three-day getaway." Kaitlyn carried the mugs over to the table, placing one in front of the detective. "Here's your tea."

———

KAITLYN AMBLED into the reception area of WPLX, whistling an aimless tune that she couldn't quite place. She crossed to the reception desk and reached her arm over it so that her hand was inches from Sammy's face. Wagging her fingers, she didn't have to wait long for a response.

"Oh my god! When did he ask? I want details! Tell me everything!" Sammy leapt up from her chair, grabbing the hand and pulling it closer to her face.

Kaitlyn's smile widened, and she wondered if her cheeks could stretch any further. "Sunday. In his kitchen. Over breakfast."

The corners of Sammy's smirk fell, a frown forming on her face. "Really? That's not very romantic. Tell me he at least got down on one knee. If he didn't get down on one knee, I'll be very disappointed."

Kaitlyn nodded and laughed. "What happened after wasn't very romantic either. If you know what I mean."

Sammy snorted. "You didn't. On the kitchen floor? No, don't tell me. I don't want to know." She made her way around the reception desk to give Kaitlyn a hug. "Congratulations. I'm so happy for you!"

As their embrace ended, Kaitlyn placed her hand on Sammy's shoulder. "I've got to ask. Will you be my maid of honor?"

"Do I get to throw you a helluva bachelorette party?"

Kaitlyn grinned, nodding her head. "If it gets you to say yes."

The receptionist spun around, waving her hand with an air of excitement. "This city's never seen a party like the one I'm going to throw for you. There'll be food. Chippendales. Alcohol. Chippendales. Did I mention the Chippendales? Or maybe we could get those Australian guys. What are they called?" Sammy thought for a second, then added, "Thunder from Down Under!"

Kaitlyn chuckled at her friend's enthusiasm. Apart from Brad, Sammy was the closest she had to a best friend. She loved Sammy's no-nonsense, "take no bullshit from anyone" attitude, and their mutual fondness for workplace gossip created an instant bond between them. But she'd kept Sammy at arm's length, never fully confiding in her. "Once we've picked a date, you can start planning your little shindig."

"Shindig? This'll be the party of the year. Maybe the century."

"Just remember, I want to enjoy my wedding." Kaitlyn folded her arms, giving her friend a shake of her head. "No hangovers."

Sammy waved her hand in dismissal. "I make no promises. Have you told your Mom yet?"

"Of course. Called her yesterday. She's thrilled."

"Who's gonna walk you down the aisle?"

A momentary pang of sadness gripped her heart. Kaitlyn hadn't given it any thought, but it was something she'd have to carefully consider. The heart attack had taken her father almost two years ago. She'd always found it ironic that he'd survived some of the fiercest fighting during the fall of Saigon only to die in his sleep forty years later. "Don't know."

Sammy leaned in close, speaking softly. "You should ask Scott. He'd be thrilled."

"Maybe." Kaitlyn pondered the suggestion. Scott had taken her under his wing when she first moved to Philadelphia. But it was more than that. He'd welcomed her into his family. During her first year in the city, Scott—along with his wife Amanda—frequently invited Kaitlyn to join them for dinner, doing what they could to help her settle into her new life. Scott was supportive of all of her ideas and was always prepared to give her "fatherly" advice.

Sammy made her way around the desk, preparing to return to her seat. The receptionist smiled. "I almost forgot. There's flowers waiting for you back on your desk."

Kaitlyn's face flushed with warmth. "Oh god, he didn't!"

"I'm afraid so."

"Brad's determined to embarrass me." She smiled. "Has anyone seen them?"

Sammy nodded. "I think Scott and Kevin are back there now."

"Damn." Kaitlyn moved toward the inner office door. "Guess I'll go face the music."

When Kaitlyn entered the bullpen, Scott was leaning back in an office chair with his feet resting on Kevin O'Neill's desk. Kevin sat on top of the desk; his legs folded under him. As she walked through the door, Scott dropped his feet to the floor. His salt and pepper shoulder length hair shifted with the movement. "There she is."

Kaitlyn gave them both a smile, crossed to her desk, and stopped to smell the bouquet of red roses that stood on her desk in a glass vase. Then, she dropped her bag on the desk and spun around to face her co-workers.

"He asked me," she said.

Kevin tilted his head to one side, looking puzzled. "Asked you what."

Scott leaned forward, slapping Kevin's arm. "To marry him, you idiot."

Hopping from the desk, Kevin crossed the room, enfolding Kaitlyn in an embrace. "Congrats!" He held her tight, his arms pulled her against him and his hands lingered in the center of her back. He reeked of cigarette smoke. As usual.

Scott waited behind him, hugging her when she pulled herself away from Kevin. "You did say yes, right?"

As they parted, she held out her hand for them to see the ring. Kevin gave a low whistle.

"That's quite a rock," he said.

Scott smiled, patting Kevin on the back. "That's what an attorney's salary gets you in this city."

Kevin gestured to the flowers on the desk. "A ring *and* flowers."

Warmth rising in her cheeks, Kaitlyn smiled and turned away to hide her blushing face. It was just like Brad to do something that would embarrass her in front of her co-workers. He'd get an earful from her tonight. She leaned over the flowers again and sniffed the sweet aroma. Catching sight of a small envelope stuffed down between the stems, she reached in to pull it out. The florist's name and address were typed on the front, as well as her name. *This had better not be something dirty*, she thought. She pulled the card from the envelope. As she read the words typed on the card, she inhaled quickly. Her hands trembled, fingers clutching the card. She staggered backward. Her hip hit the desk. The vase of roses toppled off the desk and shattered to pieces when it hit the floor.

12

THE WAITRESS LED Rodney to a booth on the far side of the restaurant. After taking his drink order, Shelli left him alone to look over the menu. The atmosphere in McGonigel's Pub was a stark contrast from the bright lights of his office. The dark wood of the paneling, floor, and booths, along with the dim lighting, cast the Irish pub's interior in gloomy shadows. A single bare bulb hung above the booth and cast a solitary cone of light onto the menu in his hands.

The pub, only a block and a half up Lancaster Avenue from the police station, had become part of his Monday and Thursday routines. An hour of firearms practice in the police station's anti-quated basement firing range was rounded off with a good meal at McGonigel's. He put the menu down. He was becoming a creature of habit. Sheppard's pie again. It'd be the fifth time in a row. Or maybe sixth. He'd lost count.

Shelli returned with his Arnold Palmer, setting the glass down before him. The young woman smiled and placed her hand on her hip. "What'll it be, Rod? Your usual?"

Rodney laughed, shaking his head. He reached for the menu. "Give me a few more minutes. I don't ever want to hear you ask again if I want the usual."

She smiled, giving her well-chewed piece of gum a loud crack. "Take your time. It's quiet in here tonight."

He watched her walk off, noticing the spider web tattoo on the back of her neck. Funny, she'd never worn her jet-black hair pulled up before. Why the change? With his attention back on the menu, Rodney was determined to find something that he'd never ordered. Perhaps he needed to broaden his restaurant options.

The shrill of his mobile phone interrupted him. He slipped it from his pocket and answered.

"Detective? It's Kaitlyn Ashe. Do you have a minute?"

He frowned. Her voice sounded distraught. Never a good sign. "Of course, Ms. Ashe. How can I help?"

"Please, call me Kaitlyn." She went silent for a few moments, leaving him to wonder if the call had been cut off. Then she spoke again. "I've had another letter. Well, it's more like a note. It came with some flowers."

"Flowers?"

"A vase of roses was delivered to the radio station. With a card. I think it's from the same person sending me the letters."

Rodney glanced up at Shelli, who had returned to the table. He gestured that he needed a few more minutes. He heard the chewing gum crack again as she walked away. "What makes you think they're from the same person?"

"Let me read it. 'Congratulations may be in order, but you'll get none from the Shallows.'"

It was Rodney's turn to fall silent. There was that reference to the Shallows again. He wanted to ask her about the drowning, and about why she'd changed her name. According to the report Julie had sent him the other day, the drowning had been accidental. He'd contacted the Woolwich Township Police on Sunday to ask for more details, but the investigating officer had retired years ago and now lived in North Carolina. Not much chance of finding out anything from him.

He opened his mouth to ask about her past but realized that

the restaurant had begun to fill up. Too many ears. Not the right place or time.

"What's the florist's name? Is there an address listed on the card?" he asked instead.

"Happy Petals Florist. Market Street."

Rodney frowned. Philadelphia's Center City was out of his jurisdiction. He'd have to liaise with the city police on this one. It'd slow things down. The GBT Strangler would make sure of that.

"Set aside everything that came with the delivery, including the flowers. I'll need them for evidence."

He heard her hesitate. "Is something wrong?" he asked.

"The vase broke."

"What? How?"

"I was startled by the card. I bumped it off my desk."

Rodney sighed; a bit louder than he'd intended. He was sure she'd heard his frustration. "Hang on to the pieces then. I'll get onto the florist and see if I can find out who ordered the flowers." He paused. "Are you going to be okay?"

There was another moment of hesitation before she answered. "Yes."

After he hung up, Rodney took a long sip from his Arnold Palmer. He should give Julie a call to give her an update on this latest development. But his eyes fell on the menu again. It could wait until he'd eaten. It would be shepherd's pie again tonight.

———

RODNEY TURNED his Dodge Challenger onto Market Street and drove slowly past the darkened storefronts. A sports car flew by him. Its angry horn blasted out a compliant from its driver. The bright streetlights shone on the wet pavement, giving the street in front of him a glossy sheen. A faint mist coated his windshield, the remnants of a passing shower. His car radio played quietly in the background. The music faded as her voice drifted through the speakers.

"It's quarter past eleven at WPLX, and Kaitlyn Ashe is here to make sure you're tucked up in bed, warm and tight. Warm is what you'll want to be. The forecast is calling for a chilly overnight. I'll give you all the details coming up next on WPLX."

Her voice, although familiar, was different somehow. There was a sultry undertone to it that Rodney hadn't heard before. He found it difficult to ascribe the voice to the woman he'd met just a few days ago. The voice of Kaitlyn Ashe on the radio exuded a strong sense of self-confidence, where the Kaitlyn Ashe he'd met had seemed anxious and afraid.

After finishing his dinner, Rodney had returned to the office and tried to call the florist who'd delivered the flowers to the radio station. They'd closed for the evening. He wasn't going to get any further information tonight. Julie had already left for the day, and he toyed with the idea of calling her, but decided against it. This new development could wait until morning.

At home, Rodney endeavored to return to the book that he'd abandoned the other day. But his mind wandered back to Kaitlyn Ashe. News of the floral delivery made him apprehensive. The letters had come on a regular routine. But, in the past week, the routine had been broken. The frequency of the messages had increased. Things were beginning to escalate.

By 10:15, Rodney had fallen into a cycle of fitfulness. His body felt like a tightly wound spring. He'd sit in his Lazy Boy for a few minutes, rereading the same paragraph in his book. Moments later, he'd jump from the chair and pace the room, hoping to relieve the interminable agitation he felt. What was it about this case that vexed him? Why did he have this nagging sense of foreboding?

As he brought the car to a halt at the corner of 20th and Market, Rodney realized that he'd never intended to come into the city. His decision to go for a quick evening drive had been nothing more than an attempt to run off some of his apprehension. He'd only meant to drive around Ardmore, not go stalking into Center City to look for Happy Petal Florist. But since he was here now . . .

He found the florist two blocks past Philadelphia City Hall—a small storefront wedged between a Dunkin' Donuts and a Game Stop. A steel security door had been drawn down over the florist's main entrance, leaving little for him to see other than a faded graffiti artist's signature. He pulled the car up to the curb out front, and stared out the windshield, first at the store, and then down the street.

The rain had done little to stop people from venturing out into the sodden evening. Rodney watched a couple exit the Dunkin' Donuts, each holding a steaming Styrofoam cup. A lone woman dressed in a dark business suit passed his car; an umbrella protected her from the mist. Her head was bowed forward, and her lips held a deep frown. *Worked late. Hates her job*, he thought. A yellow cab pulled up in front of him and deposited a pair of young men onto the curb. One of them tossed money through the car window at the driver, and then stumbled over to his companion. They embraced, kissed, and then moved off down the street, their steps wavering and unsteady. *A little too much to drink*, Rodney thought as he pulled the car away from the curb. *At least they didn't drive*.

Somewhere in this city was a man who was strangling gay, bisexual, and transgender men. The GBT Strangler. He didn't like that the media had given him a name. Raised the killer's status which, in his experience, was exactly what these sick minds craved. What were the chances that he could be the same person stalking Kaitlyn? *Probably slim to none*, Rodney figured. Kaitlyn didn't seem to fall within GBT's victim profile. His targets, thus far, had all been male. Rodney kept tabs on Philly police's investigation, just enough to be familiar with the latest updates on the case.

It was five minutes to midnight as Rodney pulled the Dodge into the parking garage of the Stetler Building. The bright lights within were a stark contradiction against the dank darkness outside. Driving up the ramp, he noticed that the concrete within the garage was dry with the exception of a single set of car tire tracks. He followed the tracks upward, rounding the corner on each level of the garage until he saw a lone candy apple red

Harley-Davidson parked near the elevator. He pulled the car into the spot nearest the motorcycle, shut off the engine and climbed out.

Rodney gazed around the garage, and, seeing all the empty parking spots, figured that it probably emptied out en masse around quitting time every night. His eyes fell onto the wet tire tracks, which appeared to have pulled into a neighboring spot, and then pulled out to proceed further up into the garage. He checked his watch, wondering how long it'd be before Kaitlyn came out to head home. Nothing to do but wait, he decided, and leaned back against his car, arms folded, and eyes fixed on the elevator.

While he waited, his mind drifted to his daughter. Kaitlyn represented everything that he hoped Carol would be when she reached that age. But he knew it would never happen. The last time he'd visited her, he could tell that prison life was taking its toll. The change in his daughter after just a year of incarceration was extreme. Gone from her eyes was the innocence that he dearly loved. It was replaced by a callous stare. The fiery hatred in her eyes as they sat across from each other was burned into his memory.

It was the way she called him "father" that hit him hardest. She'd always called him "daddy," or "dad," even up to the moment she was arrested. But now it was "father." It was a frigid, apathetic word. She must have known how it hurt him. She put a cold-blooded emphasis on the word every time she said it. When she launched into that final tirade, her words were laced with bile. His heart shattered. His little girl was gone forever.

Had he failed his daughter? Should he have hidden the evidence of the accident? He would never have been able to live with himself if he had. That thought didn't console him. How could a loving father turn in his own daughter to the police? It was a question he asked himself almost daily. Always followed by, how can a good cop ignore a crime? The paradox wasn't lost on him. He couldn't be both. He had a choice to make, and he chose to be the good cop.

Maybe Julie was right. Perhaps he was using Kaitlyn as a proxy for his daughter. What of it? This was his chance to get it right. When he looked at Kaitlyn, he saw his daughter. He wouldn't let her down this time.

He'd been standing there for twenty minutes when the bell on the elevator dinged and the doors opened. Kaitlyn stepped out and proceeded across the garage toward him. When she caught sight of Rodney, she hesitated. He caught the questioning look in her eyes. He smiled, trying to look reassuring, but feeling like he'd failed miserably. Kaitlyn's steps became more cautious and deliberate.

"Detective, this is a surprise," she said.

"I was in the neighborhood."

Kaitlyn stopped at the motorcycle, setting her leather handbag down beside it. "Is something wrong? Why are you here?"

Rodney pushed himself off the car and stepped toward her. He saw her tense up at his movement. "Nothing's wrong. I was in town looking up your florist and decided to swing by and see if you wanted an escort home."

Her shoulders were still tense, eyes questioning.

"I'm not trying to alarm you. I was just concerned for your safety," he said, again trying to be reassuring. "I doubt that you are in danger, but the flower delivery made me a little uneasy."

She thought on his remarks for a second, and then she smiled. The tenseness in her shoulders faded away. "Thanks. I don't think I've ever had a police escort before."

He wondered if she'd had a police escort the night that Jesse Riley drowned, but decided not to ask.

————

RODNEY KEPT a car length's distance between himself and the tail lights of Kaitlyn's motorcycle. The traffic on Walnut Street was nonexistent, and they both moved with ease along the wet street. The traffic lights were in sync, green the whole stretch, as was the norm in the middle of the night. The mist had turned back into a steady rain, leaving Rodney to wonder how soaked Kaitlyn would be by the time she got home.

As they passed South 20th Street, a car turned out of an alleyway and pulled up behind him, headlights ablaze in his rearview mirror. Rodney cursed and tried to ignore the blinding glare reflected into his eyes. His grip tightened on the steering wheel. He returned his gaze forward, watching sheets of water spray from Kaitlyn's Harley as she sped ahead of him.

Behind him, the car raced forward, coming far too close to Rodney's Dodge for his comfort. His shoulders tensed. *Back off, asshole*, he thought.

For a moment, he caught sight of a petite silhouette behind the wheel of the car. Then the car backed away, the bright round headlights once again shone through his back window. He had half a mind to throw his teardrop light onto the roof. But he was outside of his jurisdiction, and more importantly, stopping the other vehicle would leave Kaitlyn unprotected for the remainder of her journey home.

The car raced forward again and then darted out to his left. It accelerated up Walnut Street, overtaking Rodney's car. As they drew parallel, Rodney got his first good look at it. A Volkswagen Beetle. He peered across the narrow gap between them, trying to catch a glimpse of the driver's face. The rain and the streetlights, however, conspired against him. The wet sheen on the window glass reflected the overhead streetlights back at him and obscured his view of the driver inside. He saw nothing more than a shadowy profile leaning back into the driver's seat. *Probably just some punk ass kid*. He was only half-convinced by the thought.

But then the car sped up, passed him, and then drifted back into the right lane between Rodney and Kaitlyn. His stomach twisted as a dozen worst-case scenarios played in his mind. Rodney squinted through the windshield, trying to make out the numbers on the car's license plate. It was a Pennsylvania tag; he could tell that much. But the rain, which had become a driving downpour, made it difficult to read the letters and numbers. He leaned toward the steering wheel and thought he saw a "B". Yes, the first letter was a "B". Then, there was a "G", followed by a . . .

Suddenly, the Volkswagen pulled into the left-hand lane, speeding toward Kaitlyn. It pulled up alongside of her and matched her speed. Rodney saw Kaitlyn glance at the car, and then back at him. He watched them race parallel along the road for a few moments, powerless to help. Then the car veered sharply back into the right-hand lane and cut Kaitlyn off. The motorcycle swerved toward the side of the street, and then back toward the center, barely missing a parked car along the curb. The back end of the Harley kicked out from underneath Kaitlyn. She leaned into the fall, coming down hard on the pavement. As the motorcycle skidded on its side along the wet road, Kaitlyn tumbled over and over behind it.

Rodney slammed on his brakes and skidded to an abrupt halt in the center of the Walnut Street. He leapt from the car and threw the teardrop on the roof; the spinning red light flashed brightly in the wet darkened night. Water soaked his shoes and pant legs as he raced up the street, splashing through the small streams of water flowing toward the storm drains. When he reached Kaitlyn, Rodney dropped to his knee beside her motionless form.

"Kaitlyn," he shouted. "Kaitlyn!"

Glancing up for a moment, he caught the fading taillights of the Volkswagen as it sped along Walnut Street and disappeared into the rainy gloom of the night.

13

THE RED-LIGHT FLASHES in my rearview mirror as I race away from the accident. I don't know how injured Laura is, but I hope it isn't too bad. I only wanted to scare her, not kill her.

I can't understand why he was following her. But I hope it doesn't become a problem. I doubt he saw enough of me to make a positive ID, but I'll need to be more careful from now on. Maybe I should loop back around, leave the car on a side street, and watch from a nearby corner. No, it's too risky. There'll be police swarming the area shortly, and someone may see me. Best to get off Walnut Street, and out of the city.

I turn onto the next side street and race a few blocks down before turning again. Check the mirror. No one's following. Time to slow down. Don't want to draw attention to myself.

The rain splatters on the windshield just like the day of the funeral. I dressed in my finest and watched the ceremony pass in a haze. The green tent provided meager protection from the downpour. Water droplets rolled off the coffin, dripping into the six-foot hole beneath. She was there, along with many others. But I couldn't stop looking at her. Couldn't stop wondering what really happened. "It was an accident," everyone said. "There was nothing that could be done," I heard more than once. But I didn't believe it. Accidents don't just happen. Someone must be to blame.

Traffic is light, and I make good time returning to my house. With the car in the garage, I stand by the open garage door and watch the rain fall. I draw in on my cigarette, and the smoke feels cool against the back of my throat. I hate the fact that I've started enjoying these damn cancer sticks. I never meant to become addicted. Ha! As if anyone ever did. I just needed something to get me through the first few days after discovering who Kaitlyn Ashe really was. I'd tried cigarettes in college, a fad that lasted only a couple weeks, but now . . . days have turned into months. Soon, it will be a year.

I toss the half-used cigarette out onto the driveway and pull another one from the pack in my pocket. There's only two more left. Fuck. I'm going through these things like they're candy. Half the time I don't even finish one before I'm lighting another.

It was snowing the night I mailed the first letter. It took me hours to come up with just the right words, and then another three hours to find those words in newspapers and magazines. That asshole at the 7-Eleven raised his eyebrows when I dropped the stack on the counter.

"Can't sleep," I'd said.

I never went back there again.

Piecing together the letter was painstaking, but I couldn't risk anyone recognizing my handwriting. I knew fingerprints could be lifted from paper, so I wore gloves. I drove to Delaware that night to post the letter. A Wilmington postmark would throw off anyone who tried to track the sender. Every subsequent letter has been postmarked from somewhere different. West Chester. Philadelphia. King of Prussia. Even from towns in Jersey, like Woodbury, Penns Grove, and Paulsboro. Never from Woolwich and never from anywhere in Lower Merion Township. I'm not even sure what I was hoping for with those first couple letters. Maybe just a kindred spirit. Perhaps a shared reflection . . . of Jesse. Just to hear her play that song one more time. But she didn't. The bitch didn't.

I finish my second cigarette before throwing it out into the rain, then close the garage door and move into the house. There's a bottle of merlot in the wine rack. I grab it and a glass from the kitchen cabinet. This is another vice that has gained a bit too much of a hold over me lately.

With a filled wine glass in my hand, I drift into the back bedroom. A dim light burns in the far corner, leaving the room in shadow. I cross to the opposite wall and stare at the framed twenty-four-by-fourteen canvas. It hangs on the wall amidst dozens of smaller stills, all of her. It's a photo taken months ago. She's dressed in a sequined gown with her hair pulled up in a bun. Her hand clings to Brad's arm, who is dressed in a tuxedo. This year's Philadelphia Flower Show Black Tie event. I had a helluva time getting a ticket. But, when I heard she was going to be there, I had to be there as well. I've a dozen or more pictures just like this one.

She looks happy, so fucking happy. She's got no right to be in such high spirits. Everyone thinks she's such an angel. But they don't know her like I do. They don't have a clue what she's capable of. Of how easily she can crush someone's life and walk away without a second thought. She's a master at acting the part of the innocent while harboring the darkest of hearts. I can't stand to look at her any longer and turn toward the door. As I cross the room, I can feel her eyes on me. That smile of hers grows and becomes a sneer. She mocks me. Mocks what I've become. I can almost hear her laugh echoing through the otherwise silent room. I should've killed her tonight. Crushed her between my car and the others on the street. Maybe I would've . . . if he hadn't been there. My hand trembles, the wine splashing around in my glass. I close my eyes, picturing her years ago by the Shallows. She stands on the dock and turns to look at me. That smile. The same smile. I open my eyes, scream, and turn around, throwing the wine glass across the room at the wall. It shatters into a hundred tiny shards. A crimson trail of merlot drips down the wall.

14

RODNEY WAS UNCOMFORTABLE. Although the seat was cushioned and covered in leather, the wooden chair back felt like it was at an odd angle. Just enough to make it impossible to feel at ease. He wondered if that was why Bernie had chosen the chair for his office, to keep the occupant from ever becoming relaxed.

He glanced at Julie, who sat in a similar chair next to him. She had her legs crossed and her hands clasped together resting on her knee. No sign of discomfort. Maybe it was just him. He shifted in the chair, hoping to find a position that wasn't as hard on his back.

The Captain passed through the open office door, crossed to the oak desk along the opposite wall, and lowered himself into the chair behind it. The chair creaked in protest. The sleeves of Captain Bernie Doyle's shirt were rolled up to the elbows, and his tie hung loose around his neck. Rodney recalled his first year as a detective. Bernie—only a detective himself at the time—had become a mentor of sorts to Rodney. He'd been a good detective in his day, but Bernie had spent the past few years behind a desk running the division. Rodney wondered if the captain still had his keen eye.

Bernie's glance moved from Rodney to Julie and then back again. "I'm sorry to keep you both waiting."

Rodney studied the captain's round face, noting the dark shadows under his eyes and the greenish tinge to his complexion. A faint layer of sweat coated his bald head. "You're looking a bit peaked. You okay, cap'n?"

Bernie waved his hand to dismiss the concern. "It's nothing. The wife and I got some bad Chinese takeout last night. I'm faring better than she is. At least I made it to work."

Julie brushed a few stray hairs behind her ear. "You sure you should be here?"

"Believe me. I'm fine. What's the latest on this stalker case? I heard there was an incident last night."

Rodney leaned forward with his hands clasped between his knees. "Forensics didn't find anything useful on the letter. Just Elmer's Glue and magazine clippings. Kaitlyn . . . Ms. Ashe received flowers at her place of employment yesterday. The note reads like it came from the letter sender."

"I've called the florist. The order came in through the web," said Julie. "It was paid using a pre-paid gift card. The name on the order was Jesse Riley, and the sender's address was 1401 John F. Kennedy Boulevard in Philly."

Bernie cocked his head. "Sounds familiar."

Julie smiled. "Philly City Hall."

Bernie gave a chuckle. "Our stalker has a sense of humor." He turned his gaze toward Rodney. "Any idea what this 'Shallows' thing is?"

Leaning back in his chair, Rodney felt the hard wood press into his back. It was like leaning against plywood. "Nothing yet. We've confirmed that Kaitlyn Ashe was born Laura Hobson and changed her name sixteen years ago."

Bernie nodded. "Nothing illegal about that. Tell me about what happened last night."

Rodney gave up on trying to get comfortable and rose from the chair. The captain seemed to know what he was thinking. "Terrible, aren't they? That's the best the township will give me."

Rodney smirked, and then said, "I'd driven into the city last night—"

"Why?" said Bernie.

Rodney shrugged. "The floral delivery bothered me. We may be looking at an escalation in behavior."

Bernie folded his arms across his chest. "I'd agree."

"I offered to escort Ms. Ashe home. Just to make sure she got there safely. The rest is in the report."

"Did you get a look at the driver?" Bernie asked.

"Not a good one. It was a Volkswagen. One of the newer Beetles. Couldn't tell what color."

Bernie glanced at Julie. "You drive a Beetle, don't you?" He laughed, "Where were you last night?"

Julie returned a broad smile. "Playing naked Twister with my ex-husband."

"Again?" Rodney shook his head. "Why bother getting the divorce?"

Bernie chuckled, then returned his gaze to Rodney. "License plate?"

"It was a PA tag, but I only saw the first couple digits. BG. Julie ran a search this morning."

Bernie looked toward her. Julie shook her head. "Nothing. Hundreds of plates that start with BG, but none are assigned to Beetles."

"Faked plate?"

Rodney crossed to the door, glancing out the window at the detective office beyond, then turned back to face the captain. "That's what we're figuring."

"How is Ms. Ashe doing?"

"Bumped and bruised. She leaned into the fall, and her helmet and riding jacket took the brunt of it," Rodney said. "They released her from the hospital this morning. Nothing too serious."

Bernie nodded. "Good. Keep me informed of any progress."

Julie rose from her chair, nodding toward the captain. "Yes, sir." She crossed the room, opened the door, and stepped out.

Rodney moved to follow her, but halted for a moment, turning back toward the captain. "You really don't look all that great. You sure you should be here?"

"It's my wife that I'm worried about. She practically slept next to the toilet last night. Not the most pleasant of mornings, but at least I'm here."

Rodney laughed. "Hope you feel better."

———

JULIE WAS PERCHED on the corner of Rodney's desk. He knew why she was waiting for him. He was already running the dialog through his head. She looked pissed. A frown on her lips. A furrowed brow. Her angry eyes, cold and hard, followed him as he approached.

"Why didn't you call me last night about the flowers?" she said.

Her voice was stern, and Rodney couldn't miss the accusation behind it. "Didn't get a chance," he said.

"Bullshit."

Rodney circled the desk and lowered himself into the chair, forcing her to slide off and turn to look at him. He gave her a broad smile. "It didn't seem that important. I thought it could wait until morning."

Julie's hands landed on her hips. "It was important enough for you to go rushing into the city."

He sighed. "It didn't start to bother me until later in the evening. Then, it was too late to call."

"Don't give me that." She scowled. "You know damn well that you can call me anytime."

"Julie, there's no reason to get upset over this." He leaned back in his chair. "There's nothing you could've done with the information until morning."

"That's not the point." The sharp edge in her voice made some of the other detectives in the office steal discreet glances in their direction. She tapped her finger on his desk, punctuating each word. "I need to know everything you discover in this case."

Rodney raised his hands as a gesture of surrender. "All right. I'm sorry. Next time, I'll make sure to call you."

Her eyes bored into him, but the anger seemed to be diminishing.

"Happy?" he said.

She folded her arms and glared at him for a long moment. Her scowl dissolved into a smile. It looked genuine enough, but her still narrowed eyes told him it was forced.

"Just don't do it again," she said. Her voice was softer, more relaxed. She hitched herself up on the edge of his desk, leaning toward him. "You can't protect her, you know. It's impossible for you to be there all the time. You can't be there when she goes to work, goes shopping, or goes for her runs on the Heritage Trail. You just can't do it, so don't try."

"What do you mean?"

Julie glanced over her shoulder to see if anyone was listening, then lowered her voice. "You don't think I noticed the resemblance? I'm not blind. Don't make her a proxy for Carol." She gestured over her shoulder toward the coffeemaker in the far corner. "You want some coffee?"

Rodney nodded. Julie smiled, and then slipped off the desk, moving across the office. As he watched her walk away, he wondered why she'd come down so hard on him. He knew that Julie tackled every case with intensity, but this had been something altogether different. He recalled her reaction from earlier in the morning when he recounted the previous evening's developments.

"What were you doing there?" she'd asked, her voice filled with indignation. "It wasn't your jurisdiction."

He tried to explain the situation, but she'd cut him off with the start of what he was certain would've been a five-minute tirade. A phone call from Captain Doyle requesting their presence in his office had been the timely intervention that saved Rodney from an even lengthier diatribe. It wouldn't have been the first one he'd received from Julie. But this one felt a little over the top, even for her.

He thought about Julie's last remark. Was he turning Kaitlyn into a proxy for his daughter? It'd been so long since he'd visited Carol. He couldn't even be sure that he would recognize her. Maybe that was the issue. Kaitlyn looked and acted like he'd always hoped his daughter would. A college graduate. Successful in her career. Even a lover who seemed genuinely in love with her. She fulfilled an ideal that Carol never achieved, and he wanted to protect her in a way that he didn't with his own daughter.

When Julie returned with two Styrofoam cups of coffee, he smiled, took one from her, and took a long sip. Rodney felt the warmth on his hands. How much coffee had he consumed in the past twelve hours? He'd lost count in the wee hours of the morning while he sat in the hospital ER waiting room. He'd made it home for a quick shower and change of clothes before coming into the office.

"What now?" she asked.

"Go over everything again. Figure out what we missed."

15

KAITLYN STOOD before her bathroom mirror and gave her naked body a close inspection. Her fingers probed the large bruise on her hip. She winced at the pain. Twisting around, she caught sight of another contusion on her shoulder in the mirror. It had only just started to turn black and blue. There was one on each of her knees as well. Her whole body felt sore, and every joint was stiff. She'd taken a couple Ibuprofen an hour ago, hoping they would kick in soon. So far, no such luck.

She moved back into the bedroom and stopped to examine her riding gear, which lay in a disheveled pile on the bed. She'd been lucky. Her helmet and leather jacket had suffered the most damage during the accident. Deep gouges in the leather and a several torn seams meant she'd have to cut her losses and replace the jacket. Kaitlyn picked up her helmet and studied the cracked shield. She'd have to pick up a new one, as well as buff out the scratches along the helmet's crown. Better that it took the hit than her head. She tossed the helmet back onto the bed. She had no way of knowing for sure that the accident was related to the letters, but she felt fairly certain that it was.

Kaitlyn stood by the bed for a moment, assessing the damage

that couldn't be seen. Her anguish, the sense of an approaching reckoning. There was an uneasy quivering in her stomach as she fought back the sobs.

"Jesse," she said into the dead air of the empty room. "Why're you doing this to me?"

His face came back to her in her mind. She heard his shouts and curses. His arms flailing. Splashing. The gurgling . . . and then nothing.

Tears crept down her cheeks. She rubbed her eyes with balled up fists. "Why can't you leave me be?"

Kaitlyn collapsed onto the bed and sobbed uncontrollably. The Shallows was calling her back. Drawing her back to face her crime.

When her tears had stopped, she moved to the bathroom. As she stepped into the shower, Kaitlyn thought about her Harley. It hadn't fared well in the accident. The handlebars were bent, the rear tire blown, the left foot pedal ripped off, and the paint and chrome had been scratched up. That was the damage as far as she could tell. Her mechanic would have to determine what else was wrong.

The hot shower helped soothe her aching muscles. She should take the ER doctor's advice and take the evening off. But Kaitlyn was already taking Friday night off for her weekend getaway with Brad. Scott would've understood, and probably have insisted, but Kaitlyn didn't want to take advantage of the situation.

As she stepped from the shower, Kaitlyn heard the phone ring in the bedroom. She grabbed a towel and threw it around her body, then rushed to get the phone.

"Hey babe," Brad said when she answered. "How're you feeling?"

He sounded chipper, but she heard the weariness in his voice. She felt bad. Brad had been up most of the night with her at the hospital. He'd even driven her home after she'd been discharged. *He must be exhausted.* "Sore, but alive. What about you? You've gotta be tired."

She heard a deep sigh, and he said, "I can't say I'm not tired. At least I don't have client meetings today."

Balancing the phone between her head and shoulder, Kaitlyn placed a foot on the bed and dried her leg with the towel. "Thanks again."

"For what? Rushing to your side in the hospital? Were you expecting any less?"

She rubbed the towel over her wet hair. "I guess not. Just feel bad that you were up all night."

"You sure I can't persuade you to take the night off?"

Kaitlyn giggled. It sounded fake, but it was the best she could do. Rodney had asked her the same question when she was discharged from the hospital. "No. I'll be fine. Just gives me more reason to look forward to that hot tub in the Poconos this week-end." She went silent for a moment, then added, "I love you."

"Love you too. Be careful tonight."

After the call ended, Kaitlyn sat on the edge of the bed. She should have taken Rodney's appearance in the parking garage as an omen. But what could she have done even if he hadn't been there? She probably would've lain in the street until someone found her. Or worse, she might've been killed.

She recalled the rain splashing down on her face. Rodney refused to allow her to get up, despite her repeated attempts to do so.

"Best not to move until the ambulance gets here," he'd said. "You could've injured your neck."

She couldn't argue with his logic. Her body ached all over, making it difficult for Kaitlyn to tell what was broken and what wasn't. The water seeped through her clothes, even getting inside her leather jacket and her boots. The cold rainwater drew out buried memories of Jesse.

She remembered their first date, huddled beneath an umbrella in the bleachers, watching the Dragons—their high school football team—play a rainy Friday night game. The team lost that night, and they were both soaked by the time she got home. Their first kiss made her spine tingle.

That was a memory she wanted to keep, but it was pushed away by the dark waters of the Shallows. A hand thrust upward, breaking the surface and grasping at the air. She shuddered at the thought.

Brad met her and Rodney at the Thomas Jefferson University Hospital emergency room. Both her fiancé and the detective paced the floor of her room like expectant fathers. For her part, she endured X-rays, a CT Scan, a physical exam, and blood work, all which left her feeling not only exhausted but also a bit like some science curiosity being studied for the first time.

There had been little that Kaitlyn could remember from the accident itself. It happened too fast for her to see anything more than the flash of color and a blur of lights. She couldn't even be sure of the make or model of the car that cut her off. She thought it was blue, but she could be wrong. Even the skid was a vague memory. Leaning into the fall had been more instinct than anything else. The motorcycle safety classes she'd taken paid off after all. Kaitlyn laid the bike down and let her gear take the brunt of the impact just as she was taught. She might've been able to keep it upright if the rain hadn't slickened the road.

She remained on the bed, feeling an ache in every fiber of her body. She suddenly realized how tired she was. She'd been so concerned about Brad that she'd forgotten that she hadn't slept either. With her eyes heavy, Kaitlyn set her alarm clock to awaken her in four hours, then slipped her naked body between the sheets and drifted to sleep the moment her head hit the pillow.

———

KAITLYN TOOK her time driving into the city that afternoon. As much as she loved her Harley, she was glad to be in her Prius today. Once her motorcycle was fixed, she'd be back on it. The car offered a level of protection she needed right now. As if a car could protect her from her remorseful memories.

Kaitlyn tried to put the previous evening's accident out of her mind, but she found herself glancing at the rearview mirror far more than usual. Any time a car would linger behind the Prius for more than a few minutes, her grip on the steering wheel would tighten. She hated the fact that someone was using her deepest secret to make her afraid of her own shadow. What could they possibly gain from it all? Who could hate her so much to put her through this? Jesse's parents didn't blame her for what happened. Even if they were still alive, Kaitlyn would never believe that they would do anything like this.

Taking the parking spot nearest the elevator, Kaitlyn sat in her car for a moment. The walk to the elevator—although short—gave her pause. The parking garage appeared devoid of life, but what if someone was waiting for her? She reached for her phone and considered calling Brad. Maybe he could talk her down from her fear-fraught ledge. She stared at his name in her list of contacts; her thumb hovered over the screen. He'd still be in the office. Then, with a brisk motion, Kaitlyn slipped the phone into her bag. *No, I'm going to do this on my own.* It wasn't fair to expect him to blindly carry a burden that she refused to share with him. Opening the door of the Toyota, she stepped out, scrutinized the surrounding area, and then walked toward the elevator. Her legs trembled with each step and her pace quickened the closer she came to the doors. It wasn't until she was in the elevator that she let out a long exhale.

When Kaitlyn entered the offices at WPLX, Scott Mackay had his back to the door, his elbows leaning on the reception desk's high counter. He was deep in conversation with Sammy, who stood on the other side facing him. When she caught sight of Kaitlyn coming through the door, Sammy's eyes widened, and she let out a gasp. She rushed around the desk and grasped Kaitlyn's hands. She said, "Holy fuck! What happened?"

Scott turned as well, cursed, and crossed the office to stand beside Sammy. "My god, you okay?"

"Do I look that bad?" Kaitlyn tried to put on a smile but found it difficult. It took too much energy to make it appear even remotely genuine. "I took a tumble. Nothing's broken except the bike."

"Should've taken the night off," Scott said.

Kaitlyn shook her head. "I'm fine, really." She tried to sound convincing, but even she was having difficulty believing her own words.

"Sweetie, sweetie! You're not okay," Sammy said. "Scott's right. You should go home."

Kaitlyn held up her hand, motioning for them to stop with their fussing. "Stop it, both of you. I'm working my shift tonight. Period."

Sammy wrapped her arms around Kaitlyn, squeezing just hard enough to make her wince. Kaitlyn pushed back on the embrace. "Ow! Easy!"

"Tell you what. I'll hang out with you tonight," Sammy said. "I'll grab us dinner and keep you company."

"You don't have—"

Sammy glared at her. "Don't argue."

The phone at the reception desk rang and Sammy gave her one final stern look as if to signify that the discussion was over. Then she returned to her desk and answered the phone. Scott gestured for Kaitlyn to follow him, then walked down the hall toward his office.

Once in his office, he ushered Kaitlyn to the leather sofa along the far wall, pushed the door closed, then turned and leaned his back against it. Scott folded his arms, then frowned. "How bad is the bike?"

Kaitlyn shook her head. "Don't know yet. Terry's going to look at it later this week and let me know."

Scott sighed. "What's going on?"

Kaitlyn turned her eyes away from him and looked around the room, avoiding his stare. Scott had a long career in broadcasting, and framed photographs adorned his office walls as a testament to it. Backstage shots featured Scott with a cavalcade of pop and rock bands, from Devo, Journey, Gin Blossoms, and even Justin Timberlake. Kaitlyn's eyes lingered on the photo featuring REO Speedwagon. Her spine prickled. When she turned back to him, she smiled. "Nothing. Just an accident."

Shaking his head, Scott crossed the room and sat down next to her. "Come on. Something's up. You got a crank letter. Then flowers."

Her shoulders stiffened. How did he know about the letters? She'd been keeping that to herself. "How did—"

Scott interrupted her question. "You know what they say, telegraph, telephone, tell Kevin."

Kaitlyn allowed her shoulders to relax and slumped back into the sofa. "Yeah. There's been a couple of letters."

"A couple?"

"Like you said, it's just some crank." She shrugged, trying to make it as nonchalant as possible. It didn't feel all that convincing, and Scott's furrowed brow confirmed the feeling.

"Perhaps we should get the police involved."

She hesitated for a moment, knowing that her response wouldn't help the situation. "They already are."

Scott rose from the sofa and glared back at her. "What the hell, Kaitlyn? What's this all about?"

She'd never seen him like this before. Scott was the most composed person Kaitlyn knew. He met every crisis with the same level tone and cool stare, but now his voice cracked with emotion. His eyes were wide and a little wild. She never wanted him to know—or anyone for that matter—what was going on.

"The Lower Merion Township police are looking into it. They've got it under control."

His eyes narrowed. "Lower Merion? Why are they involved? Surely the city police should be—"

She interrupted. "A letter came to the house."

Scott ran his hand through his hair, walked across the room, then turned back to her. "Damn it. Why didn't you tell me?"

Kaitlyn rose from the sofa. She hated hiding things from Scott almost as much as she hated hiding things from Brad. The conversation needed to end before she said anything else. "Because I'll be fine. It's nothing, really." She moved toward the door. "I've got a show to prep for."

KAITLYN FOUND Kevin O'Neill at his desk when she entered the bullpen. He glanced up, then rose from his chair, mouth agape.

"What happened to you?" he said.

"Motorcycle accident. It's not as bad as it looks."

He folded his arms. "That's good, because it looks pretty bad from where I'm standing."

She crossed the office and placed her bag atop her desk. She caught sight of movement in the corner of her eye, and before she knew it, he was hovering over her shoulder. Kaitlyn stepped away from him and moved to the other side of the desk to sit down.

Kevin said, "Care to elaborate?"

She recounted an alternate version of the previous evening's crash; one that didn't include stalkers or a police escort home. Kevin was nothing more than a nosy busybody, like her elderly neighbor who always peered out of the front window. She wasn't about to give him what he craved . . . office gossip.

When she finished her story, he looked disappointed, as if her near-death experience wasn't exciting enough for him. He returned to his desk and closed the lid of his laptop. "Glad to know it wasn't serious." He grabbed his jacket from the back of the desk chair, slipped the laptop under his arm, and strode toward the door. "Have a good show."

But then he halted at the office door and turned back to her. "I didn't hear REO Speedwagon the other night. Did you forget to play it?"

Kaitlyn drew in a breath, then stammered, "I forgot."

Kevin waved his finger back and forth. "Tsk, tsk." He turned to leave, then stopped. "You know how I said that REO Speedwagon songs were all shit? I thought of a song that's even worse." He smiled. "That Christopher Cross song from the '80s. 'Think of Laura.'"

16

KAITLYN SET the warm mug of tea down beside the control console and sighed. Music drifted through the room from the ceiling speakers. She tapped the console with her fingers in rhythm with Weezer's remake of the song "Africa". Despite her best efforts, she couldn't shake the dark anxiety that hung over her. The only person who knew the truth about the Shallows was dead and long buried. There was no way Jesse was sending these letters. She refused to believe in ghosts.

She glanced over the control console to the opposite side of the studio. Sammy stood—her back to Kaitlyn—near the broad window. She'd been standing there for almost fifteen minutes, gazing down on the Philadelphia nightscape. Kaitlyn smiled, feeling certain that she knew what Sammy was thinking.

"Beautiful, isn't it?"

Sammy only responded with a nod of her head.

"You should see it when it rains," Kaitlyn added. "The wet pavement sparkles like diamonds."

Turning, Sammy crossed to the control console and took a seat across from her. "Don't think I've ever been up here at night. No wonder you like the night shift."

"It has it's perks."

Sammy sipped from the mug in her hand. "So . . . you gonna tell me what really happened?"

Kaitlyn turned her gaze toward the studio computer to avoid eye contact. She didn't want to answer these questions. "Don't know what you mean."

"Don't bullshit me. I'm not some dumb blonde." She hesitated. "Okay, I might be blonde . . . and a bit dumb, but I know when you're lying."

"It was nothing. Just an accident." Kaitlyn knew her words didn't sound convincing, but she didn't want to talk about the early morning crash. *Too many people already know too much.* The more Sammy knew, the more questions she would ask. The last thing Kaitlyn wanted was someone asking questions. She feared that— now that the police were involved—everything would come out. The Shallows, Jesse's death . . . and her part in all of it. Detective Shapiro hadn't asked too many questions. At least not yet. He appeared to accept her ignorance of the motive behind the letters. She hadn't completely lied to him. She truly had no idea why someone was sending her the letters.

"I'm not buying it," Sammy said. "You're too good of a biker."

Kaitlyn reached for the microphone and drew it close to her mouth. "Even good bikers crash."

As the song faded, she clicked on the microphone to deliver a quick station ID, and then introduce the next song. Once finished, Kaitlyn scanned the upcoming playlist, made a quick note on her notepad, and returned her gaze to Sammy.

"Fine. You don't want to tell me. That's your prerogative." Sammy turned her eyes away, feigning offense to Kaitlyn's unwillingness to talk.

"You're too much."

Sammy raised her hand and held it out. "Talk to the palm, 'cause these ears ain't listenin'."

"Someone cut in front of me, that's all. It was rainy. I swerved and lost control."

Sammy pondered the statement for a moment, then turned back to her. "Truth?"

Kaitlyn crossed her heart with her hand. "Hope to die." As soon as the words slipped from her lips, she wished she could pull them back. A shiver ran down her back as she realized what she'd said. She could've died last night. For all she knew, that might have been the objective. She smiled, hoping to not betray her concern. "Believe me?"

Sammy took a long sip from her mug, then nodded. "Yeah. How can I not?"

The irony of those words wasn't lost on Kaitlyn. She had told the truth, or at least a version of it. But she was holding back a lot from her friend. In little over a week, she'd face another anniversary, and follow her decade-long tradition of remembering the dead. She'd work her shift, return home, and open a bottle of wine. Then, she'd raise a glass to Jesse's memory, finish the bottle, and cry herself to sleep, ashamed of what she'd done. In the morning, she'd go back to being Kaitlyn Ashe, and the sins of Laura Hobson would be purged for another year.

"You gonna answer that?" Sammy's voice startled her. "Someone's calling."

Kaitlyn leaned forward and pressed the blinking button to answer the phone. "WPLX, do you have a dedication?"

"Yeah, I want to dedicate my entire night to kissing every inch of your body."

Kaitlyn felt a rush of heat on her cheeks as her face flushed with embarrassment. "Brad . . . Say hello to Sammy. She's in the studio with me tonight."

Sammy smirked and said, "Hey, Legal Eagle!"

There was a long awkward pause on the phone. "Huh, guess I should've expected that to happen one of these days."

Kaitlyn and Sammy burst out laughing. After a moment, he joined in as well. This was the second time he'd called to check up on her. The first time was around five, before she went on the air. His concern was comforting, but it made her feel guilty. She'd been lying to him for weeks, denying any knowledge of the meaning behind the letters. She was afraid of losing Brad if he discovered the truth, but was it fair to keep him in the dark?

When their laughter subsided, Brad added, "Just wanted to check on you."

"I'm fine," she said. "I've got a mug of tea and Sammy to keep me company."

"No more letters?"

Kaitlyn's eyes darted toward Sammy, who was returning her stare with raised eyebrows.

"Letters?" Sammy said.

Kaitlyn shook her head. "It's nothing." She turned her attention back to the phone. "We're good for the night."

There was a long silence on the phone, and then, "You okay getting home tonight?"

"I'll be fine. Can't imagine that lightning would try to strike twice."

"I'm not concerned about it trying. I don't want it to be successful this time," he said.

"Don't worry. Nothing will happen." She was far less certain than the words made her sound.

They hung up. Kaitlyn glanced toward Sammy and wondered how many questions were about to come her way. Sammy, to Kaitlyn's surprise, remained silent, sipping from her mug and gazing toward the window.

The request line blinked again, and Kaitlyn reached to answer it.

"WPLX, do you have a request?"

A distorted whisper replied, "Play REO Speedwagon for me. You know the song."

After she hung up the phone, Kaitlyn caught Sammy looking her way.

"You okay?" Sammy asked. "You've gone all pale."

Kaitlyn swallowed hard before answering. She nodded. "It's nothing. Just a crank."

She turned her attention to the studio computer, checking the playlist and the commercials coming up in the next break. She kept her hands out of Sammy's sight; she didn't want her to see them tremble.

17

KAITLYN CLICKED off the microphone and slid the headphones from her ears. She cleared the weather forecast from the computer screen and slid from the chair. Turning the studio monitors down until they were nothing more than a soft melody in the background, she rounded the control board and crossed to the window. A gentle rain pelted against the window. The wet roads of the city below glistened, the colorful lights creating a kaleidoscope against the moist asphalt. The forecast called for rain the rest of the evening, but things were going to clear up the next morning. Just in time for her first day in the Poconos with Brad.

She twisted her neck to the right and left, trying to relieve the stiffness. It'd been two days since the accident. She'd hoped that the aching would have subsided by now, but it seemed she was destined to be sore for another day or two. At least there was a hot tub waiting in their room in the Poconos. No matter how late they arrived, she planned to take a long soak.

She caught the reflection of the wall clock in the window. She smiled. 10:51. A little over an hour before her shift was over. Brad would be waiting for her in front of the building at midnight. They'd planned to go straight to the Poconos, but Kaitlyn only half-packed her bag before she had to leave for work earlier in the evening. Brad would be a bit irked to find that they'd have to circle back to her house before heading to the resort. But she'd make it up to him over the weekend.

She circled back around to the studio's control console and slid onto the chair. The flashing request lines caught her attention, and she leaned over to answer the first. It was a young teenage voice requesting a rap song that Kaitlyn knew would never be in the rotation at WPLX. After politely declining to play the song, she hung up and shook her head. *Don't they even listen to the station?*

She let the other request lines flash unanswered. Her mind hadn't been on the show tonight, or for most of the week for that matter. Monday evening had been the first time she'd realized how dangerous this situation had become. Until the accident, Kaitlyn had foolishly felt that she could keep things at arm's length and remain relatively safe. As frightened as she was to have a letter show up on her front door, it had never occurred to her that it might be a prelude to something more perilous.

Her thoughts jumped to a night sixteen years ago. She ran along the path in the dark. The lights burning in the house ahead were her only guiding light. She stumbled and fell, crashing into the high grass that lined the dark trail. The tears that burned her eyes and stained her cheeks flowed freely. What would she tell them? How would she explain what happened? The truth would crush the Riley family. They were such loving parents. It would devastate them. She scrambled to her feet and pressed on.

When she reached the house, she climbed the porch stairs and flung open the door. She practically fell into the living room beyond. Her blouse was torn; her jeans were dirt-stained. She gasped for air between sobs. Mr. Riley was quick to his feet, dropping his newspaper and rushing to her.

"Marion," he shouted. "Get in here." He placed his hand on Kaitlyn's shoulder and guided her to the sofa. "What's wrong, sweetheart?"

Her words came out in short bursts between breaths. "Jesse . . .

fell in . . . Shallows . . . I think . . ." and then she remembered adding one final word "Dead." Everything after that was a blur.

A lone tear escaped from her eye, raced down her cheek, and dropped onto the control console. Kaitlyn looked down and stared at the tiny puddle. She blinked a few times, hoping to stop any others that might try to liberate themselves. She'd worked so hard to bury the Shallows, bury it deep. It should've been long forgotten, a distant memory locked away from public view. What purpose could someone wish to achieve by dredging up Jesse's death? She wiped another tear from her eye before it had a chance to escape.

A quick glance at the clock told her it was time for a station ID. She reached for the headphones, cleared her throat, and clicked on the microphone. The words flowed from her lips, smooth and concise as if she hadn't a care in the world. Listeners would never know that she was trembling as she delivered her lines.

BRAD TURNED the BMW onto Garnet Lane and drifted into the driveway. The surrounding neighborhood was quiet and still, just as it was every night when Kaitlyn returned from work. Identical driveway post lights created an outline of the road as it wound deeper into the neighborhood. There were no lights in the windows of neighboring houses.

Brad had taken the news about her half-packed bag better than she'd anticipated. Kaitlyn told him as soon as she'd climbed into the car. He'd given her a smile, a kiss on the cheek, and then said, "No worries. We'll get there when we get there."

When the car halted in front of the garage door, Brad turned off the engine. Kaitlyn hopped from the car and leaned in the open passenger door. She gave Brad a broad smile. "Give me just a couple minutes. This shouldn't take long."

"You sure you don't want me to come in with you?"

"I'll be fine." She glanced around the neighborhood. *Nothing out of the ordinary.* "If something happens, I'll scream. You can rush in and be my knight in shining armor."

"If you're sure." He nodded. "Take your time. We're not in a hurry."

She pushed the door closed and dashed along the sidewalk to the front door. Inside, she flipped on the foyer light, tossed her keys on the table by the door, and sped up the stairs. The duffel bag still sat on the bed, right where she'd left it. She glanced in the bag to refresh her memory of what she'd already packed, and then grabbed a pair of jeans from the dresser, along with a beige cable sweater. She slipped into the bathroom, returning moments later with a small makeup case, which she tossed into the duffel bag.

"Hiking boots," she said aloud. "Can't forget hiking boots."

She grabbed her brown Merrill boots from the closet and set them on the floor next to the bed. She pondered what else she needed to take, then smiled. Crossing to the dresser, she pulled open the top drawer and gave the contents careful scrutiny. Her fingers dipped into the drawer and pulled out a black chiffon negligee. She shook her head, returned it to the drawer, and pulled out a similar one; this time in red. Her smile broadened as she carefully folded the delicate lace and placed it in the duffel bag. She'd never been one for wearing sexy underwear. Wearing a thong always made her feel like she was flossing between her butt cheeks. But, this weekend, she'd make an exception. Brad was in for a real treat.

Before she could close the drawer, her eyes fell on the small box near the back. She hesitated before reaching for it. She'd tried to put it out of her mind, hoping to forget that it was back there, buried beneath piles of underwear and bras. She removed the lid from the square box and reached her fingers inside. The frayed leather thread draped over her hand as she stared at the silver Celtic star knot in her palm.

"Jesse," she whispered.

The clasps were broken where they'd snapped when she pulled the necklace from Jesse's neck. It'd been a final desperate grasp as he fell backward. The leather was too thin to stand the strain. When it was all over, she clung to the broken necklace as evidence that she tried to save him. But she knew better.

A horn honked from outside, jarring her back to the present. She placed the necklace back in the box, then moved to the window. Kaitlyn pulled the curtains aside and looked down on the driveway. The honk was coming from Brad's BMW, which was shrouded in shadows. The light above the garage door was out. Funny, she hadn't noticed it earlier.

Why was he honking? He'd said they weren't in a hurry. And she was sure she hadn't been in the house more than a few minutes. A moment later, the honking stopped. She smiled at his impatience.

Kaitlyn returned to the closet and searched through her blouses, looking for a couple to take with her. Satisfied with her selection, she added them, along with a sweatshirt, to the duffel bag. Throwing in a couple pairs of socks, she took a quick inventory before zipping the bag closed. Her jaw tightened and she looked toward the window when another horn blew outside. *Enough already*. She slung the bag over her shoulder, picked up her hiking boots, and hurried from the bedroom.

When she pulled the front door closed, Kaitlyn glanced at the BMW in the driveway. She turned to lock the door, but a sense of unease gripped her. Something wasn't right. She didn't know what, but something was off. She turned the key in the lock and moved toward the car.

Each step forward became heavier, as if she was wading through molasses. She peered at the car, trying to see into the darkened interior, unable to make out anything other than Brad's motionless silhouette in the driver's seat. *There's nothing wrong*. She gulped down each breath. Her heart pounded against her chest. She fought the urge to rush back into the house, lock the door, and hide away in a dark closet. *Stop overreacting*.

"Brad?" she said, half whisper and half shout. He didn't move.

When she was feet from the car, she glanced through the windshield. The car's interior was shadowed by the streetlight behind. Beads of sweat formed on her lips. She licked them away, catching the faint taste of salt on her tongue. Why was she trembling? She wanted to call out for Brad, but the words were lost in her throat.

She reached for the car door. The light within the car flicked on as she pulled the door open.

And then Kaitlyn's scream echoed down Garnet Lane.

18

I'M WAITING for her again, but not in the garage. Tonight, I'm parked across from the main entrance to the building. I'd been circling the block for the better part of an hour, waiting for her boyfriend to show up. She didn't drive into work this afternoon, instead taking an Uber, so it was only fair to assume he was coming to get her. When I saw him pull up ten minutes ago, I pulled over and turned off my headlights.

Fifteen minutes till midnight. She's still on the air. I've been listening most of the night. She still refuses to play the song. Doesn't she understand that I need to hear it, must hear it? Laura always was audacious. Always independent, never one to bow to pressure. Not even for someone she loved. Oh, the nights we spent on the banks of the Shallows. Just the three of us. Dancing beneath the moonlight, splashing in the water, watching the stars from the dock. REO Speedwagon playing over and over on the boombox. That song was just as much mine as it was theirs. She seemed so innocent back then. We were all innocent. Laura was just a guest, just a fleeting memory compared to me. The Shallows were mine—mine and his—long before she came along.

Why won't she play the song? That one simple act could

change all of this. I might stay my hand if she would just play it once. Just once. Is that too much to ask?

I pull a cigarette from the pack in the cupholder, light it, and place it between my lips. Crack my window and blow smoke out into the night air, and then laugh. Who am I kidding? There is only one way that this will end. Only one thing that I want. Her defiance will only make her downfall all the sweeter. Laura will know my wrath and beg for mercy when I'm done with her.

Five minutes till midnight. He still sits, waiting for her. His head is bowed forward, and the car's interior is awash with a faint blue glow. Must be looking at his phone. She signs off, saying goodbye to her listeners. None of them know who she really is. None know what I do.

I flick ash out the window, watch and wait. They're heading to the Poconos tonight. A romantic weekend. Perhaps she thinks that'll put her out of my reach for a few days. She'll be surprised tomorrow morning. I've got a new letter sitting on the passenger seat, as well as a bottle of bubbly. Nothing ruins the mood more than an unexpected bottle delivered to your door.

Five after midnight. Laura emerges from the building and climbs into the BMW. They have a lengthy discussion before driving off. I toss my cigarette out the window and follow them, but something's wrong. They're heading toward Bala Cynwyd, not the Poconos. Why? Did they cancel their plans? Do they know I'm here? I don't like this. It isn't the way I envisioned things would go tonight. Maybe I should back off and regroup.

I keep his taillights in sight but follow at a distance. They couldn't possibly know that I'm following. But this doesn't feel right. I check the rearview mirror. No one is behind me. I need another cigarette. I try to pull one from the pack as I drive.

Shit. It dropped between the seats, out of my reach. My fingers search between the seat and center console. A quick glance down doesn't help. It's all darkened shadows between the seats. When I look up, the BMW is gone. Damn it. This night is starting to really suck. There's bile forming in the back of my throat. I'm as angry at myself as I am with her. Must keep pressuring her. Must not give up.

I'm guessing they're heading to her house. I might still be able to catch up to them.

I WAS RIGHT. When I pull past her house, Laura is just climbing out of the BMW. She leans in and speaks to Brad for a moment, then heads toward the house. I drive past, turn around up the road, and pull over by the curb a few houses up. His window is down and the blue glow within the BMW returns. He is so preoccupied, so vulnerable. If I wanted to, I could easily . . .

Could it be that easy? I look at the letter still sitting next to the bottle on my car seat. Its message would be appropriate. Think of the blow it would deliver to Laura. The pain it would inflict. My stomach quivers as my mind races through the scenario. How would I do it? A gun would be too loud. Don't want to draw attention to things before I'm away. My knife. A short, serrated blade I keep on my belt, hidden in the small of my back. Silent. Deadly. Perfect.

What about the risk? Any of her neighbors could look out their window and see me. Or worse, Laura could come out of the house before I'm finished. There are so many ways this could go south. Damn the risk. It's too good of an opportunity to pass up.

I slip on surgical gloves, pull out the knife, and give the handle and blade a careful wipe on my coat. Then, I return it to its sheath. I dig the cigarette pack out from beside the seat and light one up. Out of the car, my footsteps move to the beat of my racing heart. I pause at the end of the driveway and take a deep breath. My senses are hypersensitive, feeling and hearing everything. A dog barks in the distance. The breeze excites the hairs on the back of my neck. Cigarette smoke cools my throat and nostrils. I toss it away into the nearby storm drain, then bury my hands in my coat pockets and walk toward the BMW.

The driver's window is still down, and he doesn't appear to hear me approach. As I draw near, he must catch sight of me in the mirror. He turns his head toward me. "Hi. Didn't expect to see you here." He pauses, then adds, "Especially at this hour."

I shrug and position myself close to the car window. "I was in the neighborhood."

"Oh." He seems puzzled. His eyes narrow, and his mouth turns up in a crooked smile. He doesn't ask further questions.

"I thought you were going to the Poconos this weekend."

He looks toward the house. "Kaitlyn ran out of time this afternoon to pack. She's throwing a few things in an overnight bag."

That name makes me cringe. Does Laura think she's fooling anyone? What if I told him the truth right now? I could bring her whole world crashing down in an instant. But no. I have something better in mind.

I pull a pack of cigarettes from my coat pocket and light one. "Has she ever told you about the Shallows?"

He doesn't turn toward me, just keeps looking at the house. "I've tried to get her to talk, but no luck. I know there's something she's not telling me . . ."

He turns to look at me. He frowns, perhaps at the sight of my gloves. He holds me with a perplexed gaze. "Why are you wearing gloves?"

Adrenaline surges through my body, putting it on a razor's edge. There is no thought in my mind, just an uncontrollable urge that sends my head spinning. He has no idea how much danger he is in. This will be too easy.

With a slow, calm motion, I place the cigarette between my lips, and take a long drag. "Don't want to leave fingerprints."

I catch the questioning look in his eyes as I reach behind me and draw the knife from the sheath. His eyes widen with realization. He's a moment too late.

I drive the serrated blade into the side of his neck. It's a quick, hard thrust. There is little resistance. The blade pierces the skin and plunges through muscle. He gasps for breath. A gurgle escapes from his lips.

My god, I've done it. I feel lightheaded, dizzy. The thrill of feeling his blood trickle over my fingers is almost orgasmic. It's warm, thick, and I want to laugh aloud. I want to roar to the highest heavens. I'm trembling, but not from fear or shame, but from excitement. Utter exhilaration. My knees go weak. I rest my free hand on the car to steady myself.

He tries to speak, but it is just an unintelligible whisper. I tighten my grip on the knife's hilt and lean toward the car window.

With my free hand, I pull the cigarette from my lips and blow smoke into the car window. "What's that? You want to know why?"

He doesn't reply, only gasps for a breath that doesn't come. His eyes dart from side to side. I draw the knife out until only the tip remains within the wound. The skin around the wound is ripped and jagged. The blade's teeth drip with his blood.

"She never told you about Laura Hobson, did she? Too late to ask now."

I thrust the knife forward again. My pent-up anger and hatred powers the knife into his neck up to the hilt. I twist it and give it a fierce jerk forward. Blood pumps from the wound. Must have hit an artery. It is like a waterfall, pouring down his neck, soaking into his shirt. The smell is sweet and metallic. It's one I'm so familiar with, but it is somehow different this time. It is euphoric, like a sugar rush I'd get as a child. I want this moment to last forever.

His body convulses. Blood seeps from the corner of his mouth. I untangle my fingers from the knife hilt. My hand is coated with the thick, dark fluid that drips to the ground. I flex my fingers. The surgical gloves crinkle. Oh, if Laura could only see me now. To see my fingers covered with his blood. To see the pure joy on my face. To see who I am.

The BMW's horn startles me. His hand presses on the steering wheel. The final desperate action of a dead man. He gasps. Then dies. The horn goes silent.

Time for me to leave. But, there's one last thing to do. I pull the folded letter from my pocket and lean into the car. Where to put it? I don't want it found immediately. It takes a couple tries to get it to stay in place. It falls into the pool of blood once, staining the paper a dark red. When it's in position, I stand and take one more drag on the cigarette, then toss it away into the grass. One more thing to do. I reach into the car and honk the horn. Why not? Might as well wake the neighborhood. Let them all watch Laura fall to pieces. Then, I rush to my car. Need to go to the Shallows and tell Jesse what I've done.

19

RODNEY HAD ALWAYS BEEN AMAZED at how much blood there was in the human body. Ten years of viewing crime scenes had done little to dull the awe in which he often found himself. Every pool of blood was shaped differently. Every splatter had a unique motif. It was not so much a morbid fascination with gore as it was an appreciation of the unintended art of human nature. The colors, the smells, and the patterns always varied, but the wonderment that came within the first minute always remained. This amazement, however, would quickly dissipate to be replaced by a faint sense of nausea. The realization that the captivating yet grotesque composition was nothing more than the result of human-on-human violence would return him to his senses, leaving his fascination to retreat inward in shame.

He made a slow circuit around the BMW, studying it with meticulous attention. The harsh halogen lights that had been set up around the car obliterated the shadows of the night. He ignored the red lights flashing in the corner of his eyes. The three police cars, as well as the ambulance, clogged Garnet Lane and drew the attention of the neighborhood gawkers, who had come out in force. Men and women in robes stood in a small huddle under the streetlight across the lane, watching the flurry of activity and whispering amongst themselves.

Rodney walked along the side of the car and halted by the driver's door. Kneeling by the window, he peered in at the driver. He sighed loudly as he made mental notes. A knife driven straight into the side of the neck. Small spiraled handle in black and white. No other sign of injury. Must have hit the carotid. Substantial blood loss. Death was probably instantaneous. He'd have to wait for confirmation from the Medical Examiner on that last point. He returned his gaze to the knife handle. Where had he seen it before?

He glanced toward the house for a moment and wondered how Kaitlyn was coping. It was one thing to lose a fiancé to murder. It was something totally different to be the one who found the body. This had to be a terrible shock for her. Returning his eyes to the body, he studied Brad's ashen face. The bulging eyes stared straight ahead, frozen in a state of deathly blindness. The mouth gaped open, a trickle of blood creeping from the corner. The crimson fluid from the wound on his neck had saturated his shirt and flowed down onto the seat and floor. It was a brutal scene. Rodney chewed on his bottom lip. Brad didn't deserve to die like this. No one did. "I'll catch the bastard," he said quietly. "I promise."

Footsteps approached from behind him. He knew who it was without looking. The sound of her boots on the concrete was distinctive. "Took you long enough," he said.

"Sorry. I was over in Jersey when I got the call," Julie said.

Rodney rose to his feet, turned his back to the BMW, and peeled off his surgical gloves. "It's a messy business."

Julie's hands were buried in the pockets of her jacket, holding it closed as if she were cold. Her shoulders quivered, and her face looked pale. Perhaps it was just the harshness of the halogens. Rodney frowned. "You okay?"

Julie nodded. "Huh? Yeah. Just a little tired."

He stepped aside while she gave the scene a closer examination. He turned toward the street, catching sight of her blue Volkswagen parked up the road, the red teardrop adding its own light to the already kaleidoscopic flashes from the other police cars illuminating the night.

Julie gave a low whistle. "Straight through the neck. Very clean."

Rodney returned his gaze to the BMW. "Not easy to do." He motioned with his right hand to demonstrate. His arm touched the window post. "If the attack was from behind, the door frame gets in the way."

"Seems awkward. Maybe left-handed?" Julie added.

Rodney changed positions and repeated the thrust, this time with his left hand. "It works, but that means he would see it coming. Why would he not defend himself?"

"Maybe he knew his assailant. Thought there was no threat."

"Perhaps," Rodney said. "He pointed toward the cigarette stub he'd stepped around earlier. "He might've been a smoker."

Julie straightened up, turning to face him. He was surprised at her very cursory examination. It wasn't like her to give a crime scene such a brief review. He'd seen her spend an hour or more on the initial examination. He narrowed his eyes. "You've seen all you wanted to see?"

She moved around the car, hands still deep in her pockets. "I've seen enough." She turned toward the house, and then looked back at him. "What's her story?"

Rodney stared at her. Perhaps she was tired after all.

"I haven't gotten too many details yet, but they were heading for a weekend away," he started to explain.

"To the Poconos."

He raised one eyebrow. "How'd you know?"

"She told me the other day."

Rodney rounded the car to stand next to her. "They had to stop here on their way out of town. While she was inside the house, someone killed him."

Julie was quiet for an instant, chewing on her bottom lip as her gaze focused on the house. "Seems like a convenient story."

"It's a bit early to be casting suspicions, don't you think?" He frowned, folding his arms.

"Just keeping an open mind."

A crime scene technician approached with a camera to take crime scene photos. Rodney touched Julie's arm and guided her away from the BMW. "What's gotten into you? We've not even spoken to her yet, and you're already casting her as a murderer."

Julie pulled her arms into her body, wrapping her coat even tighter around her. Her eyes darted down toward the ground, and then back up at him. "Sorry. I've . . . There's been a death in the family."

He closed his eyes, letting out a long sigh. "Julie, I'm sorry. Why didn't you say?" It was just like her to be dealing with a personal tragedy and still come to a crime scene. He placed a reassuring hand on her shoulder. "You shouldn't be here. Go home."

Slipping her hands from her coat pockets, she folded her arms and shook her head. "No. I'll be fine." She paused, as if to rein in her emotions. "Just a little distracted. Work's the best thing for me. Helps take my mind off it."

Rodney frowned, then glanced back toward the car. The forensics investigator leaned in the driver's window, preparing to take another photo. He never could understand Julie's obsession with working so hard. He'd learned long ago that he needed to make a point of separating from the job lest the job tear him to pieces. Rodney had always assumed that viewing death as frequently as he did couldn't possibly be good for him. Violent or nonviolent. Accidental or murder. It didn't matter what kind of death. Finding a way to stifle his own natural tendency toward obsessive curiosity had become his upmost priority. His study of ancient philosophy was his latest purview.

"Who died?" he asked.

She was slow to answer. "My cousin."

"Damn it, Julie. Go home. Take care of your family." He glanced at the crime scene tech, still leaning in the car window.

When he looked back at Julie, he locked eyes with hers. Perhaps it was a trick of the light, they looked vacant.

"I've not seen him for years." The corner of her mouth twitched upward into a half-smile. "I'm fine."

"If you're sure." Despite his desire to send her home, Rodney didn't have the rank nor clout to do so. He knew to argue further with her would get him nowhere.

"Sir!"

The interruption came from behind him. When he turned, the forensics investigator waved frantically, beckoning him over. He nudged Julie with his elbow. "Come on, he's found something."

As they approached, the tech held a folded sheet of paper between his gloved fingers. The edges of the fold were stained crimson. "I found this on the floor, by the accelerator," the tech said. "It might've fallen from his hand or lap."

Rodney pulled on a pair of gloves, and took the paper, turning it over and over. Several smudges of blood marred the otherwise white sheet. As he unfolded the paper, he swallowed hard. His stomach quaked with queasiness. It was just as he'd expected. Another escalation. He hated being right.

The words on the paper were, like the other letters, clippings from magazines. The message, however, was shorter than the others. Concise and to the point. As his eyes read, and then reread, the missive, the grief weighed heavy on his heart.

Compliments of the Shallows

20

KAITLYN WAS in the living room, hunched over on the same sofa she'd been sitting on when Rodney had first met her. Her auburn hair had fallen forward to conceal her face from view. Apart from the presence of a box of tissue between her feet, it seemed as if he was looking back in time. It'd been what? Two weeks, almost to the day, since he'd first met Kaitlyn Ashe and heard of the mysterious Shallows. Despite the time that had passed, he knew little more than a scattering of details about her with nothing to tie any of it back to the letters.

The middle-aged woman sitting next to Kaitlyn looked up as they entered. She wore an off-white bathrobe. *Must have rushed straight from bed at the first scream.* She rubbed Kaitlyn's back with a gentle, reassuring touch. Shrugging her shoulders, the woman turned her gaze back to Kaitlyn, who sobbed softly.

Rodney and Julie remained in the doorway for a few moments, waiting for Kaitlyn to acknowledge their presence. When it was obvious that she hadn't heard them enter, he politely cleared his throat. Kaitlyn looked up, eyes inflamed and cheeks damp from a recent onslaught of tears. He was reminded of the day Carol was arrested. She'd been in his living room, crying much the same way.

Her hair had been disheveled and her eyes just as red. Why hadn't he protected her?

He crossed the room and took a seat on the sofa across from Kaitlyn. The moment eerily paralleled his first visit to this house. He sat in the same place, staring across at the same young woman. The only difference being that, last time, Brad had been seated next to his girlfriend. This time, he was dead.

Rodney always found this to be the most difficult part of the job. "Ms. Ashe. First, let me express my deepest condolences. I'm sure I speak for Detective Lewis as well when I say that we're sorry for your loss." Rodney took a quick breath and then leaned forward. "I know this is a difficult time, but we need to ask you some questions. Do you feel up to it?"

Kaitlyn reached for a tissue, and gave a brief nod. She dabbed her eyes with the tissue. The woman next to her looked at him with a questioning glance. "Would you like me to leave?" she asked.

"You are?" Julie said.

"Betsy Wilson. I live next door. I rushed over when I heard her screaming." The woman shook her head slowly. "Such a horrible thing."

Kaitlyn grasped the woman's hand, squeezing it gently. "Betsy, thanks. I really appreciate you being here, but you can go. I'll be okay."

Betsy looked at Rodney. Her gaze held the same dilemma that he'd seen in a thousand eyes before—the desire to provide comfort to someone who was in need, while wishing to be as far from a horrible situation as possible. No one wanted to be involved in a murder. Not the victims. Not the witnesses. Not the families, and certainly not the neighbors. People wanted to watch from afar without getting involved. He tried to give her a reassuring smile but wasn't certain how successful he'd been. "We'll probably want to speak to you in the near future, but you can go if you'd like."

The woman glanced once more at Kaitlyn, who gave a brief nod. Betsy rose from the sofa, placing a hand on Kaitlyn's shoulder. "If you need anything . . ."

Kaitlyn's eyes lingered on the living room doorway once the woman had departed. She was lost in thought. Rodney remained silent, not wanting to add further to her already traumatized state. He'd wait until she was ready to talk.

"Ms. Ashe, we've got those questions to ask," Julie said, "if you wouldn't mind giving us your attention."

Rodney's head jerked abruptly to the right. He glared up at Julie, who stood beside him, notebook in hand. His face grew warm with irritation at her lack of empathy. He tried to mark it up as a result of her own recent loss, but it still didn't excuse the behavior. He needed Kaitlyn to give concise and accurate answers, not be overwhelmed with grief and antagonism. "When you're ready," he said.

She turned her head toward him. Her faint smile looked forced. "How can I help?"

Rodney returned her smile. "I know this will be difficult, but can you tell us what happened?"

He listened as Kaitlyn detailed the events leading up to Brad's death. She explained how they'd planned to leave from the radio station for a long weekend in the Poconos immediately after her shift had ended. Not wanting to leave her Prius in the parking garage all weekend, she'd taken an Uber to work earlier in the day with the expectation that Brad would pick her up that night.

"I should've taken my bag with me, but I'd forgotten that I had a lot of production work to get done before my shift," she said. "I ended up rushing out of the house before I'd finished packing."

Brad had been waiting for her as planned in front of the building. He wasn't bothered at all by the need for a quick detour. Kaitlyn went on to talk about their arrival at her house, and how Brad had remained in the BMW while she went in to pack. She stopped her narrative to regain control of her emotions, which seemed on the verge of erupting at any moment. Rodney did what he could to reassure her. "Take your time. If you need a break . . ."

She gave him a brief shake of her head. "I'm fine. Just need a second." She grabbed another tissue, wiped her moist eyes, and blew her nose. Wadding up the tissue, she allowed it to fall to the floor between her feet. "Where was I?"

"You'd just arrived at the house," Julie said.

Kaitlyn nodded, and then continued to tell them how she'd gone upstairs to finish packing. Her bag had been on the bed, right where she'd left it. It hadn't been that long, Kaitlyn explained, before she'd heard the horn from outside. By the time she'd made it to the bedroom window, the horn had stopped.

"Were you irritated by the honking horn?" Julie asked.

"Of course. It was the middle of the night," Kaitlyn said. "The neighbors were asleep. I didn't want to upset them."

Rodney heard Julie scribble a brief note in her notebook. "Upset them? Have you had issues in the past?"

Kaitlyn brushed aside a stray hair that had fallen into her face. "When I first moved in, there were some . . . complaints about my motorcycle. I don't exactly keep normal work hours."

"What kind of complaints? Calls to the police?"

Kaitlyn shook her head. "No. Just a couple letters from the homeowners association."

Julie gestured toward the front door with her pen. "Betsy seemed nice. Have you resolved your issues with your neighbors?"

Rodney rubbed his forehead with the tips of his fingers. He didn't want things to drift too far astray, which is what he feared would happen if he didn't step in. "What happened after you looked out the bedroom window?"

Kaitlyn seemed startled for a moment by the sudden change in conversation, but quickly recovered. She explained how she'd finished packing and headed out to the car. She hesitated for a moment, then added, "The horn honked again."

"Was this before you left the house?" Rodney asked.

Kaitlyn shook her head. "Yes. I was still in the bedroom." She appeared to be on the brink of sobbing.

Rodney rose from his seat. "Let's take a break. Give you a couple minutes to compose yourself."

Kaitlyn, however, seemed to have other ideas. "No. We need to get through this." She waited for Rodney to be seated again before she continued. "I felt like something was wrong. I don't know why. Just intuition. I should've gone back in the house . . . I wanted to go back in the house. But . . ." Her words dropped off for a moment. "I think a part of me knew what I'd find. When I opened to the car door, I saw . . ." She waved her hand toward the window, as if she couldn't bear to say that she'd found her fiancé dead with a knife through his throat.

———

THE QUESTIONING CONTINUED for another hour, and by the time Rodney had stepped out of the house, the sun was beginning to rise. The medical examiner had long since removed the body, and the crime scene technician was busy arranging to have the BMW removed to the lab for further examination. The small crowd that had gathered earlier across the street was still there, apparently not wanting to leave until the show was over.

He folded his arms, breathing in the crisp morning air. His eyes felt heavy, a reminder that he'd not gotten much sleep the night before. He turned the past couple hours over in his mind. Kaitlyn's story fit the facts as he saw them. Someone had approached the BMW, killing her fiancé while she was in the house. But why? Less than a week ago, someone had tried to run the woman off the road. He would've expected another attack on Kaitlyn, not on Brad. Why the change from attacking her to killing her fiancé? Perhaps to hurt Kaitlyn? That seemed like the only answer that made sense.

He returned to the front of the garage, pausing to tell the tech to take the ladder as possible evidence. Then Rodney stood beneath the garage light, his back to the garage door. He hadn't planned to tell Kaitlyn about the letter found on Brad's body, at least not this morning. He wanted to give her time to get over the initial shock, but Julie had other plans. She'd broached the subject within the first ten minutes of the conversation.

"Ms. Ashe, we found something on your fiancé's body," Julie said.

Kaitlyn looked up at the detective, eyes red and tear-stained. "What?"

"A letter, similar to the ones that you've been receiving."

Rodney saw Kaitlyn's shoulders give a violent shudder and heard her take a quick breath. He wasn't happy that Julie brought up the letter, but he decided not to interrupt. Instead, he peered at Kaitlyn, studying her face and her reaction to what was coming next.

"The message was brief," said Julie. "It just said 'Compliments of the Shallows.'"

For a moment, he thought Kaitlyn was going to burst into tears. Her bottom lip quivered, but, in the end, she was stronger than he thought. Her eyes drifted from his partner to him, and then out through the window behind him. He wasn't sure if she was looking at anything in particular, and he fought the urge to turn and look himself.

"Don't you think it's about time you told us about the Shallows?" Julie's voice was stern, far more than necessary. Rodney gave her a disapproving look.

Kaitlyn continued to gaze out the window as if she hadn't heard the detective. Then, she looked at each of them in turn, and then down at the floor. "I've told you before. I have no idea. Why do you keep asking me?" Her voice wavered for a moment. She turned back to the window. "I don't have any answers for you. I don't know anything."

When he heard the front door open, he moved back up the sidewalk, meeting Kaitlyn as she stepped out of the house. A black duffel bag was slung over her shoulder.

"Julie will run you over to the hotel and get you settled," he said. "The house will have to remain sealed for a few days while we process the crime scene. Okay?"

Kaitlyn nodded, her eyes taking discreet glances toward the

empty car in the driveway. He could tell that she didn't want to look but couldn't help herself.

"You'll be safe there. I'll call later to check up on you," he said.

Julie led Kaitlyn toward a waiting police car. He watched them slide into the back seat. A uniformed officer climbed in behind the wheel, pulled the car away from the curb, and drove off up Belmont Avenue.

21

THE DARK and murky water surrounded Kaitlyn. Her eyes were fixed on the faint glow above her. Holding her breath, she flailed her arms. *Gotta swim upward toward the light.* She couldn't be too far from the surface. It was the Shallows after all. The water pressed against her hands, propelling her forward with each stroke. It was icy cold. She shivered. The light above grew brighter as she drew close. She just had to break the surface.

Suddenly, the fingers wrapped around her naked ankle. She wanted to scream. But, to open her mouth meant she'd drown. She drew back for another stroke. More ferocity behind it this time. But she was no longer moving forward.

She gazed down at her feet. The gangly fingers of the pale hand reached out from the depths. Held her in a tenacious grip. Kaitlyn kicked at the hand with her free foot. *Have to break free.* The grasp only tightened. She flailed with all of her might. *Break the surface.* She had to break the surface.

Another hand grabbed at her free ankle, and a third clamped onto her calf. Her strokes became deranged, a chaotic struggle to extricate herself from her ghostly restraints. She gazed down and saw a fourth and fifth hand stretch out from the depths. The downward pull was overwhelming. The light above her faded. When two more hands grabbed at her hips, she stopped trying to swim. She focused on freeing herself. Pried at the fingers. To no avail. She squirmed against their iron hold in a frenzied panic. Unable to control it any longer, she opened her mouth and screamed.

Kaitlyn shot up in bed, soaked in sweat. She kicked at the sheets, which had tangled around her ankles. Struggling free from the cloth, she scrambled to the head of the bed and drew her knees up against her chest. Her arms wrapped around her legs, clinging to them tightly. She rocked back and forth; her back banged lightly on the wall behind her.

The room was still dark, but a line of light shone in from between the drawn curtains. She wanted to switch on the light, but Kaitlyn didn't want to leave the relative comfort of the bed. Her eyes traced the shadows in the far corners, looking for movement that wasn't there. The cotton of her pink T-shirt—drenched in sweat—clung to her body. She shivered, not sure if it was because of chilled fabric touching her or the twinge of fear that lingered from the nightmare.

As her racing heart began to slacken, Kaitlyn unfurled her legs and reached for the bedside light. The incandescence swallowed the shadows, bathing the room in harsh white light. She slid from the bed and crossed to the window. She thrust the drapes apart, allowing the sun to flood into the room. She squinted against the bright light and gazed out at the parking lot that served as the room's view. A glance back at the clock on the bedside table told her it was 8:37.

She'd been in bed for over twelve hours, but it had been a fitful sleep, waking and sleeping in short bursts throughout the night. She scanned the hotel room, reflecting on the generic bleakness of the furnishings. Framed featureless prints adorned the walls, adding to the nondescript nature of the room. It felt bland, lifeless, and uninspired. She drew in a deep breath, and then allowed it to escape in the form of a long sigh.

After Detective Lewis had left, Kaitlyn sat on the edge of the bed for what seemed like an eternity. Loud, violent bawling had alternated with stoic silence. A glance at the ring on her finger induced uncontrollable sobbing. When the stiff mattress springs had become too intolerable to ignore any longer, she'd moved to the maroon armchair across the room. The cushion sank beneath her weight, reminding her that she was in a mediocre hotel and not at home. There she resumed her plummet into grief and anguish. At some point, she must have fallen asleep, for she awoke sometime in the middle of the night to slip between the sheets of the bed.

She'd only grieved like this once before—the night Jesse died. Kaitlyn could still feel Jesse's arms pulling her close. His lips pressed hard against hers. His hands tearing at her shirt. Damn it, she didn't want these memories. Not now. Not ever. All she wanted to do was forget.

She moved into the small bathroom. The beige-on-white decor was characterless and reminded her further that she was far from the comforts of home. After what had happened, she doubted that home would ever be truly comforting again.

She splashed a handful of cold water onto her face. It didn't help. She could almost feel the cold car door handle between her fingers as she pulled it open. She'd leaned into the car, but it'd taken a moment for everything to register. Brad's head leaning forward against the steering wheel, his hands limp in his lap. The blood in all its crimson horror. She remembered few details after that, just hazy, unconnected images.

And then, a vague sense of someone placing their arms around her shoulders and a faint voice saying, "Let go, sweetie. Let go." Did they have to pry her fingers off the car door? Yes, she remembered being forcibly drawn away from the BMW. Kaitlyn had screamed for Brad again and again and struggled to return to the car. Her biceps were still sore from her neighbors' grip. She couldn't believe he was dead. Kaitlyn wanted to grab Brad's shoulders and shake him, in case he'd just fallen asleep. As she howled with grief, she clung to the hope that it was all nothing more than a horrifying nightmare.

Somehow, she'd ended up in her living room, Betsy Wilson

beside her trying to assuage the unassuageable. Her neighbor's comforting hand had done little to stop her weeping. By the time Detectives Shapiro and Lewis arrived to question her, she'd almost come to terms with the catastrophic reality. Their appearance in her living room drove home the finality of Brad's death.

Kaitlyn gazed into the bathroom mirror, examining the dark shadows beneath her eyes. The morning after Jesse's drowning had found her in a similar state of despair, grief, and guilt. Even back then, she knew that what happened at the Shallows would someday come back to haunt her. Was this what people called karma? A life for a life?

The room phone rang from the bedroom. She exited the bathroom, walked around the bed, and picked up the handset from the end table. "Hello?" She listened to the silence on the other end of the line. No one was speaking, but Kaitlyn could tell that someone was there. "Hello? Who is this?"

The voice had a grating metallic edge to it. She'd done enough audio production throughout her radio career to recognize when a vocoder was being used to modulate a voice. "Hello Laura. Bet you never thought you'd hear from me again," it said.

She gripped the phone with quaking hands. Kaitlyn knew she was alone, but still glanced around the hotel room to make sure. How did he know where to find her? "Who are you?"

"The Shallows. Don't you remember?"

She gave her head a fervent shake as if the caller could see. "No! Why're you doing this?"

"I'm sorry about Brad, but you needed to know what it was like."

The words sounded so condescending. Listening to them made her feel nauseous. Lowering herself onto the bed, Kaitlyn's grip on the phone tightened. "Know what? What're you talking about?" Her voice grew louder, and she almost screamed into the phone. "Did you kill Brad?"

"It had to be done. He wasn't your type."

A tear ran down her face. Was it sadness or fear? She wasn't sure. "What do you mean?"

"There will only ever be one for you."

Kaitlyn squeezed her eyes closed. Her chest tightened; her breathing was rapid and shallow. "No! Jesse's dead."

"You can't fight this feeling, Laura."

The six words froze her blood. They sent her spiraling into the past, reliving those final minutes. Jesse had whispered those exact words in her ear as he'd pulled her against him. They'd been alone. *How could anyone know what he'd said? He was dead.*

"What's wrong, Laura? Has Jesse got your tongue?"

The modulated laugh that followed tore through her heart and mind. *No, no, no, this isn't happening.* Kaitlyn couldn't think straight. The laughter seemed to engulf her.

"I know where you are," the voice said. "You'll never escape me. The Shallows are coming for you."

With a gasp, Kaitlyn slammed down the receiver and stepped back from the phone. Her arms wrapped around her shivering body. Each breath was fast and furious. Suddenly, she snatched the phone off the bedside table, and hurled it across the room. It crashed into the far wall and fell to the floor in pieces. She stared at it and moved backward until her back pressed against the opposite wall.

The knock on the hotel room door broke the silence. She recoiled at the sound. How long had she been standing there? Time had passed without her awareness. She peered across the room, afraid to move. The knock was repeated, this time followed by a familiar voice calling her name. She rushed across the room, flung the door open, and fell into Rodney's surprised arms.

Kaitlyn buried her face into his shoulder, feeling his arms wrap awkwardly around her. He spoke to her, but she couldn't make out the words. After a few moments, he eased her back into the room, allowing the door to swing closed behind them. Rodney gently pushed her away from him and locked eyes with hers.

"Calm down, Kaitlyn. What's happened?"

She started to answer, and then paused. How much should she tell him? She'd hidden her past for so long. To reveal it to the police now was to open her life to the exact scrutiny that she'd been hiding from for all these years. A secret once told cannot be untold.

"I got a phone call. On the hotel phone."

His brow furrowed, and the corners of his mouth turned down into a frown. "From who?"

A sudden chill swept over her. She didn't know how to answer. *The Shallows? Jesse?* Both were impossible.

"I don't know." She shrugged her shoulders. "I don't have a goddamn clue." She clenched her fists in a mingling of rage and fear. "You're the detective. Why can't you tell me?" She ran a hand through her hair, pulling it back from her eyes.

Rodney remained silent. And calm. Then he said, "Did you tell anyone where you'd be?"

Kaitlyn shook her head and explained that she'd made no calls since arriving at the hotel. Rodney studied her as if performing an unspoken interrogation. She couldn't bear to be under his gaze any longer. She turned away from him and crossed the room to stare out the window.

"Then how did he find you?"

"I don't know." She crossed her arms in front of her chest. Why was he expecting her to have all the answers? "Maybe one of your lot told him."

His eyes narrowed. He didn't seem to like her accusation. "Maybe. Or maybe he was in the crowd at the crime scene. Could've overheard someone say where you were going."

She opened her mouth to argue, but words failed her. What right did she have to criticize his efforts when she wasn't being straight with him? "Sorry. That wasn't fair."

"What did the caller say?" he asked.

She tried to recount the call to him, but the conversation was all a fear-filled haze in her mind. It was difficult to remember what was said when. She corrected herself again and again, feeling more and more flustered as each moment passed. The jumbled narrative slipped from her mouth and she hoped it made some sort of sense. She did, however, make sure to skip the references to her childhood name, and held back the significance of the caller's final words. When she'd finished, the detective was silent for so long that she turned to make sure he was still in the room.

He studied her intensely, so much so that she wondered if he believed her. Their eyes met, and she quickly turned away. She couldn't bear his scrutinizing gaze. She crossed to the bathroom, grabbed one of the glasses from the vanity, and filled it with water. She returned to the bedroom, and took a long, slow sip.

"Why're you here?" she asked.

"Just wanted to check on you."

She lowered herself onto the corner of the bed. "An escort from work. Now you're checking up on me. Do police always give such personal service?"

His face turned a faint shade of red. He shuffled his feet and rubbed the back of his neck. His explanation came out with an uncomfortable stammer. "I . . . you remind me of someone. My daughter. You . . . you look just like her."

Kaitlyn said, "Sorry."

Rodney gave her a broad smile. "She's not dead. You just remind me of her. It's a long story." He slipped his hands into the pockets of his windbreaker. "Have you had breakfast? I know a place that does an awesome omelet."

She smiled. She didn't have much of an appetite, but she hadn't eaten in . . . she couldn't remember when she last ate. Kaitlyn nodded. "I could go for a good omelet."

"After breakfast, I'd like you to come to the station to make a statement. Just routine. Then I'll bring you back here."

She nodded again. Whether it had been his intention or not, he'd helped to relieve her fears. She'd stopped trembling, and, although she knew Brad's murderer was still stalking her, she felt safe with Rodney.

22

I'M STILL a bit buzzed from the kill. I never thought it could be so exhilarating, and the effect it has had on her is more than I could have hoped for. I look down at the pre-paid phone in my left hand and smile. It's the little things that bring the most joy. A simple phone call. Just when she thinks she has safely absconded, I let her know there's nowhere she can hide from me. I power off the phone, pop out the battery, then toss them both into the dumpster behind the hotel. Crossing the parking lot, I walk toward my car, a freshly lit cigarette perched between my fingers.

Once in the driver's seat, I turn on my iPad and pull up the surveillance video from her hotel room. The angle isn't the best, but I didn't have the luxury of optimally positioning the camera. But it shows me enough of the room. He's standing by the window, silhouetted against the sunlight. Seems he's taken a bit of a shine to her. Laura enters from the bathroom, grabs her purse, and they talk for a moment. Damn, I wish I had sound. After a moment, he opens the door and ushers her from the room.

Interesting. I wonder where they're heading. It seems a bit late for breakfast. Should I follow them? They exit the hotel and climb into his Dodge. Flicking my cigarette out the window, I start the car and wait for them to pull away. They turn left out of the parking lot and I reach to put my car in gear. Then, I pause. My hand is shaking. I didn't notice it earlier. Haven't slept much these past few days. Coffee and cigarettes have been my only sustenance for more than 24 hours. The adrenaline I've relied on since last night is gone. I can't remember when I was last home. Probably been a day or more. There's only a few more days to go, then this is all over. Can I push myself a little further? I lean back in my seat, pressing against the headrest. My eyes feel heavy. Can I . . .?

I wake with a start. Ten minutes have passed. Damn! I must have drifted off. The Dodge is nowhere to be seen. I light another cigarette. Perhaps I should head home. A shower. Some breakfast. Maybe squeeze in a quick nap. I need to have all my senses for what's coming. Can't afford any mistakes. Yes, I think I'll head home.

23

RODNEY RECLINED in his office chair and tossed a crumpled piece of paper across the desk at Julie Lewis. The wad landed on the center of her desk, and, with a single swift motion, she brushed it off into the trash can. She peered up at him for a moment, and then returned her eyes to the report she'd been reading.

"A pre-paid cell phone," she announced.

"Damn." He leaned forward, resting his hands on the desk. After he returned Kaitlyn to the hotel on the previous morning, Rodney had spent Sunday afternoon arranging to have the phone records compiled and analyzed. He'd hoped that it'd give them a desperately needed lead. But of course, the killer used a burner phone. No chance of tracing it.

"Do you feel like this guy is always a step ahead of us?"

Julie set the report down on her desk. "Why are you so sure it's a man?"

"You think it's a woman?"

"Could be," she said. "It's not unheard of. Remember the Bagby killing?"

He shook his head. It sounded familiar, but he couldn't recall the details. "Wasn't that out near Pittsburgh?"

"Yeah, his crazy ex-girlfriend stalked and shot him," she said. "Or, maybe this whole stalker thing is just a ruse."

Rodney tilted his head to one side and gave her a puzzled look. "What's that mean?"

Julie rose from her seat and rounded her desk, perching herself up on the corner of his. "Did you ever think that maybe she had something to do with all of this? Maybe Kaitlyn Ashe knows more than she's telling us?" She folded her arms across her chest. "Face it, she hasn't exactly been all that forthright about her past."

He returned her gaze and raised one eye brow. "You suggesting that she sent those letters to herself?"

She gave a slow shake of her head. "Not exactly suggesting. More like toying with the idea, which seems to be more than you're willing to do." She gestured toward him. "She claims that there've been numerous letters, but, where are they? She threw them away." She made air quotes around her last sentence.

He straightened up in his chair, glaring at her through narrowed eyes. *Why'd she always have to play the bad cop? Always finding guilt in victims where there was none.* But this was beyond even her norm. There was an edge to her voice that threw him. Was she for real? It sounded almost like an accusation.

"Hang on a sec. What are you trying to say?"

"That you're allowing yourself to be blinded to the possibility that she might have murdered her fiancé. The letters could've been all a setup to throw us off."

There was a tinge of anger in his sigh. "Are you saying I'm not being objective?"

Julie glanced around the office at the other desks. He followed her gaze, noting that most of them were empty. The only one occupied was at the opposite side of the room.

She lowered her voice. "Yes."

Rodney pushed his chair back and rose to his feet. She didn't move an inch. "That's ridiculous."

"Is it? Have you asked her yet why she changed her name?" She paused, as if waiting for his reply. "I didn't think so. And what about the Shallows? Have you pushed her for answers on that yet? For all you know, she could've been a murderer in her previous life."

He turned his gaze away from her, unwilling to look her in the eye. He refused to admit that she might be right, even though he knew she was. There were too many unanswered questions in this case, and he'd gone far easier on Kaitlyn than he normally would have with another victim.

"Rodney, I get it. She reminds you of how you failed your daughter. But you're not helping anyone by ignoring some key points in this investigation," said Julie. "What're you going to do? Camp out in her front yard? Take her out to her favorite restaurant to help her cope with her loss? Dinner at Tuscano Italiano isn't going to bring her fiancé back, and it certainly won't help us solve this case."

He picked up the coffee mug from his desk and stared at the glossy navy-colored ceramic. His eyes traced the outline of the gold Lower Township Police logo imprinted on the side. Turning away from Julie, he crossed to the coffee machine. As he filled the mug with hot coffee, he was reminded of a quote he heard once from Ulysses S. Grant: "My failures have been errors in judgment, not of intent." He considered quoting it to Julie but knew it would be lost on her.

He returned to his desk. Julie hadn't moved from her place on the corner. After gulping down some coffee, he placed the mug on the desk. "It's never been my intention to hamper this investigation." He didn't feel the need to explain himself to her, but he did, however, feel the need to defend his actions. "For Christ's sake, she's just lost her fiancé. We had her in to give a statement. What more do you want me to do? Drag her in here and grill her for hours?"

"Why not? Isn't that how we get results?"

"That may be how you get results." He lowered himself back into his chair. "I'll get more information out of her if she's cooperative."

"Whatever. You're the investigating officer on this case. I'm just here to do the shit work. You run the case however you want." Julie slid off the desk.

Rodney could sense the passive aggression ooze from her back as she returned to her chair. Her tendency towards finding guilt in every person involved in a case often infuriated him. He'd always chalked it up to inexperience, hoping that it would soften over time. It had to a point. This case, however, brought the tendency back with a vengeance.

Rodney heard the computer on his desk ding. He leaned forward and checked his email. "The ME's report. Says our victim died from a single wound to his throat. But—get this—there were signs that he was stabbed more than once in that same wound."

"Interesting. Sounds like there was some rage behind the crime."

He nodded and continued to scan the report, paraphrasing as he went. "The stab wounds went straight through his carotid artery. He wouldn't have lived long. ME estimates about thirty seconds, forty-five at most. Nothing else out of the ordinary."

Julie scratched on a notepad with a pen. At first, he thought she was taking notes, but the random shapes on the page told him differently.

He pictured the crime scene again. It was amazing how brutal a stab wound to the throat can appear. The amount of blood alone was enough to make a strong man look away in horror. Just one cut generated so much gore. He couldn't remember ever seeing so much blood in one place. Forensics had the car now and was going over every inch of it looking for clues. Somehow, he was certain they wouldn't find anything. This bastard—whoever he was—knew how to hide his trail.

Julie turned toward him. "What now?"

He pushed his chair away from the desk. "WPLX. It's time to meet Kaitlyn's co-workers."

24

RODNEY WALKED into the lobby and stopped near the reception desk. He had spent thirty minutes with Scott MacKay, the station's program director, and discovered little that would help him find Brad's murderer and Kaitlyn's stalker. He hoped Julie was having better luck with the station's sales staff. Sammy Devonport was behind the front desk, speaking softly on the phone. He had spoken to her when they first arrived. She had nothing to add except snide remarks about the incompetence of the Philadelphia police. Rodney reminded her twice that he was from Lower Merion Township Police but gave up trying to correct her as she continued her wiseass comments.

From his open notebook, he reviewed his notes from Scott's interview, despite the fact that the conversation was still fresh in his mind.

Scott Mackay had gestured Rodney to the leather sofa while he closed the office door. Scott perched himself on the desk, his legs hanging off the front and his head bowed.

"This is a terrible situation. I'm sorrier than you can possibly imagine," Scott said.

Rodney nodded his understanding. "We're confident we'll make an arrest in short order." His words sounded far more certain than the investigation thus far allowed. "I'd like to ask you a few questions."

He started by asking about Kaitlyn's employment at WPLX. Scott explained that she'd been with the station for two years.

"She's been a great addition to our line-up," he said. "She topped out the rating within the first year." There was a wistfulness in his eyes as he spoke about Kaitlyn.

"You're fond of her?"

"You've met Kaitlyn. Who wouldn't be fond of her? Sweetest woman I know."

Rodney made a point of scribbling in his notepad, more for show than to actually make a note. He wanted a second to digest Scott's remark. Was there something more there than just an employer's interest in his employee? "Apparently someone's not fond of her."

Scott slid off the desk and rounded to the opposite side, taking a seat in his chair. He opened a drawer and pulled out a bottle of Jim Beam and two glass tumblers. "You want one?" After Rodney declined the offer, Scott went on to say, "I don't normally do this, but with all this mess . . ."

Rodney rose from the sofa and stood before the desk. "How well did you know Brad Ludlow?"

Scott poured some bourbon into his glass. "Not too well." He went on to describe how Kaitlyn would bring her boyfriend to station functions and staff get togethers. Brad seemed likable but, to Scott, always a bit ill-at-ease around the station staff. "We tend to talk shop a lot. Brad probably couldn't relate."

"Ever notice any tension between Kaitlyn and Brad?"

Scott shook his head. "No. They seemed like the perfect couple. Always happy . . ." He paused. "I take that back. There was a time."

Scott described a recent staff gathering at a pub on Walnut Street. The drinks were flowing, and everyone was having a tremendous time, when Kaitlyn's face went white. Soon after, she stood, said her farewells, and with Brad in tow, made a hurried departure from the bar.

Rodney flipped his notepad closed and glanced back at Sammy, who was still speaking on the phone. The nearby door, which led toward the station offices and studios opened. A tall, muscular man emerged and headed toward the entryway.

"Excuse me," Rodney said. "Can I have a word?"

"You must be the dick, here to question us all about our alibis."

Rodney narrowed his eyes. He ignored the flippant remark but made a mental note to let Julie do any follow-up interview. She'd eat this guy for lunch. "You are?" he asked.

"Kevin O'Neill. Look, I'll talk to you, but it'll have to be out in the parking garage. I just got off the air and I've been gagging for a cig since 10 this morning."

Rodney followed Kevin to the parking garage, where the radio DJ was quick to light up. After a deep inhale, Kevin blew a long stream of smoke into the air. "Nothing calms the nerves like a little nicotine, don't you think?"

Rodney made an absent glance around the garage. All of the nearby parking spots were full. A Ford, a couple Chevys, two Hondas, and a Volkswagen. He recalled standing near this very spot a couple weeks ago, on the night Kaitlyn was nearly run down in the city. He turned back to Kevin and watched him try to blow smoke rings into the air, unsuccessfully.

"Can't say I've ever had the pleasure of trying it," Rodney said.

Kevin thrust a pack of cigarettes in his direction. "You're welcome to try one of mine."

With a wave of his hand, Rodney declined the offer.

Kevin shrugged and slipped the pack into his pocket. "How can I help you, Detective?"

"Since you mentioned alibis, can you give me yours? Specifically, for Thursday night, between midnight and two."

Kevin drew on his cigarette, seeming to savor the act. He didn't speak for a moment, staring up at the ceiling. "Midnight? I was leaving The Phoenix Bar with a real stunner I found on Grindr."

Rodney nodded, but said nothing.

"Do you know the Phoenix, Detective? It's a gay bar. The cops spend a lot of time down there these days."

"Mr. O'Neill, I'm not from the Philadelphia Police. And, I am aware of the Phoenix Bar, as well as its reputation for being a Philly hotspot. Won the Best of Philly award a couple years ago, if I remember correctly."

Kevin turned his head away and exhaled, sending vapor into the air. He remained silent for a long moment before he turned back toward Rodney. "Apologies, Detective. I've been a bit of an ass. I'm not fond of cops, and too many run-ins with some of the more homophobic ones have left me a bit sour."

Rodney folded his arms and nodded. There were still a few older officers in Philly's police force that were being dragged, kicking and screaming, into the twenty-first century. Old prejudices sometimes die hard. "Aren't you concerned about GBT?"

Kevin shrugged. "I like it a bit rough." He smiled.

"I don't want to hear about your sex life . . . unless it pertains to Kaitlyn Ashe."

After another long drag on his cigarette, Kevin tossed the still-smoking butt onto the concrete, crushing it with his shoe. "Sorry. How can I help?"

"You can start with your alibi."

Kevin kicked at the butt. "I left the Phoenix shortly after midnight. James . . . or his name may have been John—I can't remember—invited me to his place. I won't shock you with the details of how things went from there. I left around 4 in the morning."

"How long have you known Kaitlyn?"

"As long as she's been here," he said. "I was part-time, working on the weekends. Since I have a rock-solid alibi, I don't mind telling you there was some jealousy at first. I applied for that shift as well."

Rodney asked, "Why didn't you get it?"

"Guess they thought she was better."

"Were you angry?"

Kevin shrugged. "At first. I'd been here six months. Figured I'd be a shoo-in. Imagine my surprise." He brushed his hand through his hair, then folded his arms. "Worked out in the end. Five months later, I'm offered the midday shift."

Rodney was silent for a moment. *Jealousy over a job?* The motive and the timing didn't seem to fit. Why wait a solid year and a half to seek revenge? No, it wasn't right. That didn't mean there wasn't something else that the radio DJ was hiding. "You from this area?" he asked.

"Grew up out near Pittsburgh."

"Did you ever know someone named Laura Hobson?"

Kevin thought for a second, then shook his head. "Don't think so. Who is she?"

"Just a lead we're pursuing. Probably nothing."

25

JULIE WAS ALREADY at her desk when Rodney walked into the police station on Tuesday morning. She looked up from the file she was reviewing and nodded a silent greeting. He grabbed the mug from his desk, crossed to the coffeemaker, and returned moments later.

"You're late," Julie said.

"I stopped by the hotel to see Kaitlyn. I told her she could return home today." He took a sip of coffee. "I offered to drive her home, but she declined. Said she'd get a cab later this morning."

Julie set the file down. "The girl's got guts. Going back to that house alone."

Rodney placed his mug on the desk. "I got the impression it's less about guts and more about not having anywhere else to go." He slipped his gun from the holster on his belt and placed it in the desk drawer. "She's got no family in the area."

"Still, returning to the house where your fiancé was murdered takes guts. Unless . . ."

He glared at her. He knew what she was thinking. "Don't say it. She's innocent."

"Do you have some unknown piece of evidence that proves that?"

He sat down at his desk, took a long sip from his mug, and stared across the rim at her. *Ignore her.* He didn't want to go into her ridiculous theory again.

"Did those background checks come back?"

She nodded. "Got them this morning." She gestured to the file on her desk. "Nothing too surprising. Most of the radio station staff have clean records. Scott McKay had a DUI about fifteen years ago. Kevin O'Neill had a few run-ins with the law when he was younger. All juvenile offenses over in New Jersey. Around the Penns Grove area."

He thought about this new information for a moment. Something didn't sound right. "In Jersey? He told me he grew up in Pittsburgh."

Julie shook her head. "Not according to his records. He lived in Penns Grove for several years." She picked up the file and glanced over the pages. "A couple petty thefts. Some disorderly conducts." She read further down the page. "Get this. He was accused of stringing up the neighbor's cat."

"He hung a cat?"

"From a tree. Nothing could be proved, and no charges were filed."

He leaned back in his chair and clasped his hands behind his head. "Where is Penns Grove?"

"South Jersey. Right along the river."

"Is it close to Woolwich?"

She tilted her head to one side. "You thinking he knew Kaitlyn when she was young? They're about the same age. It's possible."

Rodney toyed with a pencil that was on his desk. Why would Kevin O'Neill lie about where he lived? Did he think they wouldn't run checks on everyone involved with Kaitlyn Ashe? The radio DJ had been a little too standoffish for his liking. Yes, the GBT Strangler had put the Philadelphia LGBTQ community on edge for the past several months. Yes, the Philadelphia police were under a lot of pressure to catch the bastard, enough so that there had been recent reports of some heavy-handed crackdowns on some of the clubs in Philly's iconic "Gayborhood". But that didn't explain why Kevin O'Neill might lie about his background. Unless he knew more about Brad Ludlow's murder than he was letting on.

"I'll need to speak to him again. Anything else in the reports?"

"Nothing worth mentioning."

He pulled open his desk drawer and retrieved his gun, slipping it back into its holster. "I'm going out."

Julie looked at him, her eyes questioning. "Where to?"

"Back to the radio station. To talk to Kevin O'Neill."

"Want me to come with you?"

"No. See what you can find out about Jesse Riley's family. What happened to them. Where they are now."

————

RODNEY STOOD in the corner of the radio station bullpen, making a meticulous study of Kevin O'Neill. The radio DJ sat at his desk, looking a bit agitated. His eyes were evasive and darted from side to side. His leg bounced like a piston.

"What's this about? Are you accusing me of something?" Kevin said.

Rodney shook his head. "Not at all. I just want to understand why you told me you grew up in Pittsburgh."

"Because it was the truth."

"Really? Then please explain how you have a string of petty theft arrests from New Jersey."

Kevin sighed and rose from his desk. "I was born in Pittsburgh. My family moved to Penns Grove when I was eleven."

"Did you know Laura Hobson when you lived in Penns Grove?" Rodney watched for any sign of recognition at the mention of the name. None seemed obvious.

"You asked me that before."

"I'm asking again."

Kevin paused, seeming to give the question some thought before answering. "No. Not that I can remember."

"What about Jesse Riley?"

Kevin opened his mouth as if to speak but didn't. Instead, he pondered the question. "It sounds vaguely familiar, but I don't know why. Who is it?"

Rodney wondered how much information he should divulge. He didn't want to put Kaitlyn in an uncomfortable position by telling her co-workers secrets from her private life. "He drowned several years ago in Woolwich Township. It was a fairly big deal in the area at the time."

Kevin folded his arms and leaned against his desk. "What's that got to do with Kaitlyn?"

"Possibly nothing. It's just an inquiry we're following."

"Can't say I remember it."

Kevin's attitude shifted from agitated to indifferent. He kept his arms folded and faced off with Rodney, returning a gaze that said *Are we done here?*

"Tell me about the cat," Rodney said.

"What cat?" Kevin seemed genuinely puzzled.

"The one you were accused of hanging from a tree."

Kevin let out a loud laugh. "That? My god, you cops really dig deep for dirt, don't you?" He rolled his eyes and smirked.

"What happened?"

"If you must know, that cat was feral and a whore. Every night, the damn thing was going at it. Screeching and howling. Like she was in heat twenty-four seven. Doubt there was a male cat in the neighborhood that didn't have her at least once."

"Did you kill it?"

Kevin pushed off the desk and gathered up the papers scattered on the desktop. "I know where you're headed with this. If I could kill a cat, I could kill Brad Ludlow." With the papers in his hands, he turned and faced Rodney, standing inches from him. "You cops are all the same. You find the one person who had it a bit rough as a child and blame them. You can't pin this one on me."

Rodney remained still and matched Kevin's stare with his own. "I'm not trying to pin anything on you. Just looking for the truth."

He could smell Kevin's breath. Stale cigarettes. The odor mingled in the air with a hubris that Rodney struggled to understand. Kevin had been on the defensive from the moment Rodney arrived.

With a smirk, Kevin stepped back and smiled. "Ye shall know the truth, and the truth shall make you mad."

"Aldous Huxley."

Kevin raised an eyebrow in surprise. "Impressive. A cop with a penchant for philosophy."

Rodney couldn't let the moment slide. "Truth is the breath of life to human society. It is the food of the immortal spirit. Yet a single word of it may kill a man as suddenly as a drop of prussic acid."

Tilting his head, Kevin looked at him with questioning eyes.

"Oliver Wendall Holmes," Rodney said.

Kevin nodded, checked his watch, then turned away, heading toward the door. "I'd love to stay and toss quotes back and forth all day, but I've got a show to do." He halted halfway across the room and turned back to look at Rodney. "If there's nothing else . . ."

Rodney shook his head.

Kevin started to turn toward the door, then looked back at him. "I didn't hang the cat, detective. My old man did." With that, he stepped from the room and left Rodney alone.

The conversation hadn't gone the way Rodney had hoped. He was left with more questions than answers. The radio DJ was startled to be questioned again so soon. He even appeared fearful at first. But a self-confident indignation soon emerged and was evident throughout the rest of the conversation. Rodney didn't buy Kevin's excuse for being "economical" with the truth. There was something more to Kevin O'Neill, but he couldn't put his finger on it.

He started toward the door but noticed that the top desk drawer of Kevin's desk was half open. He glanced at the door, then opened the drawer. It contained the usual assortment of items; most that he'd expect to see in any desk. He made a quick mental inventory. A box of staples, a half dozen pens, a chain of paper clips, an opened box of condoms, a pad of Post-It notes, a thick leather cord, and assorted rubber bands. Rodney pushed the drawer shut again and pulled open the drawer below the first. A stack of magazines was piled in the bottom. He fingered through them, noting each as he scanned their covers. Billboard. Time. Billboard again. He paused on the next. A gay porn magazine. *Interesting work reading.* Another copy of Billboard was below that. Then, he found the books.

26

THE CAB PULLED up to the curb in front of her house. Kaitlyn just sat for a few moments, staring toward the garage. The concrete driveway was still damp with the Tuesday morning dew. She imagined for a moment that the wet patches were Brad's blood spilt from his BMW the night he died. She shuddered at the thought and toyed with the idea of telling the cab driver to return her to the hotel. *Coming home alone, maybe not such a good idea.*

The cab driver cleared his throat, shaking Kaitlyn out of her brown study. She handed him two twenties over the seat. "Keep the change."

Kaitlyn stood at the bottom of the driveway, suitcase resting on the concrete by her feet, and drew in a deep breath. When Detective Shapiro had told her she could return to the house, her first reaction had been one of apprehension and fear. Her house, a place that had once served as a source of comfort and sanctuary, was now indelibly stained by the horror of Brad's death. Rodney had offered to drive her home himself, but his presence would've only served to remind her of what had been happening. If she was going to get through this, she'd have to do it on her own. No one, not even Rodney, could be strong for her. It wouldn't be the first time she'd had to rise from the ashes like a Phoenix.

With her bag in hand, Kaitlyn walked up the driveway, averting her eyes from the faint blood stains on the concrete near the garage door. They'd fade over time, but until then, the brown patches would remain a reminder of her loss. She let herself into her home, dropping her bag inside the door as she crossed the threshold. With the door closed behind her, she leaned back and pressed her back against it. The house was still, the air thick. All of the blinds were drawn, leaving everything in shadows. Kaitlyn moved down the hall into the kitchen. From an overhead cabinet, she withdrew a glass and filled it with water from the refrigerator.

She drew back the curtains covering the sliding-glass doors out onto the deck. Kaitlyn gazed out over the backyard, then out to the cemetery beyond. A faint morning mist still hung low across the ground surrounding the grave markers, tombstones, and mausoleums. The gray monoliths stood like silent sentries over the dead. Normally, this view would have sent a shiver up her spine, but this morning she was numb. An indistinct dark figure stood over a distant grave, a mourner paying their respects to the lost.

The mist reminded her of the night of Jesse's death. She had been determined to remain while the police retrieved his body from the water. It'd been well past midnight by the time they'd closed the zipper on the black plastic body bag and loaded it into the back of the county coroner's van. The silver thermal blanket over her shoulders had ceased to keep her warm hours before. She barely registered being placed in the back of a police car and driven through the early morning Woolwich Township country-side. When she finally arrived at home the next morning, she'd spent four hours in the police station recounting the events that led up to the drowning. They believed every word she said.

Kaitlyn moved toward the living room, picking up the cordless phone from the kitchen counter as she did. She dialed as she pulled the curtains in the darkened living room open. The morning sun brightened the room as she listened to the phone ring. Her call was answered almost immediately.

"WPLX, how can I direct your call?"

"Sammy? It's Kaitlyn."

Sammy gasped and said, "Oh my god. Are you okay? We all heard what happened. It's terrible."

"Yes, I'm—"

"And in your neighborhood, too. Is there no place safe anymore? You must be devastated."

Kaitlyn gazed out the window at her front yard. "It hasn't been—"

"And you just got engaged too? I can't believe this happened, to you of all people. I'm so sorry. Do the police know who did it yet?"

"They're still—"

"Everybody's been asking about you. Why didn't you call sooner? We've all been worried sick, especially me. Even Ben Maxwell called yesterday. Said he saw your name in Sunday's *Post-Gazette* and wanted to pass on his condolences."

Kaitlyn smiled. Maxwell was the owner of an auto dealership conglomerate called Maxwell Auto Group. She'd voiced all of their radio spots for the past two years at his express request. "That's nice of him. Can you—"

"Are you home? Don't tell me you're home. You are home, aren't you? How can you stand to be there? You shouldn't be alone. I'll come right over and stay with you. Aren't you—"

"Sammy!"

"Huh? What?"

"Is Scott in?"

There was a pause from Sammy over the phone. "Sorry, did I just verbally vomit all over you? Of course, I did. Let me get him for you . . . Before I do, I just want to say you should call me if you need anything. Okay? Anything at all. Any time for anything. You don't have to go through this alone."

The phone went silent for a moment. While she waited, Kaitlyn walked up the stairs to her bedroom. She stood in the door, surveying the dark room. Another voice came on the phone.

"Kaitlyn? How're you doing?"

She crossed to the bedroom window, raising the blinds. "I've had better days, Scott."

"I can't begin to imagine what you're going through. Don't worry about coming in. Take as much time as you need."

She moved to the dresser along the far wall, straightening a Chanel No. 5 bottle that had been knocked onto its side. She frowned. "But who's going to fill—"

"Don't you worry about that," said Scott. "You just do what you need to do. Let me deal with covering your show. Might even do it myself."

Kaitlyn laughed. "Scott, you haven't been on the air for years."

"That's what happens when you go into management. You stop doing all the fun shit."

The drawer of the end table by the bed was ajar. She pushed it closed with her knee. "Just a few days. I've got a few things to do before I come back to work."

"As long as you're coming back, that's all that matters."

"I will. Promise."

"Great. Take care. Call if you need anything," Scott said. "Do you want me to pass you back to Sammy?"

"No, she's talked my ear off enough for one day. Thanks, Scott."

After hanging up, she tossed the phone on the bed and frowned. She walked to the dresser and pulled open the top drawer. Brushing aside the underwear within, she searched the back of the drawer. There was nothing there. She ran her hand all around the drawer and pushed the contents from side to side as she did. Her chest tightened and she struggled for a breath.

She pushed the drawer closed and searched the one below it, and then ransacked the one below that. When she'd been through all five drawers, she returned to the top one again, yanking her clothes out and tossing them on the bed in an unruly pile. Kaitlyn sifted through the collection of lace and cotton but found nothing. She jerked back from the bed and ran both hands through her hair, then turned to glare at the empty drawer.

Jesse's necklace was gone.

27

RODNEY STEPPED out into the cool Philadelphia morning air. Although his interview with Kevin O'Neill hadn't gone well, he felt like he'd made some progress. Kevin was now his prime suspect. His evidence was barely circumstantial. He wasn't even sure if he had enough to justify bringing Kevin in for further questioning. But he might have found his first lead.

He checked his watch. It was closing in on noon. He glanced back up at the Stetler building. Twenty floors up, Kevin O'Neill was busy with his show. He would be off the air at 3:00. Rodney pondered his next step. *Stick around until 3:00 and question him again? Maybe.* But first, he needed to grab some lunch. He looked along the busy city street. A couple blocks down he saw a food truck. He couldn't read the name on the back, but there was a line of people—ten or twelve deep—waiting to be served. *Must not be too bad. It's worth a shot.*

As he strolled along the sidewalk—hands buried in his pockets—he thought back to what he'd found in Kevin O'Neill's desk drawer. Beneath the various magazines were three old yearbooks, all from different schools, all with different years stamped on the front cover.

He lifted the first one out and found a page marked by a Post-It note. On the page, there was a photo circled in black ink. The young face looked vaguely familiar. The name below it was Scott MacKay. Some notes were scrawled in the margin near the image. Dates as well as some illegible scribble. The second yearbook was from a high school in North Carolina. The marked page contained a photograph that Rodney didn't recognize. The name was Justin Newman. *Might be the night DJ.* There were more notes beside the image. Some dates. A few initials. He couldn't make sense out of them.

He lifted the third book from the drawer. The high school was located in New Jersey. He flipped to the page marked by the yellow Post-It Note. He gasped. The face that stared back at him was his daughter. He looked it again. No, it wasn't his daughter. He read the name below the image. Laura Hobson. It was circled in black ink, and whoever did it had gone around and around numerous times. There were more notes in the margins; the handwriting almost unintelligible.

For a moment, Rodney considered going to the studio and confronting Kevin with the yearbook. But he had no search warrant. No reason even to look in the desk. All this proved was that Kevin knew who Kaitlyn Ashe really was. It proved nothing else. It was suspicious, but nothing more. This evidence would never stand up in court. Probably would be thrown out immediately. He was out of his jurisdiction, and out of line searching the desk drawer in the first place. But he now had some direction. Something to dig into further. He finally had a suspect.

He continued to walk toward the food truck, pausing at an intersection to wait for the traffic lights to turn. He glanced around at the gathering throng of pedestrians. Some were lost in their own world, earbuds blocking out the city noise. Others were busy— heads down—thumbing away on their mobile phones. Some were in suits, some in tight Lycra fitness wear. Still others were dressed business casual attire. Dockers. Polos. Skirts.

The crossing sign indicated that it was safe to walk. The small horde of people pushed forward into the crosswalk. Rodney wasn't in a hurry, so he was slow to move. Someone smacked into his shoulder, throwing him off balance. He spun and staggered for a moment before righting himself in the middle of the crosswalk. He searched the crowd ahead of him, trying to identify who had knocked against him.

Someone in a gray sweatshirt was moving rapidly away. The hoodie was pulled up over the person's head. Rodney weaved forward through the mass of people, but his progress was slow. He tried to keep his eyes on the gray hoodie. The crowd thinned once he reached the other side of the street. He increased his pace to catch up. The figure had turned into a nearby alley between two office buildings. But, when he arrived at the entrance, there was no one in sight. Rodney stood for a few moments, looking at the passing faces, hoping to catch sight of the figure. After a few minutes, he gave up. *It was probably nothing anyway.*

He turned back toward the food truck and moved on down the street. An uneasy sensation hung over him. Was he being followed? Was he being watched?

———

AFTER LUNCH, Rodney made his way back to the radio station. It was 1:20 in the afternoon when he arrived at the entrance to the parking garage. He rode the elevator up to the twenty-third floor where his car was parked. As he exited the lift, he took a final swig from his bottle of Lipton Iced Tea. He tossed the bottle into a nearby trash can and walked toward his Dodge.

While eating lunch, Rodney had decided that he wouldn't confront Kevin O'Neill just yet with the yearbooks. He wanted to talk with Bernie first, get his opinion on how to handle the situation. The legality of his discovery was questionable. If it was legitimate evidence, it would be best to get it through proper channels.

As he approached his car, he noticed something white caught beneath his windshield wiper. It flapped in the breeze that blew through the garage. He drew closer and stared at the folded piece of paper. He opened the passenger door and grabbed some gloves from his glovebox. Rodney lifted the paper from the windshield and opened it. His eyes narrowed as he read the message composed of newspaper clippings.

Stay out of this.
The Shallows

28

AFTER FIXING herself a bowl of Cheerios, Kaitlyn sat at the
kitchen table. With her spoon, she toyed with the cereal for several
minutes before pushing the bowl away from her. She didn't have
much of an appetite. The tea in her mug had grown lukewarm. She
frowned when she took a sip.

"What do I do now?" she asked out loud.

The only answer was dead air. Kaitlyn dumped the cereal in
the trash and set the bowl in the kitchen sink. The spoon rattled
loudly when it fell into the bowl. She gazed out the window,
staring across the cemetery beyond. *How did it come to this?* She'd
been happy, successful, and in love. In a matter of weeks, it had all
come crashing down. All because of one moment in her past. So
many years had come and gone, yet she was still haunted by a
single memory. Still haunted by his face as it slipped beneath the
water. She'd changed her name, left the area for almost a decade,
undergone years of therapy, all to rid herself of the nightmare.
She'd been far along the road to recovery. Yet, somehow Jesse had
reached out from the grave to hurt her one more time.

She moved into the living room, lowered herself onto the sofa,
and grabbed the remote. She turned on the television to find the

Channel Six noon newscast, which had started a few minutes before. A reporter stood outside of Philadelphia Police headquarters. ". . . of the LGBTQ community are outraged over the police's lack of progress in finding the GBT Strangler. The unknown assailant, who has strangled seven victims, seems to prey on homosexual, bisexual, and transgender men. Police say the GBT Strangler uses a rope or thick cord to kill his victims and . . ."

Kaitlyn turned off the television and sat in silence. What kind of evil world did she live in? A strangler stalked the streets of Philadelphia and another stalked her. What could make someone take another's life? What defect within someone's psyche would lead them to kill? She recalled the blood covering Brad when she discovered his body. So red. So deeply red. His lifeless face staring through the windshield. His skin blanched white from blood loss.

Tears streamed down her cheeks. Could it be the same person? Could GBT be Brad's killer? She thought through what she knew about the strangler. It wasn't much. She'd not paid much attention to the news of late. What she did know was that Brad wasn't strangled. He was stabbed through the throat. Did serial murderers change—what did the police call it—their MO? She shook her head. It didn't make sense. None of it made sense. And what about the letters? Someone was making a point of reminding her of Jesse's death. She couldn't think of anyone who knew about the connection between Kaitlyn Ashe and Jesse Riley. Yet, someone had made the connection.

————

IN THE BEDROOM, Kaitlyn placed the laundry basket on the floor and started to pull clothes from the hamper. She picked out each item of clothing and gave it a quick once over before dumping it into the basket. A pair of blue jeans. A white frilly blouse. Pink lace panties with red hearts embroidered on them—Brad's favorite. One sock. A couple T-shirts.

When she pulled an Oxford shirt from the hamper, Kaitlyn dropped to her knees. She drew the shirt to her face and sniffed. Brad's scent still lingered within the fabric. A sweet, musky aroma mingled with Old Spice. A momentary smile formed on her lips as she remembered the last night he'd spent at her house. It had been the Tuesday before he died, less than a week ago. He'd brought Chinese takeout to the studio, then drove her home when her shift was over. He hadn't intended to stay the night, but Kaitlyn had been overly persuasive.

"Lucky I've left a couple spare shirts in your closet," he'd said as his naked body pressed against hers beneath the sheets.

The memory was too painful, and Kaitlyn broke down, pressing the balled-up fabric against her chest as she sobbed. Her tears cascaded down her cheeks and fell onto the shirt.

She buried her face in the shirt and squeezed her eyes into the soft cotton. Kaitlyn felt alone, lost in a world of despair that was out of her control. How long was she supposed to keep running from the past? All those friends she'd kept at arm's length. She didn't want to hurt them. Or was it that *she* didn't want to be hurt? Back then, she'd promised herself that she wouldn't let this happen again. Not ever. No one would ever get a chance to do what Jesse had done.

As her sobbing abated, Kaitlyn dropped the shirt back into the hamper. She wasn't ready to deal with this yet. The emotions were still too raw. What she needed was something to take her mind off everything, even if only for an hour. Rising from the floor she crossed to the dresser and rifled through one of the drawers. She tossed a T-shirt onto the bed, along with a pair of running shorts.

A good run. That's what I need.

———

A FAINT CRISPNESS still hung in the midday air as Kaitlyn stepped out of the back door into her yard. The mist that had earlier laid low across the cemetery had cleared. She could see straight across to the wooded boundary on the far side. Row upon row of stone grave markers stood like an army frozen in an eternal march across the field behind her house. She shuddered, realizing how much she hated living by a cemetery. She slipped her earbuds into place and jogged off along Belmont Avenue.

When she turned off the road onto the Heritage Trail, Kaitlyn fell into her usual cadence and was surprised at how easy it was to lose herself to the run. Between the music playing in her ears and the feeling of her feet pounding on the ground, she was able to momentarily forget.

With each step synchronized with the beat of the music, Kaitlyn continued to run along the trail. Despite her sense of calm, she kept a wary eye on her surroundings. She was alone, a thought she tried to push to the back of her mind. She pressed on, running as if nothing had happened. Running as if Brad was still alive.

As she rounded a bend, the overhead tree branches thickened, blocking the sun and casting the trail in shadows. The temperature dropped by a few degrees. Up ahead, she saw a figure hunched over on one of the benches that lined the side of the trail. The face was obscured by a chaotic mass of dark hair. The clothes looked grimy and unkempt. Kaitlyn tried not to think about the figure as she drew closer, but her hand consciously tightened around the small pepper spray canister on her keychain. She drifted to the opposite side of the trail, feeling a wave of unease creep along her spine. As she passed the bench, the figure rose and stepped toward her. The man's face was cracked with the signs of a hard life. The stubble on his chin was thick and rough. He extended his hand toward her.

Kaitlyn stumbled away from him. His lips were moving, but she couldn't hear the words. She threw her arms up as if to defend herself from his advances.

"Get away from me."

He continued to move toward her. Kaitlyn backed away, her arms waving violently at him. She knocked an earbud from her ear. "Leave me alone!"

The man said, "Can you spare—"

Kaitlyn didn't hear anything else he said. She pressed the button on the pepper spray, but nothing happened. Frantic, she pounded on it, then fumbled with the safety, releasing a giant cloud of acid rain into her attacker's face.

29

RODNEY FINISHED SPEAKING with the uniformed officer who stood near the ambulance. When he received the initial call from dispatch, he feared the worst. All they told him was that there had been an "incident" with Kaitlyn Ashe on the Cynwyd Heritage Trail. He breathed a sigh of relief when he arrived and found Kaitlyn sitting in a police car, wiping her face and eyes with a wet towel. The uniformed officer on the scene detailed what had happened. It sounded like nothing more than a misunderstanding. A homeless man had approached Kaitlyn for money. In her panic, she misinterpreted his intentions and sprayed him with pepper spray. When she realized her mistake, she called the police. It was an honest mistake.

On the drive over, he'd listened to WPLX, and in particular to Kevin O'Neill. He didn't know much about broadcasting, but Kevin seemed tongue-tied. He stumbled over his words more than once and sounded flustered on the air. Had Rodney struck an unknown nerve? There were no direct clues pointing toward Kevin O'Neill except the yearbooks. Hell, they weren't even clues. Just happenstance. But Rodney's gut told him that Kevin was not who he appeared. Something was off. Something just wasn't right.

Rodney thanked the officer and turned toward the nearby

police cruiser. He glanced around. The hairs on his neck tingled. He'd swear that someone was watching him. He couldn't see anyone in the nearby trees, or even in the cemetery beyond. He shrugged off the sensation, then walked to the police cruiser. He thought about the letter he found on his car just an hour ago. A warning. Was he getting closer than he thought? Someone seemed to think so. *Best not to mention it to Kaitlyn.*

He looked at her through the back-seat window of the police car. Her eyes were red, puffy, and held his for a moment with a vacuous gaze. She looked frail and helpless. He was reminded of his daughter as she was driven away from his home the morning they'd come to arrest her. She'd pleaded and cried, clawing at his arm as two officers handcuffed her wrists and dragged her from the house. His wife had stood behind him, not saying a word. A precursor of sorts to what was to become of their marriage. He tried again and again to justify his actions, explaining that he had a duty to uphold the law. He was only doing what he thought was right, but his wife never understood. "She's your daughter, goddammit," his wife had said more than once. The divorce came the week after his daughter was convicted and sentenced.

"To thine own self be true, and it must follow, as the night the day. Thou canst not then be false to any man," he said quietly, reaching for the car door handle.

Kaitlyn stepped from the police cruiser and stood before him; her eyes turned down toward the ground. Her shoulders hung heavy in shame. "Am I under arrest?"

"For pepper-spraying a homeless man?" He shook his head. "No. It was a mistake. He's going to be fine."

"I feel . . . so stupid. He didn't threaten me. I panicked."

Rodney slid his hands into the pockets of his trousers. He frowned, shuffled his feet, and then said, "It happens to the best of us." He realized how superficial his words were and shrugged as if to apologize for the perfunctory response.

She tried to avoid eye contact, glancing along the trail behind her. But he saw the fear in her eyes despite the detached facade she struggled to maintain. Rodney felt sorry for her. He'd seen stronger people crushed by less hell than what Kaitlyn was going through. However, his sympathy for her was curbed by the knowledge that her suffering was, in part, self-inflicted. If she would only open up . . .

He studied her carefully, noting the dark shadows beneath her eyes. This business was taking its toll on her. Even more reason for him and Julie to make some progress, sooner better than later. Rodney knew that Kaitlyn was hiding her past from him. If she would just confide in him, they could get to the bottom of this more quickly. Maybe, he wondered, it was time to get things out in open.

He gestured back toward where his car was parked. "Come on, I'll drive you home."

They walked side by side in silence for a few moments. Kaitlyn kept her head down, while Rodney glanced ahead along the trail. She coughed, probably still trying to clear the pepper spray from her throat.

"Things are getting serious. There's been an attempt on your life, and your fiancé is dead," he said. "Don't you think it's time you told me what this is all about?"

She never looked up, just kept her head bowed and continued to walk. "I've told you everything."

Perhaps Julie was right. It was time to put on a little pressure. "No. Tell me about the Shallows . . . Laura."

She gasped and halted, turning to face him. Her eyes were wide with surprise. It reminded him of his daughter on the morning he confronted her over the hit-and-run. "You know?"

"Some. I know your name was Laura Hobson, and you were the last person to see Jesse Riley alive. I think it's time we talk about it."

Kaitlyn glanced away toward the cemetery, which was just visible through the trees. She seemed to be weighing her options. He stood in silence, making a careful study of her face, looking for a hint to what she was thinking. Perhaps the fact that he knew so much already would get her to open up. While he waited, a breeze blew through the trees and swirled around them. The rustling branches sounded like a thousand distant whispers, calling out from the graves beyond. Eerie. He couldn't shake the feeling that they were being observed. He took a quick glance up and down the trail. The uniformed officer was speaking to one of the EMTs while the other EMT helped the homeless man into the ambulance. The officer looked toward Rodney and gave a nod as if to signal he was preparing to leave. There was no one else in sight. Perhaps he was wrong. Maybe Kaitlyn wasn't the only one being affected by this case.

Without turning toward him, she said, "Take me home so I can shower." She paused, then added, "Are you free to go for a drive this afternoon?"

He nodded. "Where are we going?"

"To the Shallows."

30

DURING THE DRIVE across the Commodore Barry Bridge, Rodney attempted to rouse some form of conversation from Kaitlyn. Perhaps elicit more detail about where they were headed and what it had to do with Brad's murder. But despite his best efforts, she said very little. She remained slouched in the seat next to him, her arms folded, head turned to gaze out the passenger window. He turned, at her direction, left onto Route 322 off the bridge into New Jersey. Passing the exit for Bridgeport, he recalled coming to the town's small race track once as a teenager. The roar of car engines and smell of exhaust fumes returned to him. The trip had been his father's attempt to bond with his son, but Rodney's preference had always been an evening in the library.

When Kaitlyn gestured for him to turn off onto a narrow side road, Rodney saw wooded acres interspersed among sprawling farm fields. The occasional farmhouse dotted the rural landscape. The street sign read Center Square Road.

"Turn here," Kaitlyn said, pointing to a dirt-covered road leading into an overgrown field. It was barely wide enough for his car. He'd have driven right past it if she hadn't pointed it out. He drove slow and easy, careful to steer around the deep craters that littered the road. The overgrown weeds formed a thick wall on either side of his car. *No one has plowed here for ages.* The cloud of dust that rose behind the car obscured his view in the mirror.

As he drove onward, Rodney saw a line of trees ahead, stretching the length of the field. At first sight, the barrier looked impenetrable, but, as he drew closer, he saw an opening where the dirt road passed through the center. The sunlight dissolved as he drove into the thick foliage, the overhead tree branches creating a canopy of impenetrable shadow.

"Where are we?" he asked.

"We're almost there. Just around this bend."

The road turned sharply to the left, and Rodney saw the sunlight break through a small opening in the trees ahead. Passing out of the shadowy backwoods, the road widened and circled around to the right as it entered the overgrown yard. An old farmhouse loomed out from the wild grass. The windows of the first floor had been boarded shut; a gaping black hole was where the door should have been. Most of the second-floor windows had been broken, and a portion of the roof had collapsed into the attic. The decayed wood of the weather-beaten slat siding was a sickly shade of gray.

He drew the car up to the front of the house. "Nice place." He opened his door and climbed out of the car. "Has a real welcoming feel to it."

Stepping from the car, Kaitlyn stood silent with her hands in her coat pockets, staring at the dilapidated house. "Jesse and his family lived here. The house wasn't in all that great a shape back then either." She turned to look at Rodney across the car roof. "They moved away shortly after he died. They never found anyone to take over the farm."

As he walked around the car, Kaitlyn moved toward the broken porch stairs with slow, cautious steps. Rodney touched her arm. "It might not be safe."

She glanced over her shoulder. "I'll be fine."

As she mounted the stairs, Rodney heard the wood creak in protest. He reached for the stair rail, more out of instinct than need. The railing shifted under his touch; the rotten wood broke free and fell to the ground. Treading cautiously up the remaining stairs, he stopped behind Kaitlyn. She was motionless in the doorway, transfixed by the darkness beyond, and didn't seem to notice his approach.

"If thou gaze long into an abyss," he said, "the abyss will also gaze into thee." Rodney placed his hand on her shoulder. She shuddered at his touch. "You probably shouldn't go in."

She shook her head. "Just revisiting some old ghosts." Kaitlyn turned to face him. Her eyes were moist and held a deep sadness within. "I spent a great deal of time here when I was a teenager. Almost every other night. They were like a second family to me."

Kaitlyn walked down the porch stairs and moved off along a narrow path beside the house. Rodney followed close behind, listening as she continued to speak. He wondered if she was talking to herself more than she was to him. Her words were distant, as if she was carrying on an inner monologue rather than a conversation.

"We met in high school. Jesse was a year older than me," she said. "I was always welcome here. Day or night." Rodney noticed that she kept her head bowed as she walked, never looking to the right or left. "Mr. Riley worked the farm. Jesse helped out before and after school. I remember playing in the corn fields. Running through the rows and rows of stalks. Jesse, me, and his little sister."

Rodney glanced back toward the house. They must have walked half a mile, he reckoned. Ahead he saw a sparse line of trees. Did he just hear a car rush by?

"They never had a lot of money. Just getting by on what came in from the farm," Kaitlyn said. "Jesse told me that his dream was to become a doctor. He wanted to support his parents so they wouldn't have to work the farm anymore. But they could never have afforded to send him to medical school."

They passed beneath the trees, and the ground sloped down to the water's edge. Kaitlyn halted, gesturing before her. "Detective, welcome to the Shallows."

The pond wasn't large—the length of a football field, and half as wide by his estimation. Rodney figured it would be an easy swim from one side to the other and wouldn't leave even the most amateur of swimmers winded. A dilapidated dock stretched out into the water, the front corner dipping below the surface. The pond's opposite bank sloped up to a wire fence, on the other side of which was the interstate. A blur of red flashed by along the highway, leaving behind the whoosh of a speeding car.

He stepped to the pond's edge and surveyed the algae-covered water. "This is where Jesse drowned?"

Kaitlyn nodded, then moved to a nearby bench. The pavilion that covered it looked as dilapidated as the dock. He sat down next to her, hoping the old rotted bench would hold their combined weight. In front of them was a short, sandy beach that led down to the water.

"We came here all the time. It doesn't have a real name, but we always called it the Shallows. It's not too deep, but you can't stand in the center without it being over your head. This is where you'd find us swimming every day in the summer. And in the winter, we'd come here to ice skate."

Rodney pointed toward the pond. "You'd swim in this?"

The corners of Kaitlyn's mouth curved upward. It was the first that he'd seen anything that remotely resembled a smile since they'd started this trip. "The water was clean back then. This . . ." She looked down at her feet. "Just the passing of time."

He followed her gaze back toward the scum-covered water. Green algae drifted in aimless clumps on the pond's calm surface. A dragonfly skimmed across the surface, landing on a branch that was half-submerged.

Rodney leaned forward and clasped his hands together, allowing them to hang down between his knees. "Tell me what happened."

Kaitlyn breathed in deep, then sighed loudly as she exhaled. "Jesse and I came down here one evening. April 25th. I'll never forget the date. We'd been lounging on the dock. It was getting dark. Jesse was telling me about the acceptance letter he'd gotten from the University of Delaware. He was brilliant. Could've gone anywhere, but he'd only applied to schools that were close to home. I'd like to think that he'd done it to stay close to me, but I knew it was more about his family than about keeping our relationship going."

"You were assuming it would end when he went to college?"

She shook her head. "Not assuming. I knew it would. I was planning to break up with him over the summer." She hesitated for a moment, glancing toward the interstate. "Too many of my friends got hurt when their boyfriends headed off to college. I didn't want to be one of them." She shrugged. "He didn't need some teenage high school sweetheart holding him back."

Rodney followed her gaze, catching sight of a U-Haul barreling by. "What was he like?"

"Witty. Smart. Good-looking. He was very popular in school." Her voice wavered as she pondered her next words. "But he was troubled."

Rodney looked down at his brown leather shoes, shifting them in the sand beneath his feet. "What do you mean?"

"Jesse could be a bit—what's the word—manic. His episodes were rare, and he did a good job of hiding them from most people. But I was all too familiar with his sudden outbursts. So was his family."

He glanced at Kaitlyn, noting a tear moving down her cheek. "Did he ever hurt you?"

Kaitlyn gave her head a vehement shake. "No. No. His episodes weren't necessarily violent. More like he became ultra high-strung. He had his moments of anger, but he never hit me, if that's what you're getting at."

"Did he have one of those episodes the night he died?"

She didn't answer right away, just stared at the old dock.

Rodney figured it was best to not push it, just let her speak in her own time. Her silence lingered until she finally spoke, "No. It was dark. He missed his step and fell off the dock."

"How'd he drown? You said the water wasn't that deep."

Kaitlyn turned toward him. More tears fell from her eyes. She gestured toward the beach in front of them. "Over here, the water isn't too deep." She nodded toward the dock. "It's much deeper over there. Even you would struggle to keep your head above water." She paused. "There are spots . . . by the dock. Muddy spots below the water—two or three feet of thick mud—if your feet get stuck, the mud sucks you down. Worse than quicksand."

Rodney turned "He couldn't get free?"

"He was just out of reach of the dock. I managed to grab his hand for a moment, but I couldn't pull him back up. He kept splashing and gasping for air." She clasped and unclasped her hands, her voice wavering.

"Is that how your blouse got torn and you got the scratches on your arms and legs?" Rodney said.

She looked up, as if to question him. He said, "I've seen the police report on Jesse's death. What happened then?"

Kaitlyn turned away from him. "If you've seen the police report, then you know already."

"I want to hear it from you."

She snapped at him. "Why? Do you enjoy making me relive this horror? I'll tell you the same thing now that I told the police back then."

He heard the agitation in her voice. He feared that she'd shut down completely and he'd get no further information from her. "I just want to hear it from your perspective . . . in your own words."

She sighed, crossing her arms. "When I lost my grip on his hand, I knew there was nothing else I could do. I ran back to the house for help. By the time I returned with his father, Jesse was gone."

Rodney stared across the water. It was still and silent. "Must have been tough."

"Today is April 24th."

"Yes. So?"

She turned to him. "Tomorrow is the sixteenth anniversary of Jesse's death."

31

KAITLYN once again slouched in the passenger seat as Rodney followed the signs back to the bridge and toward the city. They had sat in silence on the bench for close to twenty minutes before she rose, quietly walking back toward the house. She could tell he had more questions, but she was glad that he wasn't asking them. Tired, both physically and emotionally, she didn't want to think about the Shallows anymore. She simply wanted to go home.

He flipped on the wipers as the first signs of rain spotted the windshield. "Why'd you change your name?"

She didn't turn to look at him, not even acknowledging that she'd heard his question. She wondered if being inquisitive was a natural impulse for him, or if it was something he'd been trained to do.

When she didn't respond, he sighed and drove on, the monotonous rumble of tires on the pavement the only sound to fill the void between them. She listened to the droning, allowing it to subdue her weary mind. It was a few minutes before she spoke again. "Jesse's death was big news around here. Everyone knew what'd happened. Everyone knew who I was. It must have been a slow news month because the story kept resurfacing in the papers. The final months of my junior year of high school, as well as my senior year, were hell. I'd become an outcast. Some thought of me as a harbinger of death. A few, a murderer."

As they proceeded up the Commodore Barry Bridge, Kaitlyn glanced out at the Delaware River. The encroaching storm had stirred up the water, forming small white caps on the river's surface. It reminded her of the Shallows.

"But his death was ruled an accident," he said.

"That sort of thing doesn't mean much to a bunch of teenagers. To many of them, I'd killed Jesse." She fell silent, and then added, "I'd been accepted to Rowan University. Do you know it?"

He shook his head.

"It's in Jersey, about twenty minutes from home. Close enough that my name was known. I wanted a fresh start in college. My parents helped me change my name. By the time I got to college, Laura Hobson no longer existed."

Rodney changed lanes to pass a slow-moving truck, grunting when he found a slow minivan in the lane he'd just drifted into. "Must have been pretty traumatic for you."

"I spent the better part of four years in therapy. But you never really get over it, do you?"

"No, I doubt it."

"For a long time, I avoided relationships like the plague," Kaitlyn said. "Brad was the first person I'd been serious with since Jesse's death. That's what makes this so much harder." Her voice cracked as she fought to keep her emotions under control. "Just as I dip my foot back into the pool of love . . ."

She fell into silence. He didn't follow up with any questions, which came to her as a relief. She'd opened up far more than she'd expected. He now knew the truth, at least as much as she was willing tell. The rest, she decided, must remain locked away. Kaitlyn wasn't prepared to revisit the whole truth. Not yet. Maybe not ever. But maybe Rodney could find Brad's murderer without the whole truth.

While Rodney slowed to pass through the EZ-Pass lane of the bridge's toll booth, she kept her eyes fixed on an unseen point somewhere ahead, oblivious to scenes passing on either side. Without the distraction of conversation, Kaitlyn's mind was free to drift, and found its way into the past. Closing her eyes, she saw his face—a mix of rage and terror—as it sank beneath the murky surface of the Shallows. The water inched over his lips, filling his mouth. The gurgling had been so loud that she could hear it over the clamor of his thrashing arms. Snapping her eyes open again, she realized that the silence had become unbearable. "Tell me about your daughter," she said.

The question seemed to take him by surprise. "Huh?"

"Your daughter. You said I reminded you of her."

He hesitated with his answer. She'd put him on the spot with a seemingly unwelcome question. She'd only been trying to occupy her mind, but Kaitlyn wondered if she'd overstepped some unspoken boundary between cop and victim. His hands shifted on the steering wheel. He was uncomfortable, she could tell. "Sorry," she said. "Getting too personal."

"No. It's not that. Just not accustomed to talking about myself." He drifted the car to the right onto the onramp for I-95 North. "Carol was a good kid. That's how I like to remember her. She was smart, pretty, and had a bright future ahead of her. She made me and her mother proud with everything she did."

"You speak as if she's dead."

He shook his head. "She'd probably have been better off if she was. Her senior year of high school, she fell in with some bad influences. A month after her eighteenth birthday, she got mixed up in a hit-and-run that killed a mother and her young daughter. Carol had been driving home from a friend's house. She'd been drinking." It was his voice that cracked this time. "I found the damage on her car the next morning."

"You turned in your own daughter?"

He was slow to answer. "What choice did I have?"

He sounded like he was trying to convince himself. How agonizing the decision must have been for him? She wondered if the fatherly instinct had hesitated his hand even for a moment before turning his daughter over to the police. "Must have been tough."

"Yeah," he said. "My wife begged me to hide the evidence. There'd been nothing to connect my daughter to the accident except the damage on her car. But . . ."

His hands gripped the steering wheel, tight enough to turn his knuckles white. Although she wanted to know more, Kaitlyn decided that, like her, he had a past that was best left alone. She turned away from him and stared out the window. The mile markers along the side of the interstate flew past, white lettering on the green background was nothing more than a blur.

His voice broke the silence. "She killed them both. She hit them and left the scene of the accident. I've spent the past three years wondering where I'd failed as a parent." He sped up an onramp and merged with traffic. "She's serving two five-year sentences in the Montgomery County Correctional Facility."

"I'm sorry. It must have been rough, going through that as a cop."

Rodney let out a quiet laugh. "Yeah. Some of my co-workers didn't make it easy."

With that, the detective fell silent once again. Kaitlyn studied his profile. The chiseled jaw oscillated beneath the tightly locked lips, as if he were grinding his teeth. His eyes focused on the road ahead, and he didn't seem to notice her cursory inspection. She turned away and allowed herself to find some solace in the passing scenery.

"How well do you know Kevin O'Neill?"

She was surprised by the question. It came abruptly, as if he was desperate to change the subject. "I've worked with him for a couple years. Why?"

"How about when you were growing up? Any chance you might have met him?"

Kaitlyn was confused. Why would Rodney ask her a question like that? "What's this all about?"

"Kevin is the same age as you. He spent his teenage years in

Penns Grove. I thought you might have run into him when you were young."

She thought hard for a moment. She never knew that Kevin was from New Jersey. There were two Kevins that she could remember from her childhood, but neither were from Penns Grove. "Don't think so. I'm sure I'd have remembered. Does it matter?"

Rodney shook his head. "Probably not. Just curious."

———

KAITLYN FELT a sense of relief when she saw her house in the distance. The silence that had ensued during the latter part of their journey back from New Jersey had become unbearable. It left her feeling almost claustrophobic with an overwhelming urge to bolt from the car the moment it stopped. All she wanted was to forget. Forget the previous couple weeks. Forget the Shallows. Forget the past.

Rodney drew the Dodge into the driveway, and her hand was quick to reach for the door handle. She'd opened the door halfway before his hand clutched her forearm, stopping Kaitlyn from getting out of the car.

"Stay here."

She followed his concerned gaze, saw the envelope stuck to the center of the garage door, and drew in a quick breath. It was just like all of the others. Her name was scrawled in large block letters across the front. Rodney reached in the car's glove box and pulled out a pair of surgical gloves. As he climbed from the car, he slipped the gloves over his hands and walked toward the garage.

Rodney peeled the envelope from the door and carefully opened the flap. He slipped the folded paper from within. Kaitlyn caught the narrowing of his eyes as he held the paper before him. The grave frown that crossed his lips conveyed all that she needed to know.

She climbed from the car and met him by the garage door. "It's from him, isn't it? What does it say?"

He said nothing at first, glancing around the surrounding neighborhood with intense scrutiny. Then he turned the letter around for her to read. Cut from magazines, the letters formed a simple question:

Did you have fun at the Shallows?

32

KAITLYN CARRIED two mugs to the kitchen table, setting one down before Rodney and taking a sip from the other. Although the tea was warm and soothing, it would take more than a little sweet honey to comfort her. She set the mug on the table and opened one of the nearby cabinets. She returned to the table with a bottle of Jack Daniels and took a seat across from Rodney. He'd been on the phone for ten minutes with Julie Lewis. It had started out calmly enough, but she could hear the frustration in his voice and see it in his furrowed brow and tightened jaw.

"No, I didn't intentionally leave you out of it," he said, shaking his head. "It was spur of the moment."

Kaitlyn cracked open the bottle of whiskey and poured some into her mug. Then she raised it toward Rodney as if to ask him if he wanted some. He nodded. She poured a little in his mug, then set the bottle down on the table between them. As Rodney's conversation continued, Kaitlyn listened quietly, sipped her tea and tried not to laugh. It seemed like the detective had spent nine minutes out of the ten defending his decision to take her to New Jersey earlier that day.

"Julie, I'm trying to explain—"

Resting her mug on the table, Kaitlyn glanced toward the

window over the kitchen sink. Shadows were falling outside as the sun set. She couldn't believe that the day was almost over. Between the incident with the homeless man and the trip to the Shallows, the day felt like a whirlwind. As her thoughts returned to the most recent letter, her blood ran cold. How could anyone know they had gone to the Shallows? As Rodney had just said to Julie, the trip was entirely spur of the moment. Someone must have followed them to New Jersey. Was this person always watching her? Was every moment of her life under scrutiny? Her gaze remained on the window. Could someone be watching now?

Rodney had taken her keys, told her to stay in the locked car, and searched the house from top to bottom. He had placed the letter in an evidence bag and dropped it in the trunk. Then, he'd escorted her into the house.

"My god, that woman is frustrating." Rodney sighed as he dropped his mobile phone onto the table.

Kaitlyn turned her eyes back to him and smiled. "You two sound like an old married couple."

He laughed, then reached for his mug. "We do, don't we? Julie's a good detective, just a bit too high-strung for my tastes. She'll be here shortly."

He sipped at his tea. "What is this?"

"Apple and cinnamon tea with a dash of honey and . . ." She gestured to the bottle on the table.

He swallowed another mouthful, then said, "I'm more of a coffee drinker myself, but this isn't bad. The JD helps make it palatable."

She recalled a quote that seemed poignant and smiled. "You can't get a cup of tea big enough or a book long enough to suit me."

Rodney looked across the table at her, puzzled. "Tolkien?"

Kaitlyn shook her head. "C. S. Lewis."

"Hmmm, I've not read much of his stuff."

"You seem more like a student of philosophy."

He smiled. "How did you know?"

"If thou gaze into an abyss . . ." She giggled. "I know enough to recognize Nietzsche when he's quoted."

"At least someone appreciates it," he said. "It goes right over Julie's head."

———

THEY FINISHED their tea and moved into the living room. Kaitlyn went straight to the wide bow window. She squinted past her own reflection into the darkness beyond. Reflected in the glass, she saw Rodney pass behind her and move to the bookshelf along the nearby wall. Anyone lurking outside could observe their every move, and they'd never know. The thought sent a chill through her. Kaitlyn yanked the curtains closed with a quick jerk before taking a seat on the sofa.

Rodney drew a book from the living room bookshelf and gazed down at the cover. "I remember having to read *The Tell-tale Heart* in high school, but I don't think I've ever read anything else from Poe." He turned and held up the book for her to see the title. "Are his other works any good?"

Kaitlyn nodded. "Yeah, but you have to be in the right mood."

She sank into the deep sofa cushions as he opened the book and flipped through the pages. He scanned the text. Then he read aloud.

> *The skies they were ashen and sober;*
> *The leaves they were crisped and sere—*
> *The leaves they were withering and sere;*
> *It was night in the lonesome October*

Kaitlyn gave him a smile. "*Ulalume.*"

"Do you have these memorized?"

"No. You just happened to find one of my favorites."

He closed the book and placed it back onto the shelf. "I see what you mean about having to be in the mood for Poe." He continued to scan the titles. "You've got an eccentric taste in books. Stoker, Austen, and Plato. And then Doyle, Wells, and Dickens. You've got a veritable who's who of classic literature." He frowned and pulled a thick paperback from between two leather bound volumes. "And this? You disappoint me. *Fifty Shades of Gray?*"

Her face reddened, and she turned her gaze away from him. "My guilty pleasure."

He laughed and returned the book to its place on the shelf, then sat on the loveseat across from her. Rodney looked as if he were about to ask her a question. She knew he was only doing his job, but Kaitlyn wanted nothing more than to forget about the whole ordeal that had brought them together.

Suddenly a gunshot echoed through the house, followed by the crash of glass and a loud whoosh. Startled, Kaitlyn leapt from the sofa. Rodney was on his feet as well, reaching for the leather holster resting on his hip.

"What the hell—?"

"I . . . I don't know," she replied. "It came from the kitchen."

Kaitlyn followed him from the room and down the hall toward the back of the house. The smoke stung her eyes even before she caught sight of the bright orange flickering ahead. The kitchen table and chairs, as well as the curtains, were ablaze. The fire was young and nimble, just beginning to take hold of the objects it engulfed. Rodney charged into the room, yanking down the curtains around the shattered sliding-glass door. The fabric, which had just ignited, fell into a pile and he stomped at the burning threads.

"Water," he yelled.

Kaitlyn rushed to the pantry and flung open the door to grab the fire extinguisher. She ran across the kitchen and tugged at the orange safety pin free, then let loose a stream of white foam onto the flames. The fire shrank away in protest.

Rodney dropped to one knee and pulled up his pant leg. Strapped around his ankle, Kaitlyn saw a black holster holding a small revolver. He drew the weapon and handed it to her. Resting the extinguisher on the floor by her feet, she took the small silver gun in her hand. It was surprisingly lighter than she expected. The metal was cold against her palm.

"You know how to use that?"

She nodded, and allowed her fingers to curl around the pistol grip.

"Stay away from the windows if you can. Don't leave the house." He drew his own gun from the holster on his hip, stepped through the frame of the shattered sliding-glass door and halted. "And don't shoot me." Then he disappeared into the darkness.

She remained still for a few minutes, staring out of the darkened opening. A cool breeze blew in, fanning the smoke and smoldering embers. Kaitlyn slipped the revolver into her waistband and used the extinguisher to stifle some rogue flames. Clouds of caustic vapor rose from the charred remains of her table, causing her to cough and back up against the far wall. She dropped the now-empty extinguisher to the floor with a dull thud. Pulling the handgun out of her waistband, she held it within a tight grip. It had been more years than she could remember since she'd fired a gun. Jesse had taught her to shoot the autumn before he died.

Kaitlyn recalled the row of soda cans resting atop the trunk of the fallen pine tree out along the edge of the farm. An October wind whipped at the wilted cornstalks in the fields. Jesse stood behind her, his body pressed against hers. His arms reached around and steadied Kaitlyn's arms as she gazed down the barrel of the Smith & Wesson.

"Just relax," he'd said. "Take a deep breath. When you're ready, pull the—"

Her arm jerked upward as the explosive concussion echoed across the field. The shot reverberated up her arms. A sharp odor cut into her nostrils. It was an acrid but strangely sweet smell.

She looked at the row of soda cans. None had moved. "Damn."

"It's your first time," Jesse said. "Were you expecting to be a marksman your first time out?"

She turned and smiled. "Of course."

He leaned forward and kissed her. It was deep and passionate. Her arms went limp at her sides, so much so that she almost dropped the gun.

She pulled away from him. "Is it such a good idea to kiss me while I'm holding a gun?"

He reached for the firearm, slipping it from between her fingers. "I'm not worried. You'd never hurt me."

A sudden noise outside the darkened door startled Kaitlyn back to the present. With a steady hand, she brought the small revolver up and aimed at the center of the opening. She heard footsteps approach and drew a tight grip on the gun, her finger resting on the trigger guard just as Jesse had taught her.

Rodney stepped through the door, then stumbled back when she pointed the gun at him.

"It's me. Put the gun down."

Kaitlyn released the breath that she'd been holding and brought her arm down to her side. Rodney crossed the room and took the gun from her and placed it on the kitchen counter. Behind him was Julie Lewis, her hair disheveled, and her clothes rumpled and stained with dirt.

Kaitlyn asked, "What happened?"

"Julie had a run in with our arsonist."

"You saw him?"

Julie shook her head. "Not well enough to identify him." She tried to brush the dirt from her pants. "I arrived in time to see someone creeping toward the back of the house. I followed, but not before he shot out your porch door and pitched that Molotov Cocktail through. We scuffled, but he got away across the cemetery."

Rodney gestured at Julie. "I almost tripped over her in the dark."

33

KAITLYN STOOD in the doorway of the kitchen, surveying the damage. The table was blackened but intact and the curtains lay in a smoldering heap nearby. A chilled wind blew in through the shattered remains of the sliding-glass door. The overhead light in the kitchen made the blackness beyond the opening appear even darker, almost impenetrable. Smoke still lingered in the air like a haunting reminder of the danger she was in. She shuddered and wrapped her arms tightly around herself.

Rodney, wearing gloves, picked his way around the scorched rubble, careful not to disturb anything. He hovered over some shards of broken glass, then pointed to the floor. "Looks like a wine bottle."

Kaitlyn followed his gaze. The short bottle neck was intact, but everything below it was gone. The jagged glass edge had been blackened by the fire.

Julie, who stood near the refrigerator, came toward Kaitlyn and pointed to the nearby wall. "There's a bullet hole over here."

The round hole was inches from Kaitlyn's head. She shuddered at the sight. If she'd been standing there . . .

Rodney pulled a small flashlight from his pocket. "I'm going to look around outside." He took a cautious step through the shattered glass door and disappeared into the night.

Julie folded her arms and stood rigid and still. She eyed Kaitlyn from across the room. It was an unsettling stare, and Kaitlyn turned her gaze away.

"Rodney tells me you two went over to Jersey today," Julie said. Her voice had an accusatory tone.

Kaitlyn nodded. Exhausted, she needed something to prop herself up. The wall was the closest thing, so she moved across and leaned her back against it. "We went to the Shallows."

Julie raised an eyebrow. "I thought you didn't know anything about the Shallows."

"It's something I don't like to talk about."

Julie's eyes seemed to challenge her to fill in the details. When Kaitlyn didn't, Julie said, "Are you going to keep me in suspense? The Shallows is . . ."

Kaitlyn finished the sentence. "A pond." She wondered how much to say. "An old swimming hole from my childhood."

Julie frowned. "All this shit is over a pond?" She gestured to the blackened mess before them.

"Not exactly," Kaitlyn said.

She gave Julie an abbreviated version of the same story she'd told Rodney earlier in the day. The words didn't flow as easily as they did with him. She felt the need to be cautious with the details. There was something about the way that Julie looked at her that unsettled Kaitlyn. Maybe it was the intensity in Julie's eyes. As Kaitlyn detailed her attempt to save Jesse, she thought she noticed Julie's lips tighten, if only for a moment. When she finished her story, she remained silent and waited for a response.

Rodney stepped back through the door. He worked his way around the mess to stand between them. "Not much out there. Some impressions in the grass. Might get a footprint or two. I'll get forensics over here to process the scene."

Kaitlyn closed her eyes and shook her head. More police traipsing through the house. Another sleepless night. She wasn't sure how much more she could take. What could they possibly think they'd find in her blackened kitchen? A bullet. A broken bottle. A cheap dinette table, black with soot. There was nothing here. It looked so easy on television. A CSI collects some hair samples, and within forty minutes the police arrest the killer. All bullshit. She at least knew that much. If it were that simple, Rodney would've caught Brad's killer by now.

"Please. No crime scene stuff," she said.

Rodney turned to her and frowned. "We need to process the scene."

"Do you really think there is anything here worth processing?" She looked between Rodney and Julie. She didn't want them there anymore. Kaitlyn didn't want anyone there. The demons of her past were nipping at her heels, begging to be confronted. But all she wanted to do was run. Run away just like she did years ago when Jesse died. Run far away where no one knew her, and no one knew about her past.

Julie gave her a stern look. "We won't know until we process the scene."

Kaitlyn was silent for a moment. She thought about Jesse's missing necklace. Did the police take it? "I don't want anyone else blundering through the house." She gestured toward the pile of scorched rubble. "Can't you do it yourself?" She was shocked at how sullen her own voice sounded. How exhausted she was. How much she wished she'd been the one to die and not Brad. She trembled at the thought. Is that what she really wanted? To die in Brad's place? Funny, she never thought this way when Jesse died.

Rodney stared at Julie for a long moment. Their eyes locked in some unspoken conversation. His entreating and defensive. Hers stern and disapproving. "We could probably bag and tag the important stuff," he said.

"That's not advisable," Julie said, her voice was sharp as if condemning the merest thought.

Rodney walked toward the front of the house. He gestured for Julie to follow. "Let's talk about this . . . in private."

Kaitlyn remained in the kitchen as the two detectives stepped into her living room. Their voices were low and drifted out into the hall, but she could not make out every word, just the occasional phrase or partial sentence.

"—don't care. This isn't the way to run—," said Julie.

"—questioning me? I'm still in charge of—," said Rodney

"You're making this personal," Julie said. "You're in too deep and it's clouding your judgment."

After another few moments of unintelligible conversation, Julie stormed from the living room and out the front door without saying a word. The door slammed shut behind her. Kaitlyn stared down the empty hall, waiting for Rodney to return. When he did, he looked despondent. His shoulders were hunched forward as if under an enormous weight. Rodney shook his head as he moved back toward the kitchen.

"You okay?" she asked.

Rodney waved his hand, as if to dismiss her question. "Yeah. I'm fine." He looked back toward the front door. "She just needs to cool off."

"I'm sorry if I've caused all this."

"It's not your fault." Rodney glanced at the shattered glass door. "We need to get this closed up. Do you have any plywood in the garage?"

KAITLYN SWEPT the last of the broken glass into a pile. She leaned the broom against the wall and turned to where the sliding-glass door had once been. Rodney had found several pieces of scrap plywood in her garage and managed to cobble together a rudimentary wall to close off the opening. It wasn't pretty, but it would serve its purpose. She'd call a contractor in the morning and get an estimate on the repairs. For now, she was safe.

Safe. She rolled the word around in her head. What was safe? Was she safe in her own home? Was she safe at work? Would she be safe anywhere? Not as long as her stalker and Brad's killer were at large. There was nowhere safe for her. She tried to remember when she last felt safe. With Brad, she'd been secure. When wrapped in his arms at night, she was protected. But now he was gone. Where could she find safety and security now?

Rodney came in through the front door and walked toward the kitchen. "That should do it for now. No one's getting through there easily."

"Thank you," Kaitlyn said. "You look like you could use a drink."

Rodney smiled. "Yeah. Got anymore JD?"

Kaitlyn crossed to the cabinet. "With tea?" She smiled.

"I'd prefer Coke with it, if you have any."

Kaitlyn pulled two glasses from the cabinet, grabbed a bottle of Coke from the refrigerator, and fixed their drinks. "You're not going to get in trouble for this, are you?"

Rodney took the glass from her. "Probably, but don't worry about it." He sipped on his drink. "Damn, that hits the spot."

They moved back into the living room and continued to drink. They each took turns returning to the kitchen for refills. When the whiskey was gone, they moved onto wine. They talked into the night, mostly about philosophy and literature. Kaitlyn relaxed, feeling less anxious and, for a moment, almost forgetting about the turmoil her life had been in over the past few weeks.

Rodney pulled her copy of *Fifty Shades of Grey* from the shelf and read a few passages aloud. Kaitlyn laughed at his varying expressions as he read the more salacious bits. His words were slurred, or was she just hearing him wrong through her own drunkenness?

"How can you think this is good?" he asked, holding the book in the air. "It's not even good enough to be called erotica."

She smiled. "Do you read erotica?"

His face turned red. "Well, no."

"Then how . . ." She found herself tongue-tied. ". . . how do you know?"

"Because . . . because . . ." He stammered for a moment. "I don't know. It just isn't good enough."

"I need another drink," Kaitlyn said, rising to get another bottle of wine from the kitchen.

"I'll get it," Rodney said, jumping from his seat onto unsteady feet.

They collided near the door of the living room and Kaitlyn stumbled. He caught her in his arms and held her close for a long moment. She looked up into his eyes. A deep blue, just like Brad's. She never noticed before. His arms around her were warm and comforting. She struggled to catch her breath. Was that his heart pounding, or was it her own? She felt safe, safe within his arms. Every fiber of her being begged her to pull away, but the alcohol had gone to her head. She looked into his eyes again. Her head was swimming in those deep blue pools. It was wrong, she knew it. But her whole life was collapsing, why fight it?

She snaked her hand around his neck and drew him closer.

34

KAITLYN STOOD by the kitchen window and watched the morning mist dissipate from around the gravestones in the cemetery. Her head pounded from last night's alcoholic binge. Her heart pounded for another reason. Shame. She had allowed the situation to get out of hand. She could blame the alcohol, but that didn't excuse the behavior. In the midst of her own grief and guilt, she'd crossed the line with Rodney.

She remembered the kiss. It had been long and impassioned. She wasn't sure if it was the alcohol or the kiss that left her feeling feverish. She pulled Rodney closer, allowing herself to be enveloped by the warmth of his embrace. He seemed more than willing to reciprocate; his hands drew her into him. Kaitlyn struggled to catch her breath, heart fluttering. A tingling sensation surged from deep within her, making Kaitlyn draw in a breath and tremble with desire. Her fingers raked down the back of his shirt. She ached to feel his bare flesh. Then, the moment of clarity struck.

She pushed away from Rodney and quickly turned her back to him. "I'm sorry," she said. A tear ran down her cheek. She brushed it away. "I don't know what got into me."

"I should probably go." His voice was weak, fluttering with each word.

"No. Please stay. I don't want to be alone." She turned to look at him. "I'm scared."

Despite Rodney spending the night on the sofa, she hadn't been able to sleep. The bed was cold and desolate, like a frozen tundra of Egyptian cotton and down-filled pillows. Kaitlyn laid in bed, chastising herself for being callous and heartless. For god's sake, Brad's body was still in the county morgue and she was ready to hop into bed with the first man who showed compassion. She vacillated between fits of crying and angry self-recrimination. Could she have done anything more careless and humiliating?

What would happen now? Would he recuse himself from the case? Would another detective—maybe Julie—take over? Would another detective be as understanding about her past? Would he or she see through her lies?

Kaitlyn returned her gaze to the kitchen window. The sun breached the horizon, casting early morning shadows across the cemetery. Among the headstones and statues, the mist performed a swirling and twisting dance of death, as if it knew that with the morning came its demise. Kaitlyn clutched her tea mug and gazed at the clouds that hung low to the ground. The silhouette of the tall angel statue at the center of the cemetery was barely visible. Its outstretched arms beckoned to Kaitlyn, as if waving her to venture forth into its realm. She shivered at the sight.

Off to the right of the statue, a faint bluish glow captured her attention. The light was still too dim to see well, but she swore that there was movement nearby. Resting the mug on the kitchen counter, Kaitlyn leaned forward. She squinted through the windowpane in hopes of catching a glimpse of whatever was moving out there. A dark form emerged from between the stones, tall and thin and wearing a long, flowing coat. Kaitlyn's shoulders tensed at the sight. Framed from behind by the rising sun, its features were obscured. It remained still, and for a moment, Kaitlyn imagined that its eyes were locked with hers. Who was it?

What did they want? She glanced over her shoulder. Should she wake Rodney? No. She would face this alone. Her demons waited for her in the cemetery. She couldn't hide behind him any longer.

She turned back to find the form hadn't moved. The faint bluish glow she'd seen earlier hovered at the figure's side. Kaitlyn couldn't tear her eyes away from the graveyard and was vaguely aware of her arm reaching across the sink. When she finally looked down, she was holding the carving knife from the nearby butcher's block. She tightened her hold on the wooden handle. It was warm and comfortable in her hand. It felt safe.

Emboldened, she resolved to end this now. It was time to find out what this was all about, who was behind it. She was terrified of what she would find in the cemetery, but this needed to end. One way or another, she was going to get answers.

She turned from the window, moving swiftly to the front of the house and out the door. With the knife firm in her grip, she circled the house and started to work her way through the gravestones. Despite the rising sun, the mist still hung low across the cemetery. It made it difficult for her to see the low grave markers that littered the ground. Kaitlyn's eyes darted around, searching for the figure she'd seen earlier. At first, she saw nothing but rows of marble monoliths. Then, a dark silhouette rushed into the space between two large monuments ahead of her. It vanished just as quickly. Kaitlyn tightened her grip on the knife and forged forward, treading cautiously through the mist. She crept past the broad base of a marble angel, back and wings arched forward as if in mourning. She crouched beside the stone effigy, leaning her shoulder against its cold, hard surface.

Kaitlyn listened for footsteps, for anything to tell her she wasn't imagining things. A crow swooped down and landed on a nearby gravestone, cawing. The harsh sound seemed to be directed at her. Was it angry that she had invaded its domicile? It cawed again, this time more loudly. The crow peered down at her like a black harbinger of evil. Maybe this wasn't such a good idea. Her arms quivered, and her mouth had gone dry. She felt stupid for not waking Rodney before coming out here. She set the knife on the statue base, then rubbed her eyes with balled up fists. With a quick glance back toward her house, Kaitlyn wondered if it would be better for her to head back. That was when she heard the snap.

She made a frantic grab for the knife, knocking it to the ground at her feet. Pain raked across her palm. As she reached down, a dark form darted from behind a nearby crypt toward her. Kaitlyn threw up her arms protectively and tumbled backward. She rolled into a grave marker then scrambled to her feet, cursing. The dark figure was almost upon her. She turned to run but only took a few steps before her assailant slammed into her shoulder. Kaitlyn was thrown hard to the ground. Rolling with the fall, she reached out. Her fingers grasped what felt like a shoe. In desperation, she yanked hard, throwing the figure off-balance and to the ground. Kaitlyn lunged forward, arms outstretched. She reached for the face. Her fingers caught a handful of hair. Kaitlyn pulled hard but was surprised when the hair came away in her hand. A booted foot slammed into her face. She reeled backward; her head crashed into a gravestone. The sound of running footsteps faded with the morning sunlight as she lost consciousness.

THE VOICE that called her name was distant and muffled. It swam through the ache in her head, swirling around with the blotches of color that drifted before her closed eyes. Something nudged at her shoulder, then touched the side of her throat. She tried to open her eyes but found the light too bright. Turning her head to the side, Kaitlyn winced as a sharp pain jabbed at her right temple.

"Kaitlyn." There was an urgency in the voice that was calling her name.

She squinted against the daylight, trying to focus on the blur of gray, green, and blue. There was another nudge on her shoulder, more forceful than before.

"Come on, Kaitlyn," said the voice. "Talk to me."

It was a familiar voice. She couldn't quite place it. Closing her eyes, she tried to remember what happened. The cemetery, she was in the cemetery. Vague images formed in her mind, then a dark figure lurched out of the gloom of her memories. Her eyes snapped open and she jolted up. Her head exploded with pain; it blazed down the side of her face. Kaitlyn screamed. A hand gripped her shoulder, and another cradled her back, guiding her back down. Rodney's concerned face came into focus.

"What the hell?" she said.

"Don't move. An ambulance is on the way."

Kaitlyn stared at the blue sky above her. "What happened?"

"I was hoping you could tell me," Rodney said. "I woke up and couldn't find you in the house."

Kaitlyn fell silent, trying to make a mental assessment of herself. Her mouth was parched and her lips dry. Her palm stung and her fingers were covered with something thick and moist. There were aches in about half a dozen joints, and her face felt as if it were on fire.

"I found you lying here with a bump on your head and a gash in your hand," Rodney said.

Kaitlyn hesitated for a moment, trying to frame up the right words in her mind. Then she recounted her encounter among the graves. Her sentences were broken and short, but Rodney took in every word. "I got some hair . . . I think."

Rodney shook his head. "Sort of. You got a wig." He held it up for her to see. "Here."

Kaitlyn studied it as best as she could. The color and length were familiar. She'd seen it a lot recently. Chestnut-brown. Shoulder length. *My god*, she thought.

"It's a woman?" she muttered.

"Or a man dressed in drag."

Kaitlyn shook her head, regretting it immediately. "No. It's a woman. I've seen her a couple times over the past couple weeks."

"What did she look like?"

The shrill of approaching sirens echoed across the cemetery. Kaitlyn sighed as she tried to recall the details, any details, of the woman with the chestnut-brown hair. The hooded figure during her run a few weeks ago. And at Toscana Italiano. The woman had bumped into Kaitlyn as she and Brad were leaving. And just a few days ago in the hotel lobby, the woman had been there as well.

"She's been following me," Kaitlyn said.

Rodney's face turned grim. "She's been doing more than following you." He paused, then said, "I don't want to make things worse, but look."

He held up an iPad where she could see it. Against the morning sunlight, the screen was flushed and hard to see. However, Kaitlyn could make out four squares, each with a different image. At first, she thought she was looking at grainy black and white pictures until she noticed the constantly changing numbers in the top right corner of each square. A video feed? Maybe security cameras? Each image struck a familiar chord. A bedroom. A living room. Even a kitchen. She peered closer, then her body stiffened with terror.

"That's my house?"

"I found this on the ground a few feet from here. Your attacker must have dropped it."

Kaitlyn stammered. "But . . . that's MY house."

"Whoever this is, they've had you under surveillance. They've bugged your house for video."

35

DAMN IT! Goddammit! I have to break through the tree line and get onto the dirt trail beyond before I can stop. There is a wheeze in my lungs that was never there before. Damn cigarettes! Someone shouts her name. It echoes across the cemetery and through the trees. He's looking for her. I've got to move, and fast. It won't be long before the police arrive. I can't be caught anywhere near here. My car is parked down the trail at the old Barmouth Train Station. A quick walk and then I'm gone.

Gotta keep my pace rapid, but not so much that I might attract attention if someone sees me. What a huge blunder! Now they have my wig, and my iPad. The iPad, I'm not too concerned about. There's nothing on it that would lead them to me. They could try to trace the serial number, but I paid cash. That'll be a dead end. Fingerprints? I wore gloves . . . did I wear gloves all the time? I can't remember. Damn, that could be a problem.

What about the wig? Forensics can probably get some DNA from it. It'll be the first concrete clue that they get. I don't think that will lead them to me, at least not before I complete what I set out to do. It might thwart my future though.

Why didn't I just run when I saw her come out of the house? I could've gotten away without her ever seeing me. But, no . . . I had to do something. Had to give in to the urge to add a little mystery. To inflict a little more pain. To pour out some justice. What the hell was I thinking?

I know what I was thinking. I was thinking about Jesse and what she did to him. What was that Bible quote I learned in Sunday school? "Vengeance is mine saith the Lord." Well, what the Lord won't do, I will.

I've waited over sixteen years. Patience has been a constant companion, especially these past few months. It hasn't been easy. Every time I've been near her, I've had to curb my desire to get my hands around her neck and choke the life out of her. Maybe I was just tired this morning. Poor judgment got the better of me. Patience for twenty-four more hours is all I need. Then it'll be over.

My car is where I left it, but now there is a Ford Focus and a Chevy Malibu nearby in the parking lot. Damn, another opportunity to be identified. I scan the area, but don't see either of the drivers. If news about Laura's attack in the cemetery is released to the public, someone might remember seeing my Volkswagen and report it. This morning just keeps getting worse and worse.

Approaching sirens echo through the morning air. I climb in my car and race from the parking lot, kicking up stones and dirt behind me. From East Levering Mill Road, I turn left onto Belmont Avenue and drive away from the cemetery, the Cynwyd Heritage Trail, and my latest crime scene. Flashing red lights in my rearview mirror catch my eye. The first cop car is arriving. More will be coming in moments.

I take the roundabout way home and smoke four cigarettes in the process. They take the edge off my nerves, but not enough to stop my mind from racing through a dozen scenarios that could result from this morning's misadventure. My phone rings. Damn. Let it go to voicemail. I'm still too wound up to talk. I may get shit later for not answering, but I don't care anymore.

There are a lot of "ifs" hovering over me right now. If forensics pulls DNA from the wig and if they find mine as a match, the cops will be after me soon. But I'm confident that it'll be at least a couple days before that happens. That's more than enough time to follow through with my plan. If someone tells the police about the blue Volkswagen parked at the Heritage Trail this morning, they might put two and two together. But, what're the chances of that.

Once at home, I strip off my dirt-covered clothes and toss them in a black trash bag. Gotta ditch them somewhere so they can't be traced back to me. The dirt and grass stains could place me at the cemetery.

The hot shower is reinvigorating, soothing my aching body. There's a bruise forming on my right arm. I recall falling on a rectangular grave marker during my struggle with Laura. She put up more of a fight than I expected. Spunky little bitch. May have to be cautious tonight. Don't want to give her a chance to try for round two.

After the shower, I dress quickly. I can't be incommunicado for too long. He might get suspicious. His voicemail tells me what happened in the cemetery . . . like I don't already know. He wants me to meet him at the hospital. I send him a quick text to tell him I'm on my way.

I check my watch and smile. Twelve more hours . . . and Laura will be dead.

36

RODNEY LEANED against the nurse's station, watching the emergency room staff of Mercy Health dart from curtained bed to curtained bed. A cacophony of buzzes and beeps filled the room and the air smelt of antiseptic. Dr. Venezia had just updated him on Kaitlyn's condition.

"That cut in her palm was superficial. It should heal on its own. No concussion, but she needs to rest for a few days," the thin, sallow physician had said. "Her injuries could've been much worse. She's a lucky lady."

Rodney wondered about the doctor's idea of luck. It certainly wasn't the word he'd have chosen to describe all that had happened to her over the past few weeks. She might be lucky, but it seemed to be all bad luck.

Rodney thanked the doctor. While he waited for the okay to see Kaitlyn, he recalled the panic he'd felt when he woke earlier that morning to find her front door open. Gun drawn, he'd made a frenzied search of the first floor, then moved up to the second. He'd pulled out his phone to call for help but glanced out the window of the second-floor back bedroom before dialing. He had a clear view across the cemetery, and what he saw sent him charging down the stairs and out into the yard. A dark figure darted away through the field of gravestone and crypts. Whoever it was had too much of a head start to bother with a chase, but he also spotted a body sprawled in the grass. He hoped he wasn't too late.

While the EMTs bundled Kaitlyn onto the stretcher, Rodney barked orders to the uniformed officers who'd responded to his call. "I want that house searched from floor to ceiling. Bag and tag every camera you find."

On his way to Mercy Health, he called Julie but got no answer. He left a voicemail, giving her a brief rundown on what happened. "Call me," he ordered, just before hanging up.

As he stood in the emergency room, he tortured himself over last night. He'd been stupid, very stupid. He put his integrity, his career, and the whole damn case at risk. How could he have done that? Not only had he been drunk off his ass, but he kissed Kaitlyn. He'd become far too involved with her to remain objective in the case. It had become personal. Maybe he should recuse himself from the case. Let Julie—or someone else—take over the case. She'd been suggesting—if suggesting was really the word—that he had gotten too close to Kaitlyn. *Damn.* He hated to admit that Julie might be right. She would never let him hear the end of it. What the hell had he been thinking?

A nurse pulled a nearby curtain aside, revealing a hospital bed within the cramped space beyond. Kaitlyn sat up. She was wearing a hospital gown and looked pale and haggard. The side of her face was bruised with a trickle of dried blood on her cheek. She tried to smile, but it looked as if even that was too much for her. Rodney moved to the bedside and rested his arms on the cold bedrail.

"Feeling any better?" he asked.

"You've become my bad luck charm," she said.

He knew she was joking, but he grimaced all the same. Twice he'd been around when she was attacked. Twice he was the one who was first on the scene. It would be ironic if it wasn't so frightening. He had no clues and only one vague suspect. He felt helpless. She was in real danger, and there was little he could do to protect her.

"About last night . . ." Rodney started to say.

Kaitlyn held up a hand to stop him. "Not another word." Her voice, though weak, didn't betray any sign of anger or spite. "We'll talk about it after this is all over." She paused. "After you catch this bastard."

Rodney nodded. Last night needed to be addressed. Some part of him wanted to get it out in the open now. Clear the air and all that. Putting off the discussion meant suppressing unspoken anxieties and unanswered questions. Was she planning to report his conduct to his captain? Should he step away from the case now? He needed her to remain open to him if he was going to dig through her twisted past to find a murderer. Would she still trust him?

"What'd you find at my house?"

"Nothing good." Rodney proceeded to recount the seven cameras his officers had found. Two in the bedroom, one in the kitchen, and one each in the front hall, living room, garage, and master bathroom. "They were expertly hidden. My own officers couldn't have done better. Top notch gear, too. Same level of tech as we use ourselves."

He wondered what Kaitlyn was thinking, but her face betrayed nothing but exhaustion. It reminded him of his daughter, the way she'd looked after the trial. Exhausted and alone. Carol had refused to see or speak to him during the two-week case. His only glimpse of her was in the courtroom, and even then, she avoided eye contact. After her sentencing, he'd tried to see her again, but Carol sent him a terse message through her lawyer. Just five words. *Leave me the fuck alone.*

Despite that, he kept tabs on her through friends who worked in the prison system. Her first three months were hell. Word got around among the inmates that she was the daughter of a cop. There'd been a couple attempts to "rough her up," as Rodney's contact said. But he'd taught his daughter well, particularly in self-defense. Two hospitalized inmates later, Carol was left alone. She became the prison's resident badass. *Something any father would be proud of.* His sardonic thought both amused and depressed him at the same time.

"Got any ideas what we're going to do now?" Kaitlyn said, bringing him back from his brown study.

"We've got to get you somewhere safe," he said. "Problem is, no one can know where you go."

Kaitlyn tried to push herself up in the bed, grimaced in the attempt, then fell back onto the pillow. "I'd argue, but I don't really have the strength right now." She gave him a half-smile. "Where do you suggest?"

Rodney folded his arms and leaned against the wall. "That's the problem. I don't know who to trust, so the fewer people who know where you go the better." He scratched the side of his face, felt the stubble on his cheek.

"What about a safe house? Don't police usually have those?"

Rodney shook his head. "That shit's only in the movies. Do you really think Lower Merion Township can afford to have a safe house?" He regretted the words the moment they left his mouth. There was an abruptness in his response that revealed his frustration. This case was getting to him. "Sorry. Just tired."

"What about a friend's house?"

He narrowed his eyes. "Who?"

"Sammy. The receptionist at the radio station." Kaitlyn paused before adding, "She was going to be my maid of honor."

He didn't like the idea. Not at all. There'd been no clues to connect this with any one person, so everyone in Kaitlyn's life was still a suspect. "Can you trust her?"

"Trust her with my life."

"That's what you'll be doing." He sighed. Every part of him screamed that this was a bad idea. But he wasn't sure what other choice he had. "If you're certain . . ."

RODNEY HELD the door open as Kaitlyn entered the WPLX offices. Sammy rose from behind the reception desk and gasped. She untangled her headset from strands of long, blonde hair, dropped it, and rounded the desk, making straight for Kaitlyn.

"Oh my god, where've you been?" She threw her arms around Kaitlyn. "I've been frantic!"

"Just been a rough couple days," Kaitlyn said. She peeled herself out of the embrace and gestured to Rodney. "You remember Detective Shapiro?"

Sammy nodded and gave him a puzzled glance. Rodney watched her closely. Until he knew better, everyone was under suspicion.

Kaitlyn gestured toward a door across the room. "Is anyone in the conference room?"

Sammy shook her head.

"Is Scott in his office?"

"Yeah, but—"

Kaitlyn cut her off with a raised hand, then turned to Rodney. "I'll fill in Sammy on everything while you talk to Scott. Will that work?"

He didn't feel comfortable with her out of his sight, but he needed to have a word with the station manager. Kaitlyn had been adamant about her trust in Sammy. He wasn't wholly convinced, but he had nothing else. Another hotel was out of the question. Only a short list of people knew where Kaitlyn was previously, and the call she'd received there indicated that she was still found. This time, that list would be *very* short. He gave her a concerned look.

"I'll be fine."

Kaitlyn took Sammy's arm and led her into the conference room. He watched the door close and remained in the lobby for a few moments. What if Sammy was the killer? Was he allowing Kaitlyn to walk to her death? Rodney considered entering the conference room and monitoring the two women. Was he worrying too much?

He cursed under his breath. The memory of their kiss from the previous night still lingered in his mind. He'd screwed up . . . big time. An alcohol-induced tête-à-tête was the last thing he needed. Kaitlyn was just another victim, and this was just another case. His job was to keep her safe and find a killer. Nothing more. He looked once more at the conference room door, then strode down the corridor toward Scott Mackay's office.

The office door was open, and Scott was seated behind his desk, his face bathed in the blue glow of the laptop screen before him. Rodney gave a short rap on the door frame and leaned in the doorway.

"Mr. Mackay, do you have a moment?"

Scott looked up, smiled, and gestured for him to enter. "Sure, come on in, detective." He rose from his chair and rounded the desk, meeting Rodney in the middle of the office. "How's Kaitlyn? Any news?"

Rodney skipped the pleasantries and got right to the point. "We're relocating Kaitlyn to an undisclosed location for her protection. It's far too dangerous for her to come to work until we've identified this killer."

"How long?"

Rodney wished he had an answer. A few days. A few weeks. How long does it take to find a killer without clues to go on? Forensics was going over the wig, the cameras and the iPad found earlier in the cemetery, but it would take time to get results. "I can't say just yet."

Scott considered the answer. "I can get someone to cover her shift for a couple weeks. Undisclosed. I'm assuming I can't reach her during her absence?"

"Afraid not."

Scott returned to his chair behind the desk. "Do me a favor. Keep me informed about your progress . . . and her wellbeing."

"I'll do what I can."

"I've got a soft spot for that kid. Kind of the daughter I never had."

Rodney frowned. He knew all too well what Scott was talking about. He'd lost his daughter, and had no idea if she'd ever learn to forgive him? He had only been doing his sworn duty. His badge was more than a shiny piece of metal. It was a symbol of his commitment to uphold the law. Had it been wrong to put the law before his own family? To sacrifice his own daughter to uphold a list of rules and edicts? "She's a nice woman," he said, unsure if he was talking about Kaitlyn or Carol.

"I'd hate to lose her. She's got real talent."

Rodney glared at him. "Her life's at stake here." The words came out with an angry edge, perhaps too much so. "I'd think survival would outweigh talent in this case."

"Detective, don't misinterpret my words. I'm concerned for her safety as much as you are."

Rodney looked down at his feet. He'd spoken out of turn. "I know. My apologies."

Scott leaned forward and rested his hands on the desk. "Take care of her."

"I'll do my best."

When Rodney returned to the reception area, Julie stood by the desk, staring at her mobile phone. She looked up as he approached, slipped the phone into her coat pocket, and smiled. Compared to his own, her clothing looked fresh and clean, like she'd just pulled them out of the closet. He'd not changed since the day before; his shirt and pants were covered with "slept-in" wrinkles. Yet, dark bags hung beneath Julie's eyes, as if she hadn't slept either.

"Where's Kaitlyn?" she asked.

He pointed to the conference room. "In there. I thought she'd be out by now." He glanced at his watch. Ten minutes. It shouldn't have taken this long. Rodney's palms started to sweat; his mind raced with a dozen possible scenarios. He rushed to the door and knocked hard.

It opened just enough for Kaitlyn lean out. She smiled. "Give us a minute more."

He fought the urge to fling the door open. "Everything okay?"

"Sammy's talking to her hubby."

That wasn't what he wanted to hear. "I don't like this."

"He's going to find out eventually. An extra woman in the apartment isn't something you can easily hide." Then she stepped back into the conference room and pulled the door closed.

This wasn't how he'd envisioned things going this morning. He'd hoped to hide Kaitlyn somewhere where no one could find her, giving him and Julie time to make some progress on the case. The growing number of people who knew where Kaitlyn was going concerned him. He should've expected this. It was foolish for him to think that he could shelter her without anyone knowing where. Now, three people knew where she was going to be. It'd only be a matter of time before more did as well.

As he and Julie waited, Kevin O'Neill came through the lobby, heading toward the front door. Kevin's eyes met his. There was a darkness within the grey eyes that made Rodney shudder. Kevin turned his gaze away and seemed to consider returning into the offices from where he'd just come. Then, with a nervous smile, he nodded at Rodney and stepped through the front door. Rodney glanced at his watch. It was still before noon. *Shouldn't Kevin be on the air? Why is he leaving during his shift? Could he be making a run for it?*

He turned to Julie. "Can you run her over to Sammy's house, then stay with her till she gets settled? I've got something I want to follow up on." He glanced at the conference room door. "I'll swing by Sammy's house later to check up."

Julie nodded. "Sure. You have an address?"

"Yeah. She lives in Fishtown."

"That's out of our jurisdiction."

"I know. I'll see if the captain can get round-the-clock surveillance from the city police." The conference room door swung open, and he glanced over as Kaitlyn and Sammy emerged.

He turned back to Julie. "Let's get her out of sight. We can worry about the details later."

"Where are you going?"

"I'm not sure, but I've got a hunch it won't be good. Just make sure Kaitlyn's safe."

Julie smiled. "Of course."

37

RODNEY HAD DRIVEN for almost an hour, following Kevin first through downtown Philadelphia and then north toward Conshohocken. The midday traffic was light and made it difficult to avoid being seen. At one point, he lost sight of Kevin's Volkswagen and, in a panic, raced ahead, accidentally passing him on the highway. It took some creative driving, using a dump truck as cover, to get behind him again.

It did not escape Rodney's notice that Kevin drove a Volkswagen. A Volkswagen was the heart of this mystery. Could this be the one that ran down Kaitlyn on that rainy night on Walnut Street? What kind of VW had passed him that night? A Beetle? Kevin drove a Golf. He wondered, could his hunch be wrong?

When they exited the interstate, Kevin sped through the Conshohocken side streets, and Rodney wondered if he'd been seen. The Volkswagen turned into an alley that ran between two rows of homes. Rodney looked down the alley. A line of detached garages lined one side and a high chain-link fence ran along the other. The Volkswagen was parked about halfway down the alleyway in front of a garage. He couldn't remember the exact street address, but Rodney knew Kevin lived somewhere in Conshohocken. Could this be his house?

Kevin climbed from the car, opened the trunk, and lifted out a dark duffel bag. Closing the trunk, Kevin glanced around and then disappeared from view.

Rodney pulled the car forward and parked along the curb. He was out of his jurisdiction and had no reason to do anything other than observe. No warrant. No probable cause. Perhaps he could get in the house under the pretense of having additional questions to ask. Rodney didn't know what he thought he might find. Possibly nothing. But something about Kevin O'Neill bothered him. He wasn't at work, first and foremost. It was the middle of the day and Kevin had gone home without working his shift. Granted, he could've been ill, but Rodney doubted it. There had been fear in Kevin's eyes at the radio station. But fear of what? Being caught?

Rodney got out and made his way down the alleyway. His steps were slow and cautious. He kept close to the front of each garage he passed. He wasn't sure what he was going to do when he reached the Volkswagen. Just play it by ear, he guessed.

There was no one around when he reached the car. Rodney peered around the corner of the garage, studying the house beyond. The blinds in all the windows were drawn. It gave the impression that the house itself had drifted off for a quick nap. He wandered over to the Volkswagen, careful to always glance back at the house. He peered through the back window. There was nothing unusual in the back seat. He rounded the car, peeking in through each window, half-hoping to find something suspicious that would give him probable cause to search further. Nothing.

He moved back to the garage, stepping out of sight of the house. Was he wrong? The suspicious behavior. The lying about his childhood. The animosity toward the police. The history of violence. It all seemed to add up. He might have just found Brad's murderer and Kaitlyn's stalker. There was no known motive as of yet, but he had an instinct for this sort of thing. He was usually right. This time, however, he was starting to think he might have missed something along the way.

Rodney decided to return to his car to think over his next move.

He started walking down the alley. A metallic crash came from inside the garage. He leaned toward the door. A muffled moan was barely audible. He tugged on the door latch. The garage door wouldn't rise. He rounded the corner and found a side door, wooden with peeling paint. Locked. He listened again. Another moan. Rodney reached for his gun. Then, he drove his shoulder against the door. Hard. The wood around the frame splintered with a crack. The door swung open and Rodney rushed into shadows beyond.

The garage was a clutter of odds and ends. An antiquated push lawn mower. Several large flower pots. A stack—three bags high—of mulch. Two spare tires, one on a rim and the other rimless. And, sprawled on the concrete floor, a man. He was gagged. His arms and legs tied behind his back like a hog at a rodeo. The young man's face was battered. His right eye was bruised and swollen shut. Dried blood caked the end of his nose. He tried to speak when Rodney entered, but his words were muffled and unintelligible.

Rodney knelt beside him and pulled the gag from the man's mouth. "You okay? What happened?"

The man gasped for air, coughed, and then said, "Thank god you found me!"

Rodney slid his gun back into the holster and tried to untie the knots that restrained the man. "I'm a police officer. Tell me what happened."

"It's him. The Strangler."

The knots were tight, and Rodney struggled to loosen them. "What?"

"I met him last night at a bar. He invited me back to his house. He beat me, tied me up and dragged me out here. He said he was going to kill me."

"Who? Kevin O'Neill?"

"Yes. That's him."

Rodney worked at the knots more feverishly. He could barely believe what he was hearing. Could it be true? Was it possible that he had stumbled upon the identity of the man the Philadelphia Police had been seeking for seven months? He remembered the leather cord in Kevin's desk drawer. There were ligature marks on the victim's neck.

Rodney struggled with the knots. They were tight, expertly tied. The rope dug into the young man's wrists and ankles.

"Damn it," Rodney said.

A sudden roar of rage came from behind him. He turned toward the door. The silhouette framed in the doorway launched itself across the garage. Rodney threw his arms up in defense. Kevin O'Neill—his face red with a fevered frenzy—crashed into Rodney. They tumbled across the concrete floor. The air rushed from Rodney's lungs on impact. He gasped for breath, fighting the tight vacuum that consumed his lungs. Kevin was already on his knees and threw a punch. Rodney's head jerked back and smacked the cold floor. His head spun and a wave of nausea rose from within him. A pair of strong hands gripped his throat. He grabbed at Kevin's wrists, trying to wrestle himself free. Kevin hung over him, mouth frothed with spit and eyes filled with murderous fury.

Rodney felt lightheaded. He punched the side of Kevin's head to no avail. He couldn't get enough leverage for a good swing. He reached up with both hands and grabbed Kevin's ears. Rodney pulled hard. Kevin screamed. His grip lessened for a moment. That was all Rodney needed. With all the strength he could muster, he pulled down while lunging upward. His forehead smashed into Kevin's nose. Blood poured out. Kevin fell backward and stumbled over the young man who was still tied up on the floor. Rodney rolled away, reached for his gun and struggled to his feet. His head reeled and he fought to remain standing. Kevin was a blur in the corner of his eye. He only saw the shovel moments before it smashed into his shoulder. The gun clattered on the concrete. Rodney fell into some nearby metal shelving. Half-empty paint cans tumbled onto the floor. Some spilled open, splattering the floor with globs of blue and red.

It took Rodney a moment to get back to his feet. He turned,

expecting another assault, but none came. The garage was empty except for the young man who was half covered in paint. Still dizzy, Rodney steadied himself on the wall and searched the floor for his gun. He spotted it by the lawn mower and rushed to pick it up.

He paused over the young man. "You okay?"

"Go! Get the bastard."

Rodney hurried out of the garage. He heard faint footsteps running in the alley. The Volkswagen sat nearby. Kevin O'Neill was on foot. Rodney stepped out into the alley and glanced each way. He caught sight of Kevin down the far end of the alley. The son of a bitch was fast. Rodney wanted to give chase, but his battered body raged against him. Kevin was almost to the end of the alley, and there was no way that Rodney could catch him.

He watched as Kevin ran from the alley. But, instead of turning and disappearing from sight as Rodney expected, Kevin ran straight out into traffic. Blind frenzy or suicidal fervor, Rodney didn't know which. He heard the blare of horns, the screech of tires. Kevin disappeared from view and traffic came to an abrupt halt.

38

I PULL the car up to the curb and shut off the engine. Nightfall has shrouded the front porch in shadows, which will play to my advantage. The less the neighbors see, the better. I pick up the revolver from the passenger seat and open the cylinder. All of the chambers are loaded. I'd prefer to use my 9mm Glock but leaving the .38 Smith & Wesson at the scene is icing on the cake. It's not as if I expect him to come to the correct conclusions any time soon. I've been careful to not leave any clues that might point to me.

Raindrops start to fall onto the windshield. Should I postpone my plans? It could get messy at the Shallows. No, it is too late to stop now. It has to be tonight. Rain or no rain. Laura must return tonight, the night that Jesse died. We're going to celebrate the anniversary together. Celebrate as if our lives depended on it . . . well, at least hers.

I reach into my pocket for my cigarettes. Just need a quick one to calm my nerves. I stare at the crumpled, empty pack for a moment. Damn it! I throw it against the dashboard, then dig through the compartment beneath the center armrest. Nothing there either. I jerk open the glove compartment and yank everything out onto the passenger seat. Owner's manual. Registration. Insurance card. Penlight. Tire pressure gauge. No cigarettes. No damn cigarettes. I lean back in the seat and slam my hands on the steering wheel. The horn lets out a quick chirp. Shit. Hope no one heard that. I stare at the house. No one looks out the windows.

Got to calm myself. I need to be fast and accurate with this. No room for mistakes. I close my eyes, breathe deep and step through my plan once more. In and out in five minutes. That's my goal. The longer I linger, the greater the chance that something will go wrong. I grab the gun again from the seat and balance it in my hand. It's lighter than my Glock, but not uncomfortable to handle. It will serve its purpose.

The lights in the front bedroom come on. A silhouette appears before the window and lingers for a moment before pulling the blinds closed. It can only be Laura. That's the room where she's staying. It's time to go.

Standing outside the car, I scrutinize the surrounding street for any witnesses. No one's about on the sidewalk on either side of the road. A car is approaching from the north and I turn my face away from the glare of the headlights. What the driver can't see, the driver can't use to identify me. There'll be no connection between me and whoever the driver thought he saw standing along the edge of the street.

I climb the three steps onto the porch and pause by the door. This is the culmination of a year's worth of work and planning. Yes, I've had to adjust my plans, and things haven't quite worked out the way I'd originally hoped. But it's the end that matters—and tonight, it'll end just as I had envisioned.

I'm a little lightheaded at the thought that it will soon be over. In a few hours, a murderer will face justice, and I'll be the source of that justice. Not like the others, where someone else prosecuted, judged, and doled out the sentence. I will be prosecutor, judge, and executioner. And, there will be no appeals.

I pull open the door. The small wad of folded paper I shoved into the striker plate earlier kept the door from latching. The carpeted stairs to the second-floor apartment are dimly lit by a single light hanging from the ceiling at the top of the stairway. I unscrewed the bulb from the overhead light here at the bottom of the stairs the same time that I rigged the latch on the door. Again, the less anyone can see, the better.

While ascending the stairs, I finger the grip of the revolver in my coat pocket. The steel is cold against my skin, even through my surgical gloves. My heart races and I can almost feel the adrenaline coursing its way through my body. My muscles tighten in anticipation with each step upward.

At the door, I take a deep breath. I need a clear head. Nothing must go wrong. Once I cross that threshold, I'm on a path of no return. Everything must be just right. Taking one more deep breath, I ring the doorbell.

39

SAMMY CLEARED the dishes and carried them to the sink. The kitchen was small and cramped, with the round table that dominated a generous portion of the floorspace. Kaitlyn sat with her back to the wall, watching Sammy's husband twist the cap off a bottle of Corona. He was a tall man who looked almost malnourished. His dark curly hair was long and messy, like something straight out of the seventies. Kaitlyn had met Sammy's "old man" only once before, when she helped them move into their apartment. His name was Zachary, but he preferred to be called Zeek. All she knew about him was that he worked in the Center City and did "computer stuff."

He was taking this invasion of their small but cozy apartment in stride. Kaitlyn didn't like to impose on Sammy and her husband, but she couldn't think of anywhere else she could go. She didn't want to sleep alone in another hotel, and staying in her own home was out of the question. She hoped this wouldn't last long. *Perhaps the police—Rodney—will get a break in the case and find this bastard quick.* She could only hope.

"Kate, you want a drink?" Sammy said.

"Do you have red wine?"

Sammy pursed her lips. "Got Corona, Jack Daniels, Grey Goose, Jim Beam, and Bacardi."

"So . . . no red wine?"

"Nope. Afraid not."

Kaitlyn thought for a moment, then gestured toward Zeek. "I'll have what he's having."

"Good choice," he said.

Drinks in hand, they moved into the living room, which wasn't much larger than the kitchen. The room was sparsely furnished with an oversized sofa stretching from wall to wall on one side the room. It faced a large flat-screen television on the other. The white walls were decorated with an eclectic collection of framed movie posters from the likes of *Casablanca*, *Citizen Kane*, and *Some Like It Hot*.

Zeek took a seat at the far end of the sofa and Sammy curled up next to him, resting her head on his shoulder. Kaitlyn lowered herself onto an oversized beanbag near a black wireframe DVD rack filled with classic films from cinema's golden age. Kaitlyn took a sip from her Corona, then rested the bottle on her leg. The condensation soaked through her jeans and was cold on her skin.

"Thanks again for letting me stay." Kaitlyn had already thanked them twice over dinner but still felt as if she needed to say it once more. It was the first time she'd felt safe in weeks. Her own house now harbored dark memories that would be difficult to shake. Perhaps, when this was all over, she'd sell it and move into the city. Or maybe it was time to leave altogether. Perhaps a new city, a new job, maybe even a new name. Somewhere far from the Shallows.

"Enough already with the 'thanks,'" Sammy said. "You're welcome to stay as long as it takes to catch this asshole."

"I was talking to your old man." Kaitlyn shifted in the beanbag and laughed. It was good to laugh again. When had she done it last? Perhaps a few weeks ago. Maybe the morning Brad proposed. The memory struck her hard and hurt like hell. She wiped a tear away from her eye, hoping Sammy and Zeek didn't notice. Taking another long sip from her Corona, Kaitlyn forced a smile.

"Sam's right. Stay as long as you need to," Zeek said.

His words were reassuring. She wasn't planning to stay long, even if Brad's killer wasn't caught. She didn't want to place her friends in any more danger than she already had. But for a few nights, she could sleep soundly.

With the television on, Kaitlyn sank deeper into the bean bag. The soft corduroy fabric cradled her body. They watched the evening news, then Jeopardy. Zeek and Sammy competed to see who could shout out the question to each answer first. Neither of them got many correct, but it was fun to watch the effort. After Final Jeopardy, Kaitlyn struggled out of the bean bag and got to her feet.

"Gonna take a shower. Then crash for the night," she said.

Sammy scrambled up from the sofa and gave her a tight hug. "Good night. You'll get through this."

The apartment's spare bedroom was at the end of the hall. Like everything else, it was small, almost claustrophobic. The full-size bed was pushed against the wall. Kaitlyn's suitcase rested atop the floral comforter. She sat on the edge of the bed and slipped off her shoes. The weeks of lackluster sleep were catching up to her. Exhaustion had overrun her body days ago and she'd been running on adrenaline ever since. She was tempted to fall back on the bed and go straight to sleep, but she wanted to shower first. She forced herself up, grabbed underwear, shorts and a T-shirt from the suitcase, and moved up the hall to the bathroom.

She stripped off her clothes and turned the water on in the shower. Just before stepping under the showerhead, Kaitlyn heard the doorbell ring. She paid it no heed. The hot water pummeled her sore muscles and soothed her aches. She turned her face up into the spray, feeling the sting of scalding droplets on her skin.

Kaitlyn knew Rodney wasn't pleased with this arrangement. She had seen it in his eyes earlier at the radio station. He was suspicious of everyone, not that she could blame him. Until there was more evidence, anyone could be a suspect, even Sammy and her husband. No, not Sammy. She trusted Sammy. It had taken a lengthy discussion to convince Rodney that she was trustworthy. Even then, he still eyed her with doubt.

Julie Lewis had driven Sammy and Kaitlyn to the apartment late that afternoon. Rodney said he'd stop by later in the evening to check up on her. That was probably him at the door. Julie had been silent for most of the ride, but, when they arrived at the converted townhouse, she inquired about the neighbors who lived below.

"A half-deaf old lady. Rarely ever see her," Sammy had said.

Inside, Julie made a brisk assessment of the apartment, looking briefly into each room. She asked a few additional questions about the locks on the windows and doors. Apparently satisfied with the answers, Julie headed toward the door. She paused just before opening it.

"We'll arrange for a city police patrol to watch the apartment," Julie said. "But I doubt we can push that through for tonight. Make sure you know who's at the door before you open it."

A loud pop from somewhere in the apartment snapped Kaitlyn back to her shower. The water muffled the noise, making it difficult to make out what it was. She dipped beneath the showerhead to rinse the shampoo from her hair. Kaitlyn was startled by two more sharp pops in rapid succession. She turned off the water and listened. The apartment was silent. Stepping from the shower, she dried herself, then slipped on her shorts and T-shirt. Kaitlyn's hand trembled when she touched the doorknob.

The faint odor of gunpowder met her as she stepped into the darkened hall. "Sammy? Zeek?"

Most of the apartment was in darkness. A single light radiated from the living room. She remained near the bathroom, afraid to move down the hall.

She called out again. "Sammy?"

The stillness in the apartment was deafening. Her bedroom was a few feet behind her. Her iPhone was on the dresser just inside the door. A couple quick steps and she could barricade herself until the police arrived. But she couldn't make her legs move. Petrified, she remained still. Listening. Waiting.

Suddenly a figure stepped into the hallway, framed by the dim light from the living room. Kaitlyn drew in a deep breath. The shadows hid the face, but she knew who it was. She'd missed all the clues, ignored the nagging sense of familiarity.

"Hello, Laura. It's been a long time."

40

RODNEY GRABBED a bottle of water from the kitchen and returned to the living room window to gaze out onto the street beyond. Night had fallen, and rain coated the pavement with a wet sheen. He was tired and frustrated. His body was bruised and achy from his fight with Kevin O'Neill. He'd spent the rest of the afternoon being questioned first by the Conshohocken Police and then the Philadelphia Police. Neither of them was overly happy with Rodney's actions. The Philly Police were, in particular, not happy that the GBT Strangler was dead. Rodney simply shrugged, pointing out that impact with a bus tended to do that to a person. They weren't amused.

He'd driven back to the Lower Merion Township police station. After he updated Bernie on the case, Rodney returned to his desk, checked his email, and caught himself staring at the computer screen without actually reading a word. Did the death of the GBT Strangler mean the end of the Kaitlyn Ashe case? Bernie seemed to think so, but Rodney wasn't sure. There was no hard evidence to implicate Kevin O'Neill in the death of Brad Ludlow, but then there wasn't much evidence at all.

Something bothered him about the case. The killer had always been a couple steps ahead of him. No clues. No real suspects. Not a fingerprint. Not a DNA sample. Nothing. Was Kevin O'Neill that meticulous? He'd love to tell Kaitlyn that her stalker was dead, and she had nothing further to worry about, but he didn't really believe that this was true.

The video cameras found in Kaitlyn's house were police-grade equipment. Forensics was tracking the serial numbers. Perhaps that would give him a break in the case. He wondered how long they'd been in the house. The batteries in that particular model would only last a week or two when configured for continuous streaming. Could someone have installed them while Kaitlyn was staying at the Marriott? That meant accessing the house after Brad was murdered, slipping in while the crime scene was still secured by police. Either the killer had an extreme talent for performing covert operations right under the nose of the police, or . . .

The alternative was too concerning to think about.

He read through Brad's autopsy report and studied the photos taken at the crime scene. Nothing. The Philly police report from Kaitlyn's motorcycle accident offered up nothing of importance either. He scanned through the scant forensics report from the murder scene. A few cloth fibers had been found, but nothing else. No fingerprints. How could there be so little to go on? It was as if the killer was a ghost. He smiled, remembering a quote from Sherlock Holmes. "The world is big enough for us. No ghosts need apply."

He continued to shuffle through the various reports for another half hour. He couldn't shake the sense that he had missed something obvious. He came across a newspaper clipping about Jesse Riley's death. A small black and white photograph showed a teenage Kaitlyn—or Laura as she was known then—sitting on the back step of an ambulance. He studied the frozen apathetic look on her face. Perhaps it was shock. The indifference in her hard stare was curious. She'd just lost her high school sweetheart. He knew everyone dealt with grief in their own way, but . . .

A car turned onto his street. Its headlights arced across his townhouse window. Rodney snapped back to the present and squinted at the momentary glare, realizing that he hadn't moved for a good ten minutes. He sipped from the water bottle as the tail-lights moved on up the street. The wet pavement reminded him of the night of Kaitlyn's accident in downtown Philly. It had been raining then as well. It was a shame he hadn't been able to get the full plate number off the Volkswagen. That could have opened the whole case up. Maybe even saved Brad's life. He swirled the water bottle, watching the water roll around the clear plastic sides. Something bugged him about the Volkswagen. Something about the license plate. Julie hadn't found any Volkswagen Beetles with a plate that started with BG. He returned his gaze to the window. Then it hit him.

The report about the license plates was not in the case files. Julie must've forgotten to put it in there. He ran his hand through his hair and turned away from the window. That wasn't like her. She was always conscientious about maintaining a complete case file. He crossed to the bookcase and picked up the bust of Aristotle, staring into its white, lifeless eyes. He couldn't help but quote Shakespeare. "Something is rotten in the state of Denmark."

He replaced the bust and roamed in aimless circles around the living room. The case was a tangle of loose threads that he couldn't follow to their source. He knew they all met somewhere, but he couldn't figure out where. A decades-old drowning. Anonymous letters from a stalker. An attempt on Kaitlyn's life. The murder of Brad Ludlow. He feared that there might be one final thread still out there—Kaitlyn's murder. Everything was building to that. He was sure of it. He should never have left her at Sammy's house. It would've been better to bring her here, to his own home. Julie would've raised holy hell over that. "Getting far too close to the victim," she'd have said.

As he continued to pace, something nagged at him from the dark recesses of his mind. Something he'd seen earlier in the day. There was something in the case file . . . something important that he'd missed.

———

RODNEY CROSSED the lobby of the Lower Merion Township Police Station. He waved at the night desk officer, then climbed the stairs to the Detective Division offices. As he took the stairs two at a time, his mobile phone chirped.

"Rodney?" Bernie said.

"Yeah, Captain. What's up?"

"I've got a situation."

Rodney entered the darkened office, flicked on the overhead fluorescent lights, and crossed to his desk. He only half-listened to the conversation. "Okay. What is it?"

"Philly police called. There's been a double homicide in Fishtown."

Rodney shuffled through the papers in the case file on his desk. "Hmmm . . ."

"A sub-nosed .38 Special was found at the scene."

He pulled an old newspaper clipping he'd seen earlier from the file and scanned the article. "Hmmm . . . Why'd they call you? Can't Philly police solve their own murders?"

"The gun was registered to you."

The newspaper clipping fell from his hand onto the desk. "What?"

"Where is your spare gun? The one you usually wear on your ankle."

Rodney remembered taking the holster off before he showered earlier in the evening. It had been empty. He'd given the gun to Kaitlyn the other night for protection but forgot to get it back. "I don't have it. Where was that double homicide?"

"Fishtown. Philly police are anxious to know how your gun got there."

Rodney's eyes dropped back to the newspaper clipping. A sentence near the bottom of the article jumped out at him. In particular, a name. His mind raced, frantic to process the possibilities. Could it be the killer had been right under his nose the entire time? He grasped the various threads and began to weave together a theory, seeing the face of a killer begin to emerge.

"Kaitlyn?"

"Missing. She wasn't one of the victims," said Bernie.

Rodney flipped the lid closed on the case file. "Captain, tell them I'll give them a full account later."

Bernie protested. "I can't do—"

"Get some men over to Julie's place. Tell 'em not to knock."

"What the hell's going on?"

"I know who killed Brad Ludlow." Rodney turned from his desk and dashed toward the stairs. "And, I think I know where they're going!"

41

THE DARKNESS MADE the ride nauseating. Curled up with her knees almost pressed against her chest, Kaitlyn could barely move in the Volkswagen's trunk. Other than the occasional streetlight glare filtering through the cracks between the seats, she was enveloped in blackness, jarred by every pothole. She tugged again at the zip ties that bound her wrists behind her back. They were tight and cut deep into her skin. She pressed her feet against the side of the trunk. Tried to shift herself into a more comfortable position to no avail. The cliché about not having room enough to swing a cat came to mind. But, if she had a cat right now, it would have most likely suffocated in the cramped space. She'd considered kicking at the back of the seats. But, although her legs weren't bound, there was no room to get enough momentum to do anything useful. Kaitlyn reached the frightening conclusion that she'd have to wait it out.

The image of Zeek and Sammy's lifeless bodies sprawled on the floor in the living room, a bullet hole in each of their foreheads, was etched in her mind. Zeek's shirt was bloodstained, marking a second hole in his shoulder. Their killer stood over them with a face stern and cold.

"Turn around." The words were accompanied by the flick of a

revolver Kaitlyn recognized. She'd held it herself just a few nights ago.

She remained motionless, glaring back up the gun barrel. "Why? Why are you doing this?"

The command came again through gritted teeth. "I said, turn around."

Kaitlyn's heart pounded against her ribcage. Fear gripped her, but she fought against it. Too many people had died because of her. First Brad. Now Sammy and Zeek. "Go to hell," she said, her voice cracking. "I'm the one you want." She gestured toward her dead companions. "Why'd they have to die?"

Before Kaitlyn knew what happened, the revolver was pressed against her forehead and she was staring into a pair of icy gray eyes. "Look, bitch. Feel how cold the metal is? I don't want to have to kill you here and now, but I will. One twitch of my finger. That's all it'll take."

Kaitlyn leaned into the gun barrel and tried to keep from trembling. "Why don't you? Get it over with."

"You think I'd have gone to all this trouble just to blow your brains out? Could've done that weeks ago, months ago. Now, *turn around.*"

Kaitlyn wanted to resist, to make a stand. The eyes glaring back were cold with hatred. After a moment, she gave in to her terror and turned her back on the gun . . . and a killer.

After her arms were wrenched behind her back, wrists bound tight, Kaitlyn was shoved out of the apartment, down the stairs, and out to the waiting Volkswagen. With the gun barrel prodding at her back, she fell into the trunk and found herself shrouded in darkness as the hatchback closed. She lay face down on the carpet, listening to the silence encompassing the car. Then it shook as one of the doors was opened and then slammed closed.

"Let me out! Can't we talk about this?" she shouted, rocking so her shoulder hit the back seat again and again. It was an anemic attempt that accomplished nothing, and she knew it. But she didn't want to go out quietly. She had no idea if anyone could hear her, but she shouted anyway. "Help! Help me!"

"Shut up, Laura." The back seat muffled the reply.

Kaitlyn trembled at the mention of her childhood name. She always suspected that she'd have to face her past someday. But she never thought it would be like this. Her hope had always been that she'd someday share her secret with Brad, perhaps after they were married. Just a quiet evening over some wine. A soft-spoken confession. A few tears. An understanding embrace. And, his assurance that it changed nothing. But that dream had ended in a pool of blood on her driveway.

She shouted again. "Help!" Maybe someone would be walking along the sidewalk. "Someone, help!"

This time, there was no rebuke from the driver's seat. Just the car engine roaring to life, then pulling away from the curb and accelerating up the street.

———

SHE HAD no idea how long they'd been driving. Twenty minutes, maybe thirty. But, when the car accelerated up a long incline, she was certain she knew where they were headed. They were on a bridge, probably the Commodore Barry Bridge. Over the river to New Jersey. There was only one destination for her over there. The Shallows.

She closed her eyes tight and sobbed. Of all the nights, it had to be tonight. No other would've been more appropriate. It all made sense now. All her suffering had been leading up to this. Not just the past few weeks, but the years and years of living as Kaitlyn Ashe. Of denying Laura Hobson and what she'd done. Years of loneliness for fear of getting close to someone who would learn the truth. The denials, the guilt, the life she'd tried to leave behind. It all came back in a flood. She didn't believe in ghosts, but if there was ever a night for the dead to return, it was this one. Somehow, she knew that Jesse would be waiting. Waiting for her to return to the scene of her crime. To return to the Shallows to face the ghosts of her past . . . on the anniversary of the night he died.

Over the bridge, the car raced onward through the twilight. Kaitlyn was jerked from side to side as it whipped along the rural roads of southern New Jersey. At times, it felt as if the vehicle was out of control. She half-hoped the driver would miss a turn and crash into a ditch. If nothing else, it would prolong the inevitable . . . or perhaps hasten its inevitability. Dying in a car crash couldn't be any worse than dying at the Shallows.

The ride became rough, and Kaitlyn was bounced around the confined trunk. Her head banged against the lid, off the floor, and against the lid again. She figured the battering meant they were close to their destination. This would be her second visit to the Shallows in less than a week. She didn't know what to expect from her abductor. Perhaps torture? An attempt to get at the truth about Jesse's death? Or was this to be a plain and simple execution?

The car came to a halt, and the engine stopped. The door opened and shut. Kaitlyn waited, listening to the silence. She expected the trunk to open any second, but it didn't. One minute turned to two, and then to three. The taillights trickled a red glow through the cracks in the trunk. The headlights must still be on. But where was the driver? The air in the trunk had become stifling, and she was desperate to be free. The minutes seemed like hours, and the dark, claustrophobic space had become more than she could endure. She wondered if this was how she would die. Suffocated in the back of a car.

When the trunk flipped open, she was blinded by a bright circle of light. Kaitlyn closed her eyes and turned her head to one side to avoid the glare. A steady rain was falling. The frigid droplets touched her face and rolled down her cheeks.

"Sorry. Was that too bright?" The flashlight clicked off, leaving the trunk bathed in faint red aura. "Get out."

Kaitlyn struggled to climb from the trunk. With her legs dangling over the bumper, she fought to sit up, but with her arms bound, it was an impossible task. After a few moments, a hand grasped her forearm and tugged hard. Kaitlyn fell from the trunk into the mud. She lay still for a moment; the moist ground was cold on the bare skin of her arms and legs. She shivered as moisture seeped into the thin fabric of her shorts and T-shirt.

"Get up."

Kaitlyn obeyed the command with reluctance. As she got to her feet, she caught the glint of a knife blade against the taillight's crimson hue. Another grab at her arm and she was spun around to face the car. She breathed deep, fighting to not tremble. Was she going to die like Brad? A knife across the throat? Bleeding to death in the middle of nowhere? The cold blade touched her wrist. After a couple quick tugs, the zip ties fell to the ground. She rubbed her skin, feeling the abrasions left by her bonds.

She turned around and stared into a face that she'd thought she could trust. A face from her past. She remembered the young inno-cent child with long, flowing blonde hair. The pudgy cheeks that turned pink with every smile. The bright eyes staring up through tortoiseshell glasses. It was all gone. The eyes were now forbidding. The hair short and dark. The face thin and malevolent. She glanced around and caught sight of the dilapidated house she'd visited a few days before. "Must be tough to see the place falling apart, Julianna," she said.

"Not as tough as it will be for you. Welcome back to the Shal-lows," said Julie Lewis.

42

RODNEY TOOK the turn for the on-ramp to Route 322 at sixty-five and fought to keep the Dodge on the road. The sign above read "Commodore Barry Bridge" and pointed straight ahead. The car lurched forward when he pressed down on the accelerator. The rain reflected the swirling teardrop light on the roof, making it look like crimson drops of blood falling from the sky.

He swerved past a minivan and raced up the bridge. Could he find the Shallows again? The last time he was there, it was daylight and he had a guide. Now, he was on his own. Kaitlyn's life depended on his sense of direction. He had no address, so GPS was useless. His only hope was to find some familiar landmark. His most vivid memory was the sound of the nearby interstate. Maybe if he drove along the highway, he might stumble upon it. But what were the chances he could find a secluded pond along miles and miles of dark freeway?

His mobile phone chirped and broke his train of thought. He checked the caller ID and answered. "What'd you find?"

"It's not good, Rod," Bernie said. "We're in her house now. There's a wall full of photos of Kaitlyn. Looks like they were taken with a telephoto lens . . . without Kaitlyn's knowledge."

"Damn it."

"Some look like they're from the winter, and even last summer. Julie's been at this for a long time." Bernie paused to speak to someone else, then returned to the phone. "We found a stack of magazines. They've been clipped to shreds. Probably where the letters came from."

Rodney banged his hands on the steering wheel. "How did I miss this?" His foot pressed harder on the accelerator. They had been partners for two years. He should've known that something was amiss. She'd looked a bit tired over the past few months, but he thought nothing of it. The Dodge crested the bridge, then raced down the other side toward New Jersey.

"Don't blame yourself."

Rodney didn't know who else to blame. He had practically delivered Kaitlyn into the arms of her stalker more than once. No wonder Julie only gave Brad's murdered body a cursory review. She didn't need to look. She'd seen it when she killed him. "Bernie, what do you know about Julie's background?"

"She was married when she joined the force. Divorced about two years later."

"Her maiden name?"

"Don't know. I'll get someone to check it out," Bernie said.

Rodney reached the bottom of the bridge, skidding on the wet pavement as the lanes merged into one. "Bet it's Riley." He thought back to the newspaper clipping he'd been reading earlier in the office. The last paragraph told him everything.

The victim's parents, as well as his younger sister, Julianna, were inconsolable.

He recalled Kaitlyn saying there was a sister. He'd looked at that newspaper clipping four or five times. Why had he missed it?

"You sure she's headed to the Shallows?" Bernie asked

"Positive. Where else would she go?"

The rain was coming down harder. The drops pattered loudly on the windshield. It reminded him of the night of Kaitlyn's accident in Philly. A Volkswagen had tried to run her down. Julie drove a Volkswagen. He'd missed that, too.

"Give me an address. I'll get Woolwich police to meet you there."

Rodney leaned forward to peer through the rain-splattered windshield. "I don't have one."

The phone went silent for a moment. "Then how're you planning to find them?

Rodney scanned both sides of the road, searching for anything familiar. "Intuition."

"What? That girl's life is in danger!"

"No other choice. I've only been there once before."

The wipers flicked across the windshield, wiping away fresh drops of rain. There were no streetlights along the road, leaving it cloaked in darkness. He flew past fields and clusters of trees, along with the occasional building. He reduced speed as he approached the overpass that ran above the interstate.

"Bernie, check in the case file," he said. He remembered turning just after the overpass. He veered left onto Coontown Road. The car's back wheels slid off the pavement, kicking up dirt and gravel. Rodney jerked the wheel to one side, regained control, and sped onward. "Look for a police report from Woolwich police. You might find an address in there."

"Will do. Give me a few minutes to get back to the office," Bernie said. "You gonna be okay on your own?"

"For now. Just get that address."

As he hung up the phone, the road came to an end at a three-way intersection. He stopped the car and peered to the right and then left. He glanced up at the nearby street sign. Stone Meeting House Road. It sounded familiar, but he couldn't recall which way to turn. He wished he'd made a note of the address before rushing from the office. Hindsight and all be damned. He climbed from the car and walked to the middle of the road. The rain soaked his clothes in seconds. He looked up the darkened road and saw nothing but shadows. If he made the wrong turn, Rodney could spend hours roaming the back roads of New Jersey and never find Kaitlyn. It was a fifty-fifty chance. Did he want to risk it? Maybe the interstate was the better choice. He knew the Shallows were close to the highway but how close he didn't know. Was it obscured from view by trees or brush? Maybe he could find it from there. But which way on the interstate? North? South? And could he see anything in the dark? He stood as much chance of speeding past the Shallows as he did finding it. Perhaps more so.

Rodney glanced up toward the dark sky. He wasn't going to find the Shallows by standing here in the rain. He moved back to the car and opened the car door. Before climbing back in, Rodney pulled the flashing teardrop light from the roof. No sense in announcing his arrival. He pulled into the intersection, turned the car around, and sped back the way he came.

43

JULIE PUSHED HARD on Kaitlyn's shoulder with the muzzle of her pistol, edging her toward the steps that led onto the old house's porch. Kaitlyn noticed a flickering orange glow from the open doorway. The stairs creaked beneath her as she climbed onto the porch. Peering into the door, she saw a modest square table and two chairs, one on either side. They must have been placed there just for this occasion. The table and chairs hadn't been there on the last visit. On the table stood a single lit candle. The flickering flame cast shadows which danced around the room.

There was another nudge of cold metal between her shoulder blades. "Go in."

Kaitlyn hesitated. The last time she'd been here, the floor looked like it might collapse at any moment. "Is it safe?"

The next shove was harder. The gun's muzzle was sharp and painful in the small of her back. "It's as safe as you're going to get right now."

She took a few tentative steps forward into the house. She remembered the family room well. There had been a plaid forest-green sofa beneath the window near the door and a reclining chair off to the left. The television once stood across the room on a dark brown TV stand the Rileys had bought from K-mart. She helped

Jesse assemble it for his parents. An old throw rug—now long gone —had covered the dull, scuffed-up hardwood floors.

Now, dust and cobwebs filled the corners and covered the floor. Some of the walls had crumbled, exposing the aged wall studs beneath. Old newspapers and decaying plaster and broken lath boards were scattered in piles around the room. It all looked on the verge of utter disintegration.

Standing in the room brought forth a flood of memories that Kaitlyn had worked for years to suppress. Jesse first told her he loved her in that room while they watched reruns of Magnum P.I. on late-night TV. Often, she'd fall asleep on the sofa, always to wake up the next morning with a blanket over her, snug and warm. She'd loved Jesse and his family. His parents always treated her like a daughter. And, Julianna had been like the little sister she never had. She heard Julie approach from behind and wondered what had happened to the little girl whose hair she used to braid.

Kaitlyn spun around. "What now? Why'd you do all this?"

Julie waved her gun toward one of the chairs. "Sit."

The chair's ladder back was uncomfortable, and the woven rush seat scratched at her bare thighs. It was the same one she remembered from the Riley's dining room. The table top was covered in thick dust, so Kaitlyn clasped her hands and rested them on her lap.

Julie took a seat in the other chair and placed the flashlight and the gun on the table between them, making sure to keep her hand on the pistol grip at all times. "It's been a long time since we sat in this room together." Her eyes reflected the flickering candle, making them appear to burn with rage. "After you left for college, I never thought I'd see you again."

Kaitlyn shifted in her chair. "Julie, what's this all about?"

Julie ignored the question. "Imagine my surprise when I found out who Kaitlyn Ashe really was." Her voice was flat, emotionless. "You know how I found out?"

Kaitlyn shook her head. She decided to remain silent. Maybe if Julie talked things out, she might see sense.

"Last year's Best of Philly issue of *Philadelphia Magazine*."

Kaitlyn recalled being named best nighttime radio personality. There was a photoshoot and a short write-up in the magazine.

"I recognized you. You can change your name, but I knew who it really was as soon as I saw the photo. It didn't take much work to dig up the details." Julie lifted the gun from the table and gestured at her, as if to drive home each point. "Laura Hobson. Kaitlyn Ashe. One and the same."

The gun came back down on the table with an angry thud. Kaitlyn flinched. The candle shook and the flame quivered at the violence. Julie continued to speak. "Imagine my further surprise to find that you lived in Lower Merion Township. Right in my jurisdiction. I was worried you might recognize me. But I'm not that pudgy young girl anymore, no blonde hair. Just enough to fool you."

Silence fell across the table as Julie glared through the flame. The shadows weaved and danced over her face, further corrupting her already malicious stare. The rain outside had fallen into a droning rhythm, sounding more like white noise. From somewhere in the house, water dripped. Plink. Plink. Plink. It filled the silent space between them.

Frightened as she was, Kaitlyn was growing tired of the games. She didn't know what Julie had planned, but she could guess it wasn't going to be pleasant. The suffering she'd experienced over Brad's death was enough for a lifetime. Add to it Zeke and Sammy's murders, and Kaitlyn felt she'd endured more than her share.

She peered back at Julie and couldn't help but picture a younger Julianna Riley, sweet and innocent. One whose laugh had been infectious. One who trailed along behind her and Jesse, happy and full of wonder. "What happened to you?" she said.

"Me? I don't know. Perhaps someone killed my brother."

The spiteful words drove into Kaitlyn's heart like a spike. Only one person had ever directly accused her of killing Jesse. But it was never taken seriously. There had been whispers in high school, but no one dared point a finger at her. How much did Julie know about what happened that night? She couldn't possibly know the truth. No one had been at the Shallows that night except herself and Jesse. No one knew what happened. No one.

"How can you say that? I loved Jesse. I loved you . . . and your family."

Julie slammed her hand onto the table and leaned forward, her face inches from the candle flame. "Then why didn't you save him?"

Kaitlyn felt the first tear on her cheek. Was this where she admitted the truth? Was it the moment she'd dreaded all her life? Even if she told Julie what really happened, she doubted she'd believe her. She needed to buy herself some time. Time to find a way to escape.

"I tried. I swear."

Julie fell back in her chair. It creaked under the strain. "You didn't try hard enough!"

"How would you know," Kaitlyn said. "You weren't there!"

Julie didn't respond. Instead, she reached into her coat pocket, pulled something out and tossed it across the table. "I think you lost something."

The wad of leather and metal slid to a halt inches from Kaitlyn. She picked it up and held it to the candlelight. The Celtic star knot reflected the flickering flame. Jesse's necklace.

"Found that the night after I killed Brad. I came back to your house to make sure my cameras hadn't been disturbed when the clods I call co-workers traipsed through."

Kaitlyn closed her hands around the necklace. The points of the star dug into her palm. If she could distract Julie, maybe catch her off guard. Kaitlyn glanced around the room, hoping to find something she could use as a weapon, but there was nothing close at hand. "Why'd you have to kill Brad?"

Julie laughed. "I wanted you to suffer like my family suffered." Julie leaned forward again. "Did you suffer? Did it hurt to see his bloody corpse that night?" Julie leaned back and laughed again. It was a manic laugh that Kaitlyn recognized from her childhood. Jesse sometimes laughed like that when he had his "attacks."

While Julie seemed lost for the moment in a fit of mania, Kaitlyn saw her chance and leapt from her chair, lifting the table as she did. It tumbled over into Julie's lap, sending her falling backward onto the floor. The candle flew off the table and landed in a nearby pile of rubbish. The gun clattered on the hardwood and Kaitlyn, for a moment, considered making a dive for it. But, deciding against it, she ran for the door, down the stairs, and into rain beyond.

44

THE COLD RAIN hit her hard in the face as Kaitlyn stumbled down the porch steps. Her bare feet slipped in the mud, and only by grabbing the nearby porch railing was she able to keep from falling. The headlights from the nearby Volkswagen still blazed, piercing the downpour like two daggers of white light. Her first impulse was to run to the car, but a protracted shout of profanity from in the house convinced her otherwise. To make a run for the car would place her in the open far more than she was comfortable. She darted around the side of the house and raced toward the overgrown field behind it. If she could hide there until morning . . .

Julie shouted somewhere behind her. "Damn you, Laura! Goddamn you!"

The weeds and high grass whipped at her legs. Rocks and twigs stabbed and pierced her bare feet. Kaitlyn stumbled in the gloom, then forced herself up again and pressed onward. She glanced over her shoulder. A narrow beam of light was sweeping and searching the trail that led to the Shallows. Julie hadn't figured out where she'd gone. Kaitlyn hoped to keep it that way for another few minutes. An old crooked tree nearby loomed from out of the darkness. She ran toward it, planning to hide, rest, and regroup.

Suddenly, Kaitlyn was caught from behind by the flashlight

beam. The white circle of light cast her silhouette on the tree. She heard the crack of a shot, and some tree bark splintered off the nearby trunk. Kaitlyn dipped her shoulders and ran the final few yards to the tree. She hid behind it with her back pressed against the wet bark. Another shot hit the trunk near where she had been only moments before.

Kaitlyn's chest heaved with every breath. Her morning runs along the Cynwyd Heritage Trail had never prepared her for this. Her bare feet felt like they were in shreds. Pierced, cut, and torn. Her hair hung in front of her face, laden with rainwater. She closed her eyes and wished for a miracle. When she opened them again, she was disappointed to find that none had appeared.

The flashlight's beam swept from one side of the tree to the other. The squish of footsteps in the mud approached, slow and steady. Kaitlyn knew it would only be moments before Julie reached her. About twenty yards from her, the wild grass grew tall, probably enough to conceal her . . . at least for a while. She closed her eyes, took a deep breath, and launched herself off the tree, sprinting toward the high grass. She covered five yards in seconds. Her feet burned and stung with every step. Ten yards. She was halfway there. Fifteen yards. The flashlight swept in her direction. A shot rang out. A searing pain ripped through her upper arm, near the right shoulder. She crashed to the ground, just shy of the high grass.

Rolling onto her back, Kaitlyn grit her teeth against the pain. She gripped her arm and writhed against the fiery burning in her flesh. Blood oozed from a gash in her arm. It mixed with the falling rain and flowed off her arm, dripping onto the ground.

A bright light shone in her eyes and Kaitlyn turned her head away. So much for her escape. "You shot me."

Julie shifted the light to the wound, then moved it back to shine in Kaitlyn's face again. "Flesh wound. I'm not ready to kill you . . . yet."

"Why do you want me to die?"

Julie's reply came like an icy dagger. "Justice."

DURING THE HALF-MILE walk to the Shallows, Kaitlyn's bare feet went numb to the rocks and branches that jabbed and perforated her skin. She didn't want to think about how bloody they must be. The mud along the trail seeped between her toes as she marched toward the Shallows. The cold raindrops pummeled the ground around her. Her clothing—meager as it was— was soaked and mud-covered. It offered little protection from cold. She shivered and kept her wounded arm pressed against her body. The gunshot wound wasn't severe—more of a gash through the fleshy part of her upper arm— but still hurt like hell. Her fingers alternated between tingling and losing feeling altogether. Every few moments, Julie pressed the gun into Kaitlyn's back as a reminder that she was still there.

An overwhelming sense of hopelessness pressed on her heart. She'd never get another chance to escape. She chastised herself for even making the attempt in the first place. Now Julie was on her guard and wouldn't leave anything to chance. Her only hope was that the police were quick to discover the murders of Zeke and Sammy, put two-and-two together, and race to her rescue. What were the chances that would happen? Rodney was the only one who knew what—and where—the Shallows were.

They emerged from the wooded path. Kaitlyn peered at the dark waters of the pond before her. Up the hill across the pond, the glow of headlights from the occasional passing car on the interstate interrupted the darkness. Kaitlyn knew that no one on the highway would ever notice a pair of women standing in the dark beside a pond. No chance that a stray passerby would call the police.

Julie made a sweep of the perimeter with her flashlight. "Brings back memories, don't it?" She spoke loud so that Kaitlyn could hear her over the roar of the pouring rain.

"Yeah."

"All those summer nights. Just the three of us. Splashing around in the Shallows. Good times."

Kaitlyn turned to face Julie. "Yes, those were wonderful times. I'll never forget them. Julie, I loved him . . . and I loved you. Why spoil these memories with further bloodshed?"

"You know why I became a cop?"

Julie shone the flashlight in her face. Kaitlyn squinted, turning her head to one side to avoid the glare. She shook her head.

"Justice," Julie said. "I wanted to ensure that justice was served." She pointed the flashlight back down at the ground. "Years ago, I watched an abhorrent miscarriage of justice. A killer walked free from her crime. Got away with murder."

Looking down, Kaitlyn studied her bloodied feet. "I didn't murder Jesse."

"What would you call it then?"

She was tired of defending herself. To Julie. To herself. "An accident. It was just an accident."

"Even in an accident, someone has to take the blame."

Kaitlyn looked up again, staring into Julie's eyes. "Is that what this is about? Blaming someone for Jesse's death?" A faint rage was building within her. "You want me to take the blame?"

"No, Laura. I don't want you to take the blame. I want you to die." Julie stepped forward and pushed her gun into Kaitlyn's stomach. "Move. Out on the dock."

45

KAITLYN TURNED, remembering the state of the old dock from her last visit to the Shallows. The boards had splintered and looked unstable. One of the corners had already dipped beneath the water's surface, with the rest on the verge of following. It hadn't looked like it would hold her weight. Now, she could barely see it in the dark. She took a few steps forward and followed the flashlight's beam toward the graying hulk that hovered over the water. Kaitlyn stepped cautiously onto the dock. The wood planks were rough beneath her feet. A nudge of cold steel in her back urged her forward. She took a few more steps. The dock shifted beneath her. Even over the sound of the pouring rain, she heard the boards creak.

"Keep moving," Julie said.

Kaitlyn made slow progress along the dock, pausing every time it swayed. The slope grew worse the further along she went, forcing her to lean to the left to keep her balance. The rain pounded the pond water. The inky blackness was stirred by thousands of tiny ripples. She moved as far along the dock as she could without stepping into the water, then turned to gaze back toward the beach. Julie stood at the water's edge with the gun hanging down at her side.

"Is this where you shoot me?" Kaitlyn shouted.

Julie laughed again, just as she had earlier in the house. "Shoot you? No. That's not justice. You'll die in the Shallows, just like Jesse."

The dock swayed as a gust of wind blew across the water. Kaitlyn shifted her feet for better balance. She glared through the rain at Julie. "You're a cop. How can you justify any of this?"

Julie's face contorted into a sinister smile. "You're the reason I became a cop. I watched you get away with murder and wanted to make others like you pay for their crimes." She laughed. "I never thought I'd get to be your executioner, but here we are. Now you pay."

The thought of drowning in the Shallows terrified Kaitlyn. She almost would prefer a bullet to the head. She recalled the horror on Jesse's face as he slipped beneath the surface more than a decade ago. His eyes wide, filled with rage, surprise, and fear. Jesse shouted—begged—her to give him her hand, to pull him back up. The mud at the pond's bottom had an iron grip on his feet and its drag was slow and agonizing. The water was already up to his chin and encroaching on his mouth second by second. Jesse tilted his head back to keep it from filling with water. His struggles to free himself only accelerated his descent.

Julie waved the gun, trying to direct Kaitlyn further along the dock. "Keep moving."

Kaitlyn didn't move. She barely heard Julie's words. Her thoughts were still deep in the past. Thinking of her torn blouse, of the scrapes on her knees and arms from their struggle. She remembered his painful grip on her arm and how hard she fought to break away. The sting of his slap on her cheek. The roughness of the dock's planks on her back as he held her down. His groping hand forcing its way into her pants.

"Move!" Julie's command was more forceful this time.

Tears ran down Kaitlyn's cheeks, mingling with the rain drops. She'd hidden these memories deep for years, not even telling her therapist the whole truth about that night. Jesse's episodes had grown in intensity over that last year. Maybe undiagnosed bipolar. Perhaps schizophrenic. She knew very little about mental health, and as far as she knew, he never saw anyone about it. His violence that night had been unlike anything that Kaitlyn had ever experienced. Luck, and a swift knee to Jesse's crotch, had been her saving grace. As he was bent over in pain, she pushed away from him. That was when he lost his balance and fell off the end of the dock. The neck-deep water wouldn't have been a problem if it had been anywhere else in the Shallows, but that mud . . .

Julie took an angry step forward onto the dock. "Are you deaf? Move it."

The dock swayed beneath the additional weight. The water breeched the wooden planks and lapped at Kaitlyn's toes.

"He tried to rape me," Kaitlyn said. "That night, on this dock."

Julie stopped moving and glared. "Liar!" She jerked the gun forward as if to punctuate the accusation.

"He had another episode. The worst I'd ever seen."

Julie pointed the gun at her. "Shut up!"

"He held me down. Tore my blouse. We struggled." Kaitlyn saw the burning rage in Julie's face. "He fell in during the struggle. But you knew that already, didn't you? After all, you were there."

The truth hung between them within the drops of the rain. The gun shook, as if Julie was cold, scared, or both. Kaitlyn waited, half-expecting the bullets to fly, fast and furious.

"What? Why would you think I was there?" Julie stammered.

"I just figured it out. How else would you know what Jesse said to me that night?" Kaitlyn bowed her head and stared at the warped boards beneath her feet. "I remember now. You disappeared for a couple hours that night. No one knew where you went. Were you in the bushes spying on us?"

"I . . . I was—"

Kaitlyn turned her eyes back up toward Julie. "Why didn't you help me? You must have seen what he tried to do."

Julie's gaze was vacant and dark. "I was frightened . . . of him."

"So was I. He'd never assaulted me before. It broke my heart.

But . . . all I could do was kneel on the dock and let him drown," Kaitlyn admitted. "I watched him sink into the water." After a pause, she added, "And so did you."

"Shut up, you bitch!"

Kaitlyn flinched and waited to be shot. But nothing happened. She looked again to find Julie still pointing the gun at her with a trembling hand. The Glock's muzzle no longer holding a dead-on aim at her.

Kaitlyn continued her confession. "I could've saved him. I just needed to grab his hand, and all would've been different. But, I didn't."

Julie's hand wavered; the gun lowered.

"Julie, believe me. I never meant for him to die."

Julie lowered the gun to her side and bowed her head. Her shoulders gave a violent shudder. There might have been tears streaming down Julie's face, but Kaitlyn couldn't be sure through the rain. She felt a sense of relief. She'd hidden the truth about Jesse's death for so long that to finally reveal it was like a burden lifted. If this was to be her deathbed confession, it was a comfort knowing that she had finally spoken the whole truth.

With Julie's attention distracted, Kaitlyn took her chance. She closed the distance between herself and Julie with slow, deliberate steps. With every step, she watched Julie for reaction, but none came. She crept forward until she was a mere few feet away. With a sudden swift movement, Julie's arm leapt forward, bringing the gun inches from Kaitlyn's face.

"Going somewhere?" Julie said.

Surprised, Kaitlyn stammered an unintelligible answer.

Julie took a step forward and forced Kaitlyn to back up along the dock. "I won't let you blemish my brother's reputation with your lies."

"I swear, Julie. It's the truth. I loved him." The dilapidated dock swayed as Kaitlyn continued to back her way along it. "But I was so scared. He tried to rape me, Julie. That's all I could think about. He tried to rape me, and he'd do it again."

"Shut up! I don't want to hear your lies anymore."

"Damn it, Julie. You know it's the truth. You saw it!"

Kaitlyn reached the far end of the dock. The pond's water lapped at her feet. She was exhausted—both physically and emotionally. She had no fight left within her. "What do you want from me? I can't change what happened!"

Julie moved along the dock toward her. "I want you to die."

46

RODNEY DOUBLED BACK to the interstate in hopes of finding the old pond from there. The pavement was slick, and his tires spun as he sped down the onramp. He fought to keep the Dodge in the lane and nearly clipped the backend of a passing tractor trailer. He raced north up I-95, searching the darkness along the shoulder for any sign of the Shallows. He would have missed it if the glare of a distant flashlight hadn't caught his eye as he raced past. Slamming on the brakes, he skidded the car to the shoulder and doused the headlights. The rain crashed against the windshield. Thick trees lined the slope leading down from the side of the highway. The car had come to a stop a hundred yards from where the light had caught his attention. A bit of a hike getting back to the Shallows. It was a miserable night to be traipsing through the woods, but Rodney had no choice. There was a flashlight in the glove compartment. He checked the magazine in his Glock to make sure it was full, then stepped from the car into the rain.

As he made his way around the car, a truck raced past, horn blaring. He cringed at the thought that his advantage may have been lost. Could they hear the horns and traffic through the downpour? He stepped off the pavement into the grass. Climbing the fence that lined the interstate had been his first big hurdle. Chain-linking snagged at his shirt and trousers as he fell over the top.

Rodney scrambled down the muddy slope through the under-brush. One hand held the extinguished flashlight and the other gripped his gun. The saturated ground made for treacherous foot-ing. More than once, he stumbled, falling backward onto the drenched earth. In the distance, he could just make out the outline of the pond he'd come to know as the Shallows. He kept his eyes focused on the solitary flashlight beam near the dock. He could only see the silhouette of the person holding the flashlight, but he knew beyond doubt who it was. The light shone on Kaitlyn as she teetered over the water near the end of the dock. Another step back and she would end up in the pond, right where Jesse Riley drowned. He had to get closer to have any hope of saving her.

As he crouched in the underbrush, he picked up bits and pieces of the conversation between Julie and Kaitlyn. He heard Kaitlyn say something about rape, then an angry outburst from Julie in response. The words were garbled by the rain. Was he close enough to get off an accurate shot at Julie? Between the dark and the rain, he wasn't certain he'd get a clear enough aim on Julie to take her out if things went south. He had to get closer, but there was nothing but open ground between him and the pond. He couldn't let Kaitlyn die . . . wouldn't let her die.

Then Kaitlyn's voice echoed through the rain, ". . . and let him drown."

Rodney closed his eyes and felt his heart fall. He'd worked under the assumption that Kaitlyn was innocent of wrongdoing. The police report on Jesse Riley's death painted the picture of a girlfriend who had tried in vain to rescue her drowning lover. But the truth was different. She'd watched him die, which meant Kaitlyn was guilty of manslaughter. He couldn't help but think of his daughter. He'd turned her over to the police after her hit-and-run. He'd never been able to turn a blind eye to crime, no matter who was involved.

When he opened his eyes again, Julie had inched forward

along the dock, her gun raised and pointed at Kaitlyn. The dock swayed beneath their combined weight. Kaitlyn had backed to the very edge of the dock, but Julie kept moving closer.

"I want you to die," shouted Julie.

Kaitlyn yelled through the rain, "How does this make you any better than me?"

Rodney crept forward to the edge of the trees. He tightened his grip on the gun.

Julie yelled, "I'm not the one who's confessed to murder."

"I didn't murder Jesse. You're a cop, you know that murder takes intent. But killing me like this, planned like this. That makes you a murderer for sure."

Julie waved her gun from side to side. "No! I'm the executioner!"

Kaitlyn spread her arms out before her. "Execution? Without a trial?"

Rodney had heard enough. He rose from the ground and moved toward the Shallows.

47

KAITLYN INCHED BACK along the dock until her bare heels hung over the edge of the last plank. There was nowhere left to go. If she couldn't get past Julie, she would end up in the Shallows. There was no way she could free herself from the murky depths with a wounded arm. And Julie would most likely shoot Kaitlyn if she tried to escape. What would it be like to drown? To be swallowed up by the water. Would it hurt? Would it be quick? She stared up the barrel of the gun at Julie. She saw nothing but a dark silhouette, the glare of the flashlight obscuring almost everything behind it. Maybe Kaitlyn could rush her. Try to tackle her and wrestle the gun from Julie's hand. Probably wouldn't succeed, but at least she would go down fighting. The soaking rain and the damp cold had sapped most of her energy. It was too hard to tell if her trembling was from fear or the weather. She didn't stand a chance against Julie, she knew that. But she had to do something.

The second beam of light came as a surprise. It shone across the Shallows and outlined Julie in its bright spotlight. She felt a sudden rebirth of hope as she recognized the voice that accompanied the light.

"Drop the gun, Julie!"

Kaitlyn glanced to her left and caught sight of a silhouette rushing toward the dock from the tree line. Julie turned as well, swinging the gun in the direction of the approaching figure. The gun barked twice; the muzzle flash lit up the water beside the dock. The second flashlight went dark. Julie's shots were answered with a single blast, which struck the dock nearby.

Seeing her chance, Kaitlyn leapt forward and made a grab for the gun. Under the sudden movement, the dock lurched and sent them both off balance. The flashlight fell from Julie's grip. It bounced off the dock and rolled into the water. A ghostly glow illuminated the sediment that was disturbed by the flashlight's plunge into the depths. Kaitlyn's fingers wrapped around Julie's wrist, but she couldn't get a good hold. Julie spun from her grasp and swung her backhand into the side of Kaitlyn's head. The butt of the gun smacked hard on her temple. Kaitlyn lost her balance and fell onto the dock. She landed on the edge; her legs plunged into the water. The warped boards and rusty nails dug deep into her stomach. Her fingers scrambled for a handhold.

Julie, standing astride the skewed dock, fired a few more shots across the water into the darkness. "This is between Laura and me," she shouted. "Stay out of it, Rodney . . . if you don't want to die with her."

Kaitlyn got a couple fingers in between two planks. Her shoulder raged with pain from her earlier wound. Splinters speared deep into her skin. Despite the agony, she held firm and tried to heave herself back up.

From somewhere in the dark, Rodney yelled, "I can't let you do this."

Julie fired another shot. "She killed my brother. Don't I deserve justice?"

Hoisting her legs onto the dock, Kaitlyn rolled over and stared up into the dark sky above. Her chest heaved with every breath. Her fingers ached, her wounded arm throbbed, and her stomach burned where she'd dragged herself across the abrasive wood and nails. She barely had any strength left, but she couldn't remain where she was. She tried to scramble to her feet.

"It's not your job to dole out justice," shouted Rodney. "Come on, Julie, I don't want to shoot you."

"That's the difference between you and me," Julie said. "I do what's necessary." She fired some more shots toward the sound of his voice.

Julie shifted her gaze and sneered. Kaitlyn had managed to get to her hands and knees. The pointed toe of Julie's boot slammed into Kaitlyn's stomach. Pain ripped through her abdomen. Kaitlyn doubled over and fell on her side. Another kick landed in her lower rib cage. She heard a crack and felt a sharp pain. Maybe a broken rib. She rolled onto her back. The dock's rough edge pressed into her spine. She dangled for a moment, half hanging in the void above the murky water. With what little strength she had left, Kaitlyn reached out and clawed at the planks. Two fingers hooked on a bent nail. She prayed it would hold. Fire tore through her hand and arm as muscles strained to keep her from teetering into the abyss.

"Don't do it!" shouted Rodney.

Kaitlyn turned her head and saw him charge toward the dock. Julie turned and raised her Glock. It would be a clear shot. There was no way she could possibly miss at that range. Kaitlyn flung her free arm forward and clamped onto Julie's nearby ankle. She gave it an abrupt tug. Julie stumbled and fell onto one knee. Kaitlyn clawed at Julie's coat, pulling her off balance. The gun clattered onto the dock, lost from Julie's grip in the fall. Scrambling over her, Kaitlyn made a dive for the gun. A fist out of the darkness slammed into the side of her head. She fell face-first into the planking of the dock. Pain ripped through her cheek, and she screamed. Julie was already on her knees, lunging at Kaitlyn, who rolled over to block any further blows. Hands clamped around Kaitlyn's neck and tightened around her windpipe. The sharp splinters of the dock's rough edge gouged into her back. She pried at the fingers that dug into her throat. They refused to budge. Any strength she had left abandoned her. Kaitlyn flailed her arms, trying to land a lucky punch. Anything to garner even a moment's reprieve. Her hands thrashed as she struggled to free herself. Her fingers found something cold and metallic on the dock. Julie leaned forward increasing the pressure on Kaitlyn's neck, completely closing off her windpipe. Rushing toward unconsciousness, Kaitlyn made a final desperate move. She brought her hand up and pressed the barrel of the gun into Julie's abdomen. Then, her world exploded.

The sneer on Julie's face faded to a look of surprise. Her shoulder jerked back, and she spun around. She fell forward, the full weight of her limp body came crashing down onto Kaitlyn. The dock heaved to one side, jolting Julie toward the edge. Her momentum pulled Kaitlyn with her. The gun fell from Kaitlyn's hand, and she reached in desperation for a handhold on the dock. Julie fell off the dock, leaving Kaitlyn unbalanced on the edge.

Kaitlyn's fall seemed to take a lifetime. Her fingers scraped along the planking. The rough surface scraped the skin on her fingertips. Her nails chipped and split. Utter exhaustion had taken hold, and she no longer wanted to fight. Perhaps Julie was right. It was time to pay for her crime. It was better this way. No more judgment. No more guilt. The dock's sharp edge dug deep into her back as she rolled off. Somehow, she always knew she'd end up in the Shallows. Her plunge into the water barely registered. Perhaps Jesse would be waiting for her. Would he forgive her?

She thought she heard another splash, then a hand clasped hers. *Is that you, Jesse?* she wondered. An arm wrapped around her waist and lifted her back upward. As her head breached the water's surface, the cold night air bit at her face. She took a deep inhale and started to cough.

Someone spoke near her ear. "Grab ahold of the dock."

The voice was familiar. "Jesse?" Then, all went dark.

48

KAITLYN SAT on the back bumper of the ambulance and watched the firefighters hose down the smoldering remains of the old house. The rain had died down to a faint mist. The blanket over her shoulders took the chill off the pre-dawn morning. There was little that she could remember after falling into the water. A vague sense of being carried some distance. Someone telling her to hang on. Nothing else. She wasn't even sure where the ambulance or the firefighters had come from. In the distance, she saw the glow of white light down by the Shallows. She wondered if Julie had survived. Kaitlyn remembered the gunshot and Julie falling into the water. Had the shot been fatal?

She'd have to answer some difficult questions before this was all over. There was no chance she could hide the truth any longer. Maybe that wasn't such a bad thing after all. She'd lived with her actions for years, her only punishment a self-imposed isolation. Perhaps it was time to face up to what she'd done. Would she end up doing jail time? She didn't know the legal ramifications, but whatever they were, it would be a small price to pay considering how many lives had been lost because of her lies. Brad, Zeke, and Sammy . . . and maybe even Julie. Their deaths could have been avoided if she had faced up to the consequences of her actions years ago.

A silhouette made its way up the path from the Shallows. The light from the pond surrounded the hunched figure as it approached. When Rodney came closer, she saw the deep frown lines on his face in the flash of the ambulance's red lights. He took a seat next to her on the bumper. His clothing was damp, and his hair was still matted down and wet.

He was quiet for a moment, staring back toward the pond. Without looking at her, he asked, "How are you?"

"I'll survive. Did they find her?"

Rodney nodded.

Kaitlyn didn't want to ask, but she had to know. "Is she . . ."

Rodney cut her off. "Julie didn't make it. They're pulling her body out now."

There was a sudden chill in the air. Kaitlyn pulled the blanket tighter around her. "I'm sorry." She felt a pang of guilt at the news of Julie's death. She wanted to remember Julianna Riley as the innocent teenager who'd tagged along with her and Jesse on the Riley farm. Yet Julie's vengeful malice would forever corrupt the memory. She tried to lay the blame for all that had happened on Julie, but Kaitlyn's guilt refused to let go. Another Riley dead because of her.

"I didn't have any other choice," Kaitlyn said. "I barely remember pulling the trigger. But I must have."

Rodney bowed his head, staring at the ground beneath his feet. "You didn't shoot her. Her gun was empty."

"I don't understand."

He shook his head. "I shot her."

The sense of relief she felt was bittersweet.

"What really happened that night?"

Rodney's question came abruptly and threw Kaitlyn off her guard. Her shoulders tightened and she drew in a quick breath. Was this it? Her moment of confession? If she told him everything, would he arrest her, charge her with murder? Maybe she should refuse to talk until there was a lawyer present. The thought of a lawyer brought Brad to the forefront of her mind. Brad. He didn't deserve to die, not for her and her secret. *No, time to tell all.*

"You probably heard most of it," she said.

Rodney looked again toward the ground. "Tell me."

Kaitlyn took a deep breath and stared out at the Shallows. "Jesse had a personality disorder. Most of the time, he was fine. But there were moments when he became agitated, angry, violent. It never amounted to much, and he'd never hurt me before." She remembered a similar moment years ago when she sat on an ambulance bumper telling the police officer that fateful lie.

"It was around sunset," she continued. "We walked down to the Shallows. When it was too chilly for a swim, we'd sit on the dock together. Just dangle our legs over the water. Listen to the cars speed by on the highway."

The blanket slipped from her shoulder, but she barely noticed. She told Rodney how Jesse held her hand as they stepped onto the dock. The sudden tightness in his grip had told her something was wrong. Jesse turned on her and pulled her close, forcing his lips against hers. His aggressiveness sparked some concern, but she was soon taken in by the passion and returned the kiss with fervency. But, when his hands started to wander, she knew things weren't as they should be.

"Jesse was the one who wanted us to abstain from sex until we both graduated," she said. "That night when he tried to unhook my bra . . ."

Rodney nodded. "What then?"

Kaitlyn told him how she'd pushed away from Jesse only for him to grab her arm and pull her back. She saw the look in his eye and knew he wasn't himself. She fought against him, but Jesse dragged her onto the dock and shoved her down onto the planking. She kicked and punched, but he was too strong for her. His hands pawed at her, making rough grabs at her breasts and buttocks. He tore at her blouse, ripping it open and exposing her bra. His hand fumbled with the buttons on her jeans. Kaitlyn screamed and pleaded for him to stop, but Jesse smacked her across the face.

"Jesse told me I was a tease, and he wasn't going to play games anymore. His voice was different. It wasn't Jesse. It was someone else. I got in a lucky kick. Hit him in the groin. I tried to get up and push away. That's when he lost his balance."

She described the look on Jesse's face as he tumbled backward into the water. The mix of surprise and anger. She'd tried to grab his shirt, but only got her fingers tangled in his necklace. As he plunged beneath the surface, Kaitlyn scrambled to her feet, ready to run back to the house. When Jesse's head emerged from the water, he seemed like his normal self again.

"Maybe the fall snapped him out of it, I don't know," she said. "The water was up over his ears. He had to tilt his head back to keep from swallowing any water. Jesse reached out for the dock but was a foot or two short. He asked for my help."

Kaitlyn recalled how she shook her head at Jesse's request and took a step back. He pleaded with her, but she refused to go near the dock's edge. Her body trembled, and she drew her arms tight around herself. For the first time, she was afraid of him. She couldn't bring herself to go closer. Then, a rising panic entered his voice when he started to sink in the mud. At first, he begged for her help. But as the water encroached on his mouth, his demeanor changed, and he cursed. "You whore! Fucking bitch!"

Kaitlyn remembered moving to the dock's edge and dropping to her knees. As the tears streamed down her face, she watched Jesse sink, his arms flailing and splashing. His descent was slow and agonizing to watch. He spat and sputtered when the water breached his lips and raced down his throat. She sobbed as his face slipped beneath the surface of the Shallows.

When Kaitlyn finished her story, she turned to look at Rodney. He was silent, staring off toward the Shallows. She reached into her pocket and pulled out the thin leather necklace. She looked down at the silver Celtic Star resting in her palm as if it could absolve her.

"You didn't deserve this. No matter what happened to Jesse," Rodney said.

"But I killed him. Maybe I didn't stab him or poison him. But I watched him die, doing nothing."

He turned toward her. "You never could've pulled him out of there on your own. And if you'd run back to the house for help, he'd surely be gone by the time you got back."

He turned his gaze back to the pond. "No. The Shallows killed him."

49

RODNEY SWITCHED off the engine of the Dodge Challenger and stared up at the gates of the Pennsylvania State Women's prison. It'd taken him more than two hours to drive to the facility in Lycoming County. He hoped it wouldn't be a wasted trip.

He'd spent the last two weeks tying up the few remaining loose ends in the investigation. The inquiry into Julie's death had been opened and closed quickly. He guessed they were trying to sweep everything under the rug. A bit of an embarrassment to the department to have one of their own officers turn out to be a stalker and a killer. Rodney half-smiled at the thought. She wasn't the first cop to cross the line, and she certainly wouldn't be the last.

A journal found in Julie's house had documented a yearlong spiral that started when she discovered Kaitlyn's true identity. She chronicled every twisted part of her plan to punish Kaitlyn for her "crime." The letters, the surveillance, even the murder of Brad Ludlow was in the journal. Although she had intended to harm him, Julie admitted that Brad's murder had been more about opportunity than strategic planning. She'd followed them to Kaitlyn's house that night, and his vulnerability was too good to pass up.

The degree to which she was willing to go for revenge was

disturbing. She'd gone days without sleep, going straight from work to stalk Kaitlyn's house or the radio station. It became a depraved obsession that consumed her life. The journal detailed her delight in misleading the investigation. Rodney found his name mentioned several times within the pages. Her comments about him were far from complimentary. The book revealed a heartless, spiteful woman hellbent on raining a twisted form of justice upon Laura Hobson. It was a Julie Lewis he didn't recognize.

Julie did state, once, on one of the first pages, that she'd witnessed Jesse's death. She'd recounted one of Jesse's episodes during which he'd pressed her against a tree and held a lit lighter an inch from her face. Julie had been terrified. She confessed that she felt a mixed sense of guilt and relief when she watched her brother drown. Rodney surmised that the years of guilt had taken its toll on Julie, eventually pushing her toward vengeance against the only person she could blame for her brother's death, Laura Hobson.

The day after Julie's death, Rodney had been on a walkthrough with Bernie Doyle. Bernie led him through the living room, which was in a state of disarray. Clothes were aimlessly tossed on the leather sofa, looking as if Julie had rushed in, changed, and rushed out again. The kitchen table and counter were littered with fast food bags and takeout containers.

"The worst is yet to come," Bernie said, leading him toward a room near the back of the house.

Rodney wasn't prepared for what he found. The small room was sparsely furnished with a desk and folding chair. A single brass lamp provided the only illumination. The computer, which had sat on the desk, had already been removed by forensics. The only thing left on the desktop was an HP printer. It was something else, however, that took Rodney's breath away. Three of the room's four walls were covered with photographs. Large 8x10s were inter-mixed with small snapshots. All of them of Kaitlyn. Some were taken of her running, some were taken through windows of her house, and others were in what looked like the parking garage at the radio station. Some were in shreds, as if Julie had taken out her unrelenting fury on the photographs.

Rodney made a slow circuit of the room, taking in the varying images. "Damn. Talk about obsession."

"That's not the half of it," Bernie said. "We found almost three months' worth of surveillance video. Looks like it came from those cameras you found."

Rodney gave a distracted nod. He stopped to stare at a photo on the far wall. It featured Kaitlyn seated on the rickety bench near the Shallows, and he was in the frame as well, sitting next to her. If he had to guess, it was probably taken from the interstate with a telephoto lens. He stared at the black-and-white image and seethed with anger. This invasion of his privacy was more like a betrayal.

In her journal, Julie admitted to stealing department surveillance equipment and breaking into the house to place the cameras. She'd written repeated rants about Kaitlyn's daily life, as well as venom-filled remarks about Brad's frequent visits. Her words made her sound like a deranged voyeur angered by the sight of the couple making love. The often-grotesque entries made for difficult reading.

He'd returned to the Shallows twice since that night, drawn there for a reason that he couldn't quite put into words. Rodney sat on the bench and looked out across the water. Occasionally, the yellow police tape that still hung from the dock would flap in the wind and catch his eye. Then he'd recall the blood stain on Julie's blouse where his bullet had entered just below her left shoulder. It had been a lucky shot. He hadn't had time to aim. Just lifted his gun and pulled the trigger, hoping to, if nothing else, delay her.

He also recalled the moment he decided to let Julie die. He hadn't hesitated to leap in the water and lift Kaitlyn back onto the dock. It hadn't been easy. The mud along the bottom of the pond was indeed like quicksand. He now understood how easy it was for Jesse Riley to drown. Every move Rodney made dragged him deeper, and only through his own sheer determination had he been able to free himself. But when he pulled himself back onto the dock, Julie's head broke the water's surface. She looked barely alive, but her eyes locked with his, almost pleading for help. He could've saved her. He could've have reached for her outstretched hand. Instead, he turned away, picked up Kaitlyn in his arms, and walked along the dock toward the shore. He glanced back for a moment just in time to see Julie's hand slip back beneath the water.

The house, which had collapsed into a massive heap of burnt timber, was being torn down by the township. A precaution to keep wandering kids safe. Funny how they didn't care about that before the house burned down. Woolwich firefighters determined that the fire had started by a lit candle landing in a pile of old newspapers during Kaitlyn's attempt to escape. It sounded plausible enough.

His gaze returned to the prison's entrance. He hadn't been here in almost two years. Nothing had changed. The gray stone walls looked cold and uninviting, as if to tell him that he was not welcome here. During his last visit, Carol had been adamant that she never wanted to see him again. Her words had hurt him more than he was willing to admit.

He fought the urge to start the car and return home. The impulse, however, was fleeting. Two years had been too long, and he wanted nothing more than to see his daughter. Perhaps even to begin to chip away at the walls that had gone up between them. If nothing else, the Shallows had opened his eyes to what was important.

As he walked toward the prison entrance, he thought for one more moment about Kaitlyn. She'd returned to the airwaves earlier in the week, and Rodney had listened every night. Maybe her other listeners couldn't tell, but he heard something different in her voice. There was grief lingering beneath her words. A heartache that was going to take a long time to heal. He'd seen her once since that night at the Shallows.

"It's over," she'd said. "I keep telling myself that, but . . ."

He'd tried to be comforting, but his words seemed clichéd and shallow. "It'll take time. You're strong. You'll survive."

Before parting, she embraced him. The action came as a

surprise. But when he thought about it later, he realized they shared a common bond that bound them together for life. It wasn't something that either of them was proud of. They'd both killed someone at the Shallows.

One other thing had nagged at him over the past two weeks. The yearbooks in Kevin O'Neill's desk. Little news about the aftermath of the GBT Strangler investigation had been made public. The Philly Police kept avoiding questions from the media, simply saying that it was an ongoing investigation. But yesterday, Rodney finally heard from a friend close to the investigation. During a follow-up interview, Scott MacKay admitted that Kevin had tried to blackmail him over something from his past. His friend wouldn't tell Rodney any further details. Apparently, blackmail could be added to Kevin O'Neill's growing list of sins.

Rodney entered the prison and approached the front desk. It appeared as cold and uninviting as the prison's exterior. The woman behind the thick plexiglass spoke through a small embedded speaker. "Can I help you?"

Rodney cleared his throat. "I'm Rodney Shapiro. I'm here to see Carol Shapiro . . . my daughter."

50

KAITLYN STARED down on the kaleidoscopic Philadelphia cityscape from the broadcast studio window. The cloudless night gave her a clear view straight across the river to the Camden waterfront. The myriad colored lights from the city streets below mesmerized her, their twinkling mimicking the stars in the sky. It was a beautiful night, perfect for her midnight ride home. Her Harley had been dropped off at her house earlier in the day. They'd finally been able to repair it. She couldn't resist riding it into work. Now it sat in the parking garage, waiting for her to finish her shift. Maybe she'd go home. Maybe she'd just ride through the night and see where it took her.

She thought about home. About the pain that still lingered within the walls of her house in Bala Cynwyd. Perhaps it was time to move. A new house. A new life. Somewhere that didn't remind her of Brad, Jesse, or the Shallows. She could head west. She'd never been out to the West Coast. There was bound to be a radio station out there that she could call her new home. Perhaps it was time . . . to run.

Kaitlyn turned from the window and crossed the room to the control console. She slid onto the stool and glanced at the computer. Three more minutes until the song ended. It'd be a quick weather forecast into a commercial break, then she'd guide things into the ten o'clock hour. The dedications had been rolling in throughout the evening. She wasn't sure she could get them all in.

She'd have to update her resume and air check, then start sending them out to stations looking for talent. The house would have to be put on the market. That would have to wait until the repairs to the kitchen were finished. The ceiling above her table was still blackened from the fire, and the patio door was still boarded up with plywood. A contractor was coming later in the week to give an estimate.

In the two weeks since that night at the Shallows, Kaitlyn had thought a lot about Julie Lewis. There had been a sense of recognition, but she'd never put the pieces together. It felt like nothing more than a case of déjà vu. Now, though, it all seemed obvious and she wondered how she could have missed it. Her last recollection of Julianna had been a dinner at the Riley's farmhouse a few months after Jesse's death. In the middle of dinner, the twelve-year-old had pointed across the table and accused Kaitlyn of murdering Jesse. The Rileys sent Julianna to her room and apologized. It was all so surreal now.

As the song ended, Kaitlyn grabbed her headphones and flipped on the microphone. She spoke briefly about the upcoming weekend forecast and how great it would be to see the sun again. The rainy spring would finally give way to the first pleasant Saturday in a month. When the commercial started to play, she pushed the microphone from her mouth, allowed the headphones to rest around her neck. *Yes*, she thought, *it was time for a change*.

One of the request lines started to blink. She considered not answering it, but, then leaned over and pressed the blinking button. "WPLX. Do you have a dedication?"

"Hey. It's Rodney."

Kaitlyn smiled. It'd been almost two weeks since they spoke. The last time had been in the Lower Merion Township Police Station when she'd given her statement about the night Julie Lewis died at the Shallows. Several times since, she'd tossed around the idea of calling him, just to see how he was doing. "This is a surprise."

"Just wanted to call to see how you're getting along."

"Surviving. It's pretty much day by day right now," she said.

"You sound good. I've been listening all week."

She smiled at his compliment. Despite all that had happened, it felt good to be back on the air. It brought a sense of normalcy. "It's been a good week. Being back here is what I needed. How're you doing?"

There was a moment's hesitation before he responded. "I'm okay." The words carried a touch of unease. Was he really okay? Two weeks prior, he'd shot his partner and let her die. She knew what he must be going through.

"Is the investigation closed? Did you get into any trouble?"

"No. Julie's journal was essentially a written confession. It was an open-and-shut case."

His statement surprised her. No one had ever mentioned a journal. "Julie had a journal?"

He hesitated again. "Yeah. I probably shouldn't have mentioned that."

"Have you read it?"

Another hesitation. "Yeah."

Kaitlyn smiled, sensing that she was making him uncomfortable with her line of questioning. "I suppose you won't tell me what she said."

"Probably for the best if I don't."

She understood. She was certain Julie hadn't been very complimentary of her. But Kaitlyn had questions that were left unanswered. She wanted to understand what drove Julie to such extremes. How long had she been harboring such an intense hatred for Kaitlyn? Did it go back to their childhood? Back to the night Jesse died? Had this been festering for that long? The answers might hurt, but true closure would never become reality without them. "How about just a summary?"

"Maybe someday," he said. "But not right now."

"Promise me."

He laughed. "I promise."

Kaitlyn glanced at the computer, shrieked, and scrambled for her headphones. "Damn! Dead air!"

"Dead what? Kaitlyn—"

She cut him off with the mute button and switched on the microphone. "It's ten o'clock at WPLX." She reached for her dedication list. "Let's kick off the hour with Journey, going out to Steve from Jenni, Brenda from Natalie, and Mark from Kim. Here's 'Open Arms.'"

When she unmuted the phone, Rodney was still calling her name. "Sorry about that. Had some dead air."

"I was seconds from racing up there."

There was a mix of concern and irritation in his voice. She giggled. "How sweet."

The phone fell silent again. What was there for them to say? Together they'd been through hell and back, coming as close to death as she'd ever been. They'd bonded in that fire. But, with everything now over, there was nothing more for them to say.

He was the first to break the silence. "I visited Carol today."

"Really? How'd it go?"

"Could've been worse," he said, the exasperation evident in his voice. "But at least she was willing to talk to me. She's changed a lot in two years. She's got a buzz cut now. I hardly recognized her. She's involved with this program in the prison, training service dogs."

Kaitlyn said, "Good. Is she still angry at you?"

"A bit. But she asked me to come see her again. She never did that before."

She smiled. "Good news then."

"Yeah," he said. "We still haven't had that talk. You know, about that night." He paused. When she didn't respond, he added, "I'll let you go. You've got a show to do."

After making a promise to stay in touch, Rodney ended the

call. Kaitlyn sat with her eyes fixed on the window across the studio. Rodney was making a new start with his daughter. Why couldn't she do that, too? And, why not here in Philly? Maybe she just needed time. Time to heal. Time to forget. She decided to postpone her plans to move, at least for now. *Give things some time to settle and then reevaluate*. Perhaps she'd stay . . . perhaps.

The song was coming to an end. Kaitlyn slipped on the headphones and turned on the microphone. "It's five past ten at WPLX. I'm Kaitlyn Ashe with another dedication. This next song goes out to Brad and Jesse. You'll both be missed." She ignored the tear that ran down her cheek as she hit the button to play the next song. Then she turned around to watch the Philadelphia skyline as the sound of REO Speedwagon filled the air.

AUTHOR'S NOTE

When writing this book, I was faced with a dilemma that is inherent in any story set in the world of radio broadcasting. What call letters should I use to identify my fictional radio station? Every broadcast radio station has a unique set of call letters assigned by the Federal Communications Commission (FCC). Sometimes station management will request a specific set of letters that reflects the city in which they broadcast or the station's format. With a Philadelphia setting, I felt that the call letters WPLX were appropriate while not being too close to any real radio station in the area. At the time of writing this story, those call letters were assigned to a low-power FM radio station in Pelham, Alabama.

This note is the longwinded way of saying that this is a work of fiction. Names, characters, places, incidents, and radio station call letters are products of the author's imagination or are used fictitiously and are not construed as real. Any resemblance to actual events, locales, organizations, radio stations, or persons, living or dead, is entirely coincidental.

ACKNOWLEDGMENTS

First and foremost, I'd like to thank my wife, Diane, for all of her love and patience. She has been so gracious in allowing me to indulge my "hobby" of writing, which takes up so much of my time. I don't know where I'd be without her support.

Thanks to my editor, Helga Schier, for putting the polish on this book. She wields a red pen like King Arthur wields Excalibur. Her efforts have helped turn what started as a disjointed little tale into a solid piece of storytelling.

I'd like to extend my deepest gratitude to the members of my critique group: Sara Badaracco, Joan Hill, Ellie Searl, Christine Schulden, and Paul Popiel. Their criticism—good and bad—has been outstanding throughout the writing process.

Thanks also to Matty Dalrymple, Laura Fiorentino, Frannie Edwards, Jo Adams, and Craig Beible for being early readers, and for providing feedback that was critical to the further development of this book.

Thanks to the folks at Dalton Farms for inadvertently providing the inspiration for this book in the form of a small pond off I-295 in New Jersey. I hope I haven't forever tainted the farm's reputation with this little tale.

Finally, thanks to Sue Arroyo, Dayna Anderson, and the rest of the crew at CamCat Publishing for investing in me and my book. It has been a tremendous joy working with them.

ABOUT THE AUTHOR

Michael Bradley was born and raised in southern New Jersey, a fact that he hopes no one will hold against him. He started life as a radio disc jockey, working at stations in New Jersey and West Virginia. He has been up and down the dial, working as an on-air personality, promotions director, and even program director. His time in radio has provided him with a wealth of fond, enduring, and sometimes scandalous memories that he hopes to one day commit to paper.

After spending eight years "on-the-air," he realized that he needed to get a real job. He spent the next twenty or so years working in Information Technology as a consultant. And yes, he has said "try turning it off and on again" more times than he wants to admit.

When he isn't camping, working, or writing, Michael hits the waterways in his kayak, paddling creeks, streams, and rivers throughout Delaware, Pennsylvania, Maryland, and New Jersey. He lives in Delaware with his wife and their two furry four-legged "kids," Preaya and Willie.

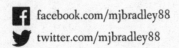

facebook.com/mjbradley88

twitter.com/mjbradley88

CamCat Books

Visit Us Online for More Books to Live In:
camcatbooks.com

Follow Us:

CamCatBooks   @CamCatBooks   @CamCatBooks